Hearts Don't Steer Us Wrong

By Caz May

Book 4 in The Always Only You Series

First Published 2020
ISBN 9780648499879

Published by Caz May

To anyone who has experienced a struggle to find out who they are, whether a sexual struggle or an identity struggle.
Kaden's story is for you.

Table of Contents

Hey lovely readers!

How exciting that we're ready to dive into book four together.

If you have not read the first three in the series, the I'd suggest you do that before diving into this story. These stories are interconnected romances that follow the same timeline focusing on a different characters part of the overall story.

This story is definitely steamy and angsty so strap yourselves in and get ready to fall in love with Kaden.

At the end of the book you will find a slang glossary which contains most of the Australian slang references you will find in the story.

This story is told in first person alternating point of views. If there is only a chapter title then the chapter is told from the main protagonists' point of view. If another name is underneath the chapter title that chapter is narrated by another character.

Lastly, I leave you with some pronunciations for my characters names.

Kaden/Kad: Kay-den & K-ad-d(main protagonist)

Elyse/Ely/Lys: El-lease, El-e & L-is

Austin/Aust: Aus-tin & Aus-t

Dana/Dan: Day-na & D-an

Travis/Travy: Trav-is & Trav-e

Bella/Bel: Bell-a & Bell

Annika/Anni: Ann-ic-a & An-e

Jairus/Jai: Jye-rus & Jye

I've loved Kaden from when we met him in book two and throughly enjoyed the dirty trip of writing his story.

I truly hope you enjoy the story as much I enjoyed writing it.

Caz May

xx

Always Only You Series

Bk 1-Roommates Don't Kiss & Tell
Bk 2-Friends Don't Say Goodbye
Bk 3-Feelings Don't Play Fair

The Mackenney Family Saga

Bk 1-Country Secrets

A Holiday Romance Duet

Bk 1-Take Flight

Follow your heart.
Your brain is stupid.

Unknown

Prologue | Wild Boys

March 2020

Having Austin back in my life has been super grouse.

Yeah, seeing him so in love with a chick hurts like some cunt had grabbed my balls and cock and was ripping them off my body. But all I really want is to see my mate happy, which he clearly seems to be. After all the shit that went down with us, when we fucked the first times whilst he worked out his sexuality and then again this past year I feel beyond honoured that he still wants me in his life and that I'm going to be best man at his wedding.

Firstly though I organised the bachelor shindig we are now enjoying. It's a simple affair; having drinks at mine, but Austin is clearly enjoying himself, beer in hand and chatting to some of our boxing mates.

I'm anxiously waiting for the knock on the door, for the naughty entertainment I'd ordered to arrive. I'd decided on a Male and female strippers show, to appeal to not only my own fantasies but Austin's lack of male attention since we had a dirty afternoon with his fiancé together.

I quickly grab a beer, and head over to Austin to chat.

"Hey man, enjoying yourself?"

"Of course, Kad...but there's a bit too much testosterone in here at the moment."

"Yeah, got something special organised. Should be happening in a few. Wanna another drink?"

"Yeah, might as well. Dana isn't expecting me home tonight."

"You gonna crash here?"

"If it's cool, yeah?"

"Why would it not be cool with me?" I ask winking at him.

"We can't Kad, not unless Dana knows we're hooking up. That was the deal."

"I know," I reply, running into the kitchen to grab some more beers when I get distracted by the doorbell ringing.

Racing to open it, the strippers barge in, a chick dressed in a naughty maid outfit and a guy dressed in a cop uniform.

They're both gorgeous as fuck and I beckon them towards the lounge room where they instantly start performing, stripping their clothes off in time to the music playing in the room.

I watch Austin out of the corner of my eye; he's definitely enjoying himself and I reach down to cup his cock in my palm.

He shifts back and pulls me aside.

"Seriously Kad? Don't tempt me."

"Sorry Aust. I just miss being with you sometimes. And seeing you getting turned on by the strippers, I just couldn't help myself."

"I know. I miss you in that way too Kad, but you know the deal I have with Dan."

"Yeah, you really love her, huh?"

"More than anything. And um...thanks for this mate. I appreciate it."

"No worries. How did you know you wanted her?"

"What do you mean?" He asks with an odd tone in his voice like my question makes no damn sense.

"That you just wanted to be with a girl after realising you were bi and we hooked up?"

"I don't man. I'm worried sick every damn day I'm going to fuck up, but I can't imagine my life without Dana in it."

"Yeah, I get you," I muse, thoughts of Elyse popping into my head.

I want her more than anything, but she doesn't deserve someone who can't love her back.

"Why you asking? Are things not good with you and Elyse?"

Shaking my head, I reply, "They're better than good in the bedroom, but I..."

"What Kad?"

"I don't know if I can just be with a chick all the time."

"You'll work it out, mate. Just trust ya heart and ya gut, not ya cock."

"Easier said than done," I mutter, heading back into the lounge room where our mates are getting lap dances from the strippers.

I laugh, watching our straight mate Ethan grimacing as the male stripper grinds on him.

"Kaden," he screams out, "get this fucker off me. I'm gonna chunder!"

Stepping up behind the stripper I grind my crotch into his arse and he steps back from Ethan's lap.

The stripper eyes me, and Ethan sighs in relief.

"You down?" The stripper asks in a super husky voice.

"Nah, mate. Not this time," I reply walking away to go deal with my hard-on in the bathroom whilst thinking about Elyse.

One | Fatherly Advice

Christmas Day 2018

There's something about Christmas that brings out the best and worst of us all and in my family it's usually the worst.

I love my parents, but their constant helicopter parenting, on my back so much even though I skipped out of their house years ago, the minute I turned eighteen still bugs me.

Sometimes I want to get far, far away from Melbourne, as even though I'm living in Hawthorn and they live an hour or more drive away in Yarra Glen, it's at times still to close.

Thankfully, the roads are quiet on Christmas Day and heading to their place for lunch I have my music in the commodore blaring and the windows cranked at half-mast, letting the cool morning air into the cabin.

After the events of the past year I know I should be telling my parents about my sexuality, but it's not exactly polite dinner conversation, and especially not Christmas lunch conversation.

I've told Brennan some things, like the first time I hooked up with a guy in year twelve—some tosser who wanted to hide from everyone he was gay even though it was clear as day.

He'd loved having my cock shoved down his throat, but I'd loved being with my girlfriend just as much.

Granted, being with her wasn't enough and when she realised I was sitting on the fence with my sexuality she dumped me and I've not been in a relationship since.

It makes me think of Austin, and how much I still want him, how much I'm still hopelessly fucking in love with him.

Fuck, I wanted him to be my damn boyfriend, but he fell in love with a chick and cut me out of his damn life like I meant nothing to him.
Pulling into mum and dad's driveway I sniff back tears, to stop myself from crying, as no doubt Brennan will give me shit, and tease me with words like *'stop crying, you gay fucker'.*
I don't want my sexuality to come out to my parents through the crass, stupid teasing words of my fucktard of a younger brother.

It shits me that Mum thinks he's a damn angel when she has no idea the shit he gets up when he stays at mine on a Saturday night.
I don't doubt that he's had at least double the pussy I've had since losing his virginity at sixteen in the back of my first car.
My brother is a bad boy, a player and super annoying.
We're close though, only being two years apart.
Getting out of the car, I grab the presents from the passenger seat and stride up the footpath, plastering a fake arse smile on my face.

I don't bother knocking, just turn the doorknob and head straight into the living room, calling out, "Merry Christmas family!"
I hear Mum's excited shriek at my arrival, and I barely get to put the presents down under the Christmas tree before she's hugging me so tight I'm robbed of breath for a moment.
Anyone would think she'd not seen me in years, let alone a month ago when we had family dinner or in other words, *'when are you going to get your life in order Kaden dinner'.*
"Merry Christmas, dear," she says kissing my forehead. She gives me a look, that annoying mother is about to say something to annoy the fuck out of me look.

"You need to cut your hair, dear, and shave that stubble off your baby face."

She grabs my cheeks, her mouth curling up in disgust when she touches my prickly stubble.

"Thanks for caring Mum, but I'm good. I happen to like my hair and a bit of stubble never hurt anyone."

"Yes, dear, so when are you going to bring a nice girl to Christmas lunch?" She berates loudly as she heads back to the kitchen.

I follow, scoffing when I sit down at the table where Dad is seated at the head and Brennan is across from me.

He laughs at Mum's question.

"Yeah, big bro, where is that pretty girlfriend of yours?" He taunts me, super loud and I swear I can hear Mum taking a breath in, in anticipation.

"Probably somewhere with your ugly arse girlfriend, little bro," I taunt him back, kicking his shin under the table for opening his big gob.

Dad is staring at me.

"Is Brennan making face? Or do you have a girlfriend you haven't told us about son?"

"He's talking shit, Dad, as usual."

I swallow the lump in my throat, hoping that Dad isn't going to call me out for swearing.

I don't doubt he'd still wash my mouth out with soap if I say fuck or cunt around him.

His gaze shifts to Brennan, staring him down with daggers in his eyes.

"Brennan Abbett, you will apologise to your brother and not speak like a bogan."

"Seriously Dad, tell Kad off for once!"

"You both need to watch your language in this house. It's Christmas Day."

"Yeah, yeah, who gives a fucking shit, " Brennan mumbles under his breath.

Dad hears, and I have to hold back my laughter when Dad clips him round the ear with the back of his hand.

"Speak like that again boy and you'll be eating a mouthful of soap for lunch."

I feel Bren kick my shin under the table when Mum comes into the room putting a large roast lamb on the table in front of Dad for carving.

He stands up, slicing it with the knife Mum hands him.

Mum has left and come back with roast potatoes, her famous broccoli cheese bake, beans, carrots and gravy.

I lick my lips in anticipation and Bren gives me a greasy.

Once Mum takes her seat next to Brennan, we all take each other's hands and Dad says grace, a thanks for the beautiful food Mum has prepared and for being together as a family.

We eat in silence for a bit before Dad rubs his belly, putting his fork down on his empty plate and looking at me questioningly.

He berates me, "So Kaden, son, in all seriousness when are you planning on settling down?"

I look up at him, looking in his dark eyes that mirror my own.

"Can we talk about it in the cave, Dad?" I ask trying to remain calm.

"Fine. Brennan, help your mother with cleaning up," he instructs Brennan when standing up.

Again Bren gives me a greasy as I follow Dad to the man cave set up in the garage.

He sits down in the armchair in front of the tv, opening the mini-fridge next to him, and grabbing us both out a beer.

"So, son, what's bothering you? Clearly you didn't want to speak about it around your brother and mother."

"Yeah, I'm not happy doing the tradesman work anymore. And I've not got a girlfriend. Haven't since Jane in year twelve."
He takes a big sip of his beer, nodding his head. "You need to follow your heart, Kaden."
"I don't know how Dad. I'm not sure what I want to do but I'm not happy at all."
"Well, son, you need to find something and someone you feel passionate about and don't let go."
I contemplate his words, gulping down a few sips of beer.
It's a little awkward talking to my Dad sometimes, and even though I want to tell him I'm bi I can't get the words out.
I'm scared as hell that he'll hit the roof, so instead, I ask, "Is that how you feel about Mum and the police force?"
"Yes, son, so you need to do the same. And while you're at it, knock some sense into your brother. He's off the rails again."
I stifle a laugh.
Dad doesn't even know the half of it with my playboy younger brother.
"Sure, Dad," I reply, putting my beer down, "Thanks for the chat. I'll leave you be to watch the cricket."
"No worries, son. Merry Christmas."
"Merry Christmas Dad," I reply, kissing his forehead before I leave.

Heading back out to the kitchen I think about Dad's words, about following my heart, but I'm too damn scared to take such a big risk, to go after what I really want to do and my heart is to shattered to pursue a relationship, let alone love anyone else.

Two | Not New

For the whole damn week I've had Dad's words of advice tumbling in my head. And his words only brought up thoughts of Austin, making my heart and my cock ache for him.

I'd tried texting him, but got no response and he'd completely gone MIA with boxing as well. Coach had cracked it big time when we had to forfeit a major match because Austin hadn't bothered to turn up for training in well over a month. I asked if I could double hit, but coach wasn't down for it.

The shittest thing is seeing Austin everywhere, even though he's not actually there. It's especially shit in the change rooms where we'd shared countless pashes and fucked in the shower for the first time. I'm trying not to think about him as I shove my gloves in my gym bag and get dressed.

No one else is around and I could probably head into the showers for a wank thinking about him, but I decide otherwise.

It's New Year's Eve after all and I know Milk has a massive shindig going on that seems super grouse and is sure to be hot hookup central. Grabbing my phone, wallet and keys out of my bag I smash my locker shut and shove my wallet in the back pocket of my jeans, the keys in the front.
There's no point going home first, as its already seven pm and the line outside Milk will be huge so I head straight there on the tram, thankful I didn't drive today.

Fifteen minutes later, I'm standing in line outside Milk, practically sweating my balls off, as it's still hot as a tin roof outside.

I survey the guys standing around me, but the talent is rather lacklustre and getting to the front of the line I hand over my cover charge hoping there are some hotter dudes inside because I need to hook up with someone, and someone preferably hot.

Sauntering up to the bar I order a whiskey straight up and down it quickly, signalling for another when I feel someone step up behind me. He grinds his cock into my arse, whispering into my ear, "What's your poison gorgeous?"
His voice is husky, so fucking deep and it sounds like a purr in my ear.
I can feel his cock is huge and hard against my arse, and steadying myself I turn around resting my arse on the barstool behind me.
My breath hitches when I look at the stranger in front of me.
He's gorgeous as fuck, cock hardening gorgeous with dark chocolate brown hair, up in a man bun and equally dark eyes that burn into me.
Gulping I reply to him, "Whiskey."
He licks his lips, glancing down at my lip that I can't help but take between my lips, already thinking about kissing him.
"Mmm, my favourite," he moans, not giving me a second to say anything else or think before his lips are on mine and he's pashing me like I'm his new high.
His kiss becomes frantic, making my cock throb as he grabs me around the waist and pulls me onto the dance floor.

The song ends, and he breaks the kiss. "Fuck, man. You're gorgeous and kiss like heaven."
"You too. What's your name?" I yell as a new song starts.
"Dexter, and yours?"
"Kaden," I tell him, licking my lips suggestively.

"Mmm, sexy name. You down tonight?"
I don't reply, instead kiss him hard, reaching down between us to grab his cock through his jeans. I can tell he's turned on, hard as fuck and no doubt his cock will be long and spring out of his jeans if I dak him.

For another couple of songs, we pash and tease each other with our hands but I want more. And what better night to have a bit of fun.

A New Year's Eve fuck is in order with the hot as Dexter.
I just hope he's not a serial killer, like his tv show namesake, because before I can think otherwise I'm dragging him out of the club and back to mine.

Three | Dirty Times

Dexter leads me out of Milk, holding my hand rather possessively as though he doesn't want to lose me in the crowd.
My heart is hammering in my damn chest in fear, panicking that he maybe is a serial killer, that I've met the real Dexter Morgan.

Outside Milk, he pushes me against the wall, again crushing his plump lips against mine and I hate that even in my panic my body reacts to his hot kiss.

Breaking the kiss, I'm panting for air, my voice coming out huskier than usual, "Fuck, man. You sure can kiss."
"Back at you. Come back to mine?" he asks, his eyes pleading me.
I'm being sucked into his spell, afraid if I say, *'yes'* I'm going to be fucked hard and then slashed into fucking pieces. But his eyes are mesmerising and his hands are touching me everywhere.
The one on my throbbing cock is the most convincing and against my better judgement I find myself replying, "Yeah, why not."

I step towards the curb, hailing a taxi and surprisingly one pulls up to us almost immediately. Together we slide into the back seat and he quickly rattles off his address to the cabbie, before he turns to look at me, again kissing me so hard I'm breathless.
I'm scared, but fucking excited to get naked with him if his kisses are anything to go by he's going to suck hard and I'm sure to come more than once.
My whole body is aching to be fucked by him.

It seems like barely ten minutes passes when the cab pulls up in front of a townhouse, that looks a little out of place among the high-rises around it in South Yarra.

I feel a little better, that maybe he isn't a serial killer, because a serial killer would have a house that would blend in and not stand out, right?

After paying the cabbie, Dexter pulls me out of the cab, straight up the steps of his townhouse and opens the door with one hand.

On the couch in the small lounge room, a young woman sits watching 'tv'.

Dexter smiles at her and she nods, winking at me.

I drop his hand, feeling like I should be running out the door. He's probably not a serial killer, but he has roommates or maybe it's his sister?

Fuck...whoever she is, she's going to get an ear full of noise coming from Dexter's room whilst we fuck.

He leads me up the stairs, stumbling a little and we fall against the wall at the top of the stairs, our lips crashing together again.

"Who's the chick?" I ask against his lips.

"My kid sister. Don't worry, she won't come knocking if I've got a guy over."

"Um, sweet, right. But we should be quiet, yeah?"

"Nah, all good. Live in the moment, Kaden," he replies pulling me into a bedroom and shutting the door behind us.

I barely have a moment to think, panic or react at all before he's stripping off his clothes whilst he stares at me eagerly.

Once he's down to his jocks, I stare at his body appreciatively. His abs are rock solid, his chest smattered with dark curly hair from his tits in a trail down to his cock.
The 'v' of his muscles points right to his cock, that is straining against his tight white jocks.
The tip is clearly visible through the white fabric and his cum has made a wet spot, showing me he's clearly attracted to me.
It feels fucking good to be wanted again.

He's about to pull the jocks down, but I shake my head at him.
"Damn, man. Just...um...give me a minute."
"Of course," he replies in his husky voice. It makes my cock throb, ready for his mouth to be on it and ready to be fucked by him.

I've only ever fucked one other stranger before, so he was going to be the third guy to fuck me.
I can't help but let my mind drift to Austin, and our hot shower fuck as I strip from my clothes in front of Dexter.

Thinking of Austin makes my cock painfully hard, and locking my eyes on Dexter's I dak myself, pushing my white Calvin Klein boxers to the floor.

"Fuck, Kaden, your cock looks delicious man. Can I suck you off?"
I don't reply, a throaty groan escaping from between the smile on my lips. He daks himself and my eyes gaze over his hard thick cock before he bends down in front of me, falling to his knees before he takes my cock into his mouth.
My cock has a mind of its own, throbbing in his mouth as his tongue swirls over my engorged flesh, into the tip and along the length.
It's fucking ecstasy, but I don't want to come in his mouth.
I want his cock in my arse whilst I come.
Why? I've got no fucking idea.

Grabbing his man bun I pull out of his mouth. He looks up at me confused.

"Not good, man?"

"Yeah, Nah, ecstasy man, but I'd rather fuck if you're down."

"Thought you'd never ask. You cool if I top?"

"Yeah, fucking oath," I moan as he stands up, kissing me hard as we stumble back towards the bed.

Falling against it, we madly pash, our hard cocks teasing each other.

His hands have a mind of their own, roaming my body, one finding it's way to my hair that he grabs in a fist and the other is making circles on my arse.

Slowly, as we pash, he inserts a couple of fingers into my arse, moaning against my mouth as we continue to pash.

His whole fingers are inside me when I gasp, pulling back from his kiss.

"You ok, man? You wanna top instead?"

"Nah, it's just been a while."

"Yeah, I get ya," he replies with a chuckle rolling over and opening his bedside drawers.

He produces a condom, ripping it open and rolling it onto his cock effortlessly.

After watching him for a moment, I crawl onto all fours staring at the rather erotic picture of two guys fucking on the wall above his bed.

I hear the click of the lid of the lube, and gasp when his fingers are at my arse again and he's slathering my hole in the cold gel.

Bending over my back I can feel his cock pressing against my arse, and I turn my head back to kiss him as he penetrates me, completely filling me.

And fuck does it feel good.

He rocks back and forth, his pelvis slapping against my arse cheeks.

Last time I hooked up with a guy, other than Austin, it certainly didn't feel this good.

It's so good, I can feel my orgasm creeping up fast.
Sitting up I lean back against his chest, kissing him as he slams harder into my body.
Palming my own cock, I come hard, ropes of cum seeping out all over his sheets.
He curses against my lips, tearing his mouth from mine and withdrawing his cock from my body.
I collapse against the sheets and he yanks the condom off, fisting his own cock and coming all over my arse and back, moaning and cursing.

I'm about to get out of the bed, to clear off, feeling content but angry at myself for fucking someone to block out my feelings when he lays down next to me and pulls me against his sweaty body.

"You down to stay the night?"
"Um, Nah, I should get home."
"Come on Kaden. You're fucking hot, and I want more of you."

He's practically begging me, glaring at me with his fucking mesmerising eyes and even though I know I shouldn't I give in, kissing him.

Four | Morning Regretfulness

Waking up my head feels groggy, and glancing at the body in the unfamiliar bed next to me regret hits me hard in the chest.

I shouldn't have fucked him. I feel like shit because a random hookup is the last thing I need.

The guy rolls over, smiling at me.

"Morning gorgeous, down for a morning quickie?"

Gulping I try to remember the night before, my mind feeling hazy like I've drunk gin which I never do. And the worst thing is the cologne that wafts up from this strangers sheets.

Tommy Hilfiger.

I knew I could smell it the night before, but I tried to tell myself it was in my head and that this hot stranger didn't smell like him, didn't smell like he'd been with Austin.

I need to get out of his bed, and out of his damn house before I break down and cry.

Yeah, fucking cry.

I can feel the tears stinging my eyes already smelling the cologne and thinking of Austin.

"Nah, I can't. I...have to..um...get to work."

"Are you sure man? Can I see you again?"

"I...um...don't think that's a good idea," I reply, flipping my legs over the edge of this bed.

Stupidly I look back at him as I get dressed. He looks cut. And it's my fucking fault. As if I could feel any worse.

"You seeing someone else? I won't be upset if you are."

"Nah, but I'm not over my ex," I tell him, biting my lip to stop more lies spilling from my mouth.

"Right, yep. Well, he's a lucky bugger. Maybe I'll catch ya at Milk another night."

"Yeah," I mutter opening his bedroom door.

He follows me out, pulling his jocks on and racing down the stairs after me. At the front door, he kisses me and I try not to gag.

I was all down for kissing him last night, but morning light brings regretfulness and my heart aches because I don't want to be with someone new. I still desperately want to be with Austin.

~~

At home, the second I walk in the door the house feels lonely.

Living by myself has some perks, like being able to walk around starkers and being able to eat and do whatever I damn well want to do, but it just makes the heartache of losing my best mate even harder.

I have so much I want to say to him, but the way he'd just shut me out when he got with Dana infuriates me. My blood boils hot with anger and lust every time I think of him, and the last conversation we had. A conversation that wasn't even face to face.

Flopping down on the couch with my phone in hand I open up messages, scrolling down through the list to his name.

Opening the messages my heart crashes against my ribcage reading what I wrote to him and his reply that ripped my heart out.

Kaden: Aust, I'm sorry. Please. Please just come over and hear me out. I want to be with you. You and me together is everything man. I'm so in love with you.

Austin: I'm with Dana. I love Dana. I'm bi Kaden, but we're never going to be together. So leave me be.

I start typing a text back, even though that last text was months ago.

Kaden: hey man. I know you said I should leave you be but I…

I stop writing halfway through, angry at myself that thinking about him is making me horny as hell. Even though I desperately want to contact him I've got to let go and let him move on whilst making myself move on as well.

Putting my phone down I get up off the couch, undressing as I head down the hallway to the bathroom for a shower.

Just thinking about him was enough to make my cock hard and standing under the shower I stroke myself, gripping my cock hard, fisting it as I lean against the shower wall.

My mind again wanders to when I fucked Austin in the shower, how fucking amazing it felt to be inside him and lose myself in the pleasure. Last night with Dexter had been the first time I fucked a guy since being with Austin.

I'd hooked up, kissed a couple of guys on nights out and gotten a couple of hand jobs, but I'd not fucked anyone and now pumping my cock to release I kinda wish I'd not gone there.

Regret is the only emotion I can feel right now, and when I come screaming Austin's name I sink to the floor, hot angry tears streaming down my cheeks.

I never should have fucked my best mate.

Five | Hit It

After laying around in bed for the entire first day of the year, I feel like a slob, as though I haven't worked out in weeks. It's only been a couple of days, but I've downed too much alcohol and eaten way too much bad (but good) food.
Sliding out of bed I pull on some gym shorts, not bothering with any jocks or boxers. Going commando always makes me feel ready for anything.
Jocks are so restrictive, especially when being at boxing surrounded by hot fit guys often makes me sport a fatty.
Granted that hasn't happened in months since Austin decided to not face seeing me.
Boxing just hasn't been the same since Austin stopped turning up. The other guys are piss weak compared to Austin, and I feel like it isn't even worth coming to fight them when I can take them down in five minutes.

After grabbing my gloves I'm out the door in a rush, getting in the commodore and gunning it down Glenferrie Road. Driving through the city streets I crank up the radio to try and block out thoughts of Austin from my mind. It doesn't help when 'Closer by Nine Inch Nails' starts playing and it makes me think of fucking him.

Thankfully the traffic is light and I get to Richmond in record time. Parking the commodore effortlessly I race inside, quickly shoving my bag in my locker, to not spend more than a minute in the change rooms.

Thoughts of fucking Austin always surface when I'm in there, even more than every other fucking second he's on my mind.

I haven't set foot in the showers since we'd fucked in them. I'd probably cry like the pansy I am if I did.

Pulling on my gloves, once out in the main room I'm kinda happy the place is practically deserted, except for one of the heavyweight guys squaring off with coach in the ring.
I smile at them, a smile I'm honestly not feeling, before punching the bag so hard I feel the jolt through my glove. Pounding the bag harder, I let out all the anger I'm harbouring.
Anger at myself for ever thinking that kissing and fucking my best mate was a good idea. The anger at myself for not separating the sex from love and falling for him when he was confused about his sexuality.
To say I'm confused again, about my own sexuality is an understatement.
Confusion often plagues me, still, even though I've known about my attraction to chicks and guys since I was fourteen.
I'd always thought that I was bisexual, but having only been with guys of late, and subsequently falling for Austin I did wonder if I was kidding myself. Kidding myself to the fact that I'm gay, and not bi at all.
The only answer, to find out for sure is to head out and find a willing girl to sink my cock into.

Six | Attraction Confusion

After boxing I rush home, quickly dress, sporting dark jeans and a white buttoned shirt. Shoving my keys, phone and some cash in my pocket I head out, jogging to the tram stop. It feels good to get my legs moving, as they feel like jelly.
I should get back into running. I always feel better when I'm out pounding the pavement. It's different to the rush I get when boxing and clears my head in a completely different way.
When I get to the tram stop, thankfully one is pulling up and I board, hanging on to the railing as it rattles away.

Rivera is only about five stops away, so the trip is short and when I get off it's a relief to see no line outside the club. It's only just gone six pm, so that would probably explain the absence of people.
The minute I'm inside the club I saunter up to the bar and order a beer.
Sipping it, the cool liquid feels so good sliding down my throat.
Leaning back on the bar top I glance around the club.
There's hardly a guy in sight, and for some fucked up reason it makes me feel so lonely.
I turn back to the bartender.
"What's with all the chicks in here tonight?"
"Ladies night, man. Fucking sucks."
"Yeah," I moan, downing the rest of my beer.
"You looking to hook up?" he asks me with a wink.
"Yeah."
"I get off at nine if you're still down then."
"Sweet, man. I'll see," I reply gulping and looking back towards the dance floor.

In the middle of the dance floor I spot a group of chicks, dancing together and grinding against each other to the thumping beat.

One of the chicks locks eyes with me and licks her lips before beckoning me over.

Crossing the dance floor I keep my eyes on hers, and reaching her I grab her around the waist pressing our bodies together.

"Hey gorgeous," I purr into her ear. She doesn't reply, instead, she smiles at me, a sexy smirk that makes my cock jolt.

Pulling her away from her friends, and the dance floor I drag her towards the booth at the back of the club.

She just stares at me, licking her lips and it's a bit of a turn on.

"So gorgeous, you just gonna stare at me all night?"

"No, sexy," she replies giggling before her lips crash against mine.

Her kiss is fierce, her lips teasing mine by breaking back from mine just an inch before she's kissing me again and licking my lips with her tongue.

It feels fucking good to be kissing a chick again, so different from kissing a guy. My cock is starting to tent my jeans and I tear my mouth from hers when she reaches between us and grabs it in her grip.

"Can I?"

"Oh yeah, gorgeous." I groan when her fingers easily unzip and unbutton my jeans. She daks me to my boxers, and before I can think she pushes me down onto the booth seat, slipping her mouth straight onto my length. She's definitely got skills and knows how to give a damn good gobby. Her tongue glides over the tip, swirling it and lapping up my precum eagerly. I watch her head bob up and down on my cock, enjoying the feeling until I shoot my load down her throat.

She looks up at me, smiling and I kiss her so we don't have to talk for a bit.

"That was great," I tell her with fake sincerity.

Yeah, I'd just come down her throat but I don't feel satisfied.

I'm feeling even more fucking confused than ever and I wonder if it's
because it was a girl who just sucked me off.
I touch her pussy through her jeans.
"Want me to return the favour?"
"Nah, it's ok. I need to get home before my boyfriend."
I'm sure I gape at her words, and I gulp at the sexy wink she gives me
when she slides out of the booth leaving me dumbfounded.
My head is spinning and I'm wondering if I'm actually gay, not bi.
Her reaction to my kisses and sucking my cock, and walking away from
me without wanting anything in return, even though she's supposedly
got a boyfriend makes me question myself, makes me wonder if I'm
giving off gay vibes. I have to get out of here and work out who I'm
attracted to, somehow.

Seven | Brothers Jeer

A couple of days have passed since the chick sucked me off in the club, and all I've done is lie around like a slob downing beers and eating pizza, Chinese takeaway and any other greasy takeaway option I could order via Deliverlog.

I've only gotten off the couch or out of bed to go to work, and I'm barely hanging on making it through a day.
I fucking hate my job, hate that I'm spiralling into a pit of despair.

My life is going down the shitter.

Shoving another hot chip in my mouth, I nearly choke on it when someone pounds hard on my door in some weird morse code knock.
I know who it is, so I take my time getting off the couch to head to the door.
Opening it a couple of minutes later I laugh at the scornful look on my younger brothers face.
"Seriously Kad? Are you trying to kill me?"
"Nah, you're practically immortal Bren. It'd take a lot more heat to kill you."
"Yeah true, but still. Can I come in before I sweat my balls off out here?"
"Yeah, sure. I could do with a chat."
He follows me inside, picking up the gym bag at his feet. He drops it by the couch when he sits down.
"Bro, want a beer?"
"Yeah, got any good shit? Not that pansy stuff you usually have?"
I look at him spread out on my couch, making himself at home.

"I've got Carlton draught if you're good with that?"

"Better than Vic Bitter. Throw one over," he replies laughing.

I grab two beers out, throwing him one when I sit down on the opposite end of the couch.

He flicks the top off, throwing it onto the pile on the floor.

"So bro, clearly something's up cause this place is a fucking shitstorm."

I gulp down half my beer, unsure if I want to confide in my brother about what's been plaguing my mind since that chick sucked me off.

I sigh, taking in a deep breath.

"Bro, I think I'm completely into dudes," I blurt out suddenly.

My brother laughs, nearly choking on his sip of beer.

"Why? I thought you got plenty of pussy."

"Well, yeah, I do and I feel bi...but..."

"Yeah, don't get that, but you like being with chicks and guys?"

"Yeah, I like being with both...but I'm in love with Austin still and being with a chick lately hasn't done anything for me."

He takes a final gulp of his beer, putting the bottle down before he replies, "Well shit bro. I don't know. Can't help...I'm 100% for the pussy."

"I know...you disgust me, little bro," I jeer at him, laughing.

He laughs. "You love me."

I laugh at his stupid remark because the Abbett brothers don't tell each other their feelings and as much as I do love him I'm not going to admit that.

This conversation isn't really helping me clear my mind, but I do like having Brennan around. He speaks again, "Just hook up with both and see what happens. Ya dick comes to the party or it doesn't."

His words are kinda wise for my playboy younger brother, and I wonder for a minute if he's finally going to settle down before I reply, "True bro."

He nods, laughing. "I may be a douche but a chick will always know I'm into her when my dick says, 'hello'."

And there he is.

"Seriously, Brennan. You're a man ho."

"Thanks, big bro. Glad you love me so much."

"Oh yeah, heaps," I reply laughing.

"So is it cool if I stay for a few? Mum and Dad are on my fucking back again."

"Yeah, cool bro. But don't go bringing any skanks back here."

"Never," he laughs, giving me a salute.

I don't trust my brother in that department, but I like having him around. The house will at least not feel as lonely whilst he's here. I'm still lonely though, and going to see 'him' is the only thing that's going to help me move on, facing 'him' the only thing that's going to heal the gaping hole in my heart.

Eight | Pretty Tomboy

I can't get Brennan's words off my mind. What he'd said about being with both chicks and guys, and seeing if my dick comes to the party certainly has appeal. But what I really want to do is be with Austin, to just see him again.
Not talking to him about everything that happened between us, and ultimately him falling for Dana even when I confessed my feelings for him has made a gaping hole in my heart.
I want to confide in him, just talk to him again as a friend, because I miss having a mate to confide in about my feelings.

Brennan is still asleep, so I get dressed in trackies and a tank, deciding to head to his house and confront him. I just hope I can actually get the words out that I want to say, and that I keep my dick contained in my boxers when I see him. Thoughts of kissing him are already running through my mind, and I need to squash those fuckers down into my fantasies because kissing Austin again is not going to happen.

Twenty minutes later I'm sliding out of the commodore I'd parked crookedly on the curb outside his apartment in nervousness.
Sliding out of the car I walk quickly up to the front door, knocking hard and tapping my foot on the concrete as I wait for someone to answer the door.

It opens slowly, and someone peers out between the gap.
It's not Austin, and it's not Bella, but definitely a chick with long dark hair and a fit sexy as sin body.

I'm about to say something when she opens the door wider standing against the door frame.

And fuck me, does she look gorgeous.

I'm practically salivating, looking her up and down. And my dick is throbbing in my trackies. I'm afraid it's going to spring forth to say, 'hello'.

God, who is this fucking gorgeous chick?

"Um, hi," I say, my words catching in my throat so they come out a little husky, "I'm just wondering if Austin is home?"

She gulps like she's trying to find the words to answer me. We're both completely dumbstruck by each other.

"Is he here?" I ask again.

She shakes her head.

"Um, no. He moved out months ago."

She rushes the words out so quickly I'm not sure if I actually heard her right.

I look at her confused, running a hand through my hair, pushing it back off my face.

She's still eyeing me, and I can see my presence is effecting her just as much as I'm being effected looking at her.

"Oh shit, um...are you sure?" I stammer.

"Yeah, didn't he tell you?" she asks giving me an odd look that I can't read. I feel like I know her but I can't work out from where.

Surely I'd remember if I'd hooked up with her because from the reaction my dick is having to her I would have gone back for seconds, thirds and countless other servings.

I want to push her inside and pash her on the old brown couch in the lounge room.

"Nah I haven't seen him for a couple of months. He's skipped out on everything lately," I tell her, a little forlorn and looking down at the ground so she doesn't have to see the pain in my eyes that saying those words brings.

"Well, I can let Bel know you dropped by and to let Austin know."

My mouth drops open at her words and I ask, "Sorry, do you mean Bella?"

"Yeah, Bella, she's my sister. I'm living here now with her and her daughter Nora. I started uni a month or so ago." Again she rushes out her words in a crazed panic. I look her up and down again, biting down on my lip a moment when the dots connect in my head.

"Oh, shit…fuck no…um…you're…fuck!"

The recollection hits us both at the same time. And she shrieks, "No way! You're the guy Austin was pashing last year when I came to stay with Bella?"

I feel my cheeks heat with a blush.

"Yeah…names Kaden," I tell her stretching out my hand to her to shake.

"Elyse," she replies, blushing when she takes my hand and shakes it apprehensively.

An electric tingle rushes up my arm and my dick jolts in my boxers threatening again to tent my trackies with excitement.

"Nice to meet you, Elyse," I reply, "I should probably head to boxing but I'll catch ya later."

She nods, stammering, "Um, yep, later."

Turning to walk away I wave at her before she closes the door behind her.

I never thought I'd see her again. The thought of a comment I made about wanting her after my threesome with Bella and Austin crashes into my mind and for a moment I want to rush back to kiss her.

I shouldn't want her, considering she's Bella's sister and she's clearly younger than me, but fuck I've not had that reaction to a chick in ages.

I want Elyse, but if she knows anything about me she'll never even go near me with a ten-foot pole.

Nine | Caught Out

Since my encounter with Elyse I've thought of nothing else but kissing her and wondering what her body looks like under her boyish clothes. What she was wearing when I met her the other day left enough to my imagination that I'd wanked thinking about her when I got home.

And fuck did I come hard, so hard Brennan rapped his fist on the wall between the bedrooms cursing at me for being a dirty fucker.

I shouldn't want Elyse. Wanting her is so wrong.

I need to fuck some random skank to rid my mind of her.

Thankfully Brennan has headed out, for what I don't fucking know, but I don't care.

Lying back on the couch, I open 'Tinder' on my phone, looking at the random hookups available now in my area. Almost immediately I find a chestnut-haired chick nearby. Her profile pic is her leaning over showing off some ripper cleavage and she's pouting; a come hither kinda pout.

I swipe right and a match message pops up.

Quickly I type a message to her and she agrees to come over.

~~

Twenty minutes later the chestnut-haired chick is straddling me on the couch, kissing me so hard she's sucking all the breath out of my lungs. I'm honestly not feeling it, but kiss her back, faking moans of pleasure. I'm glad when the door crashes open and Brennan rushes in, laughing when the chick jumps off my lap. She's pissed we've been caught out, but I'm fucking grateful.

"Hey bro, I can leave if you want? But if you wanna pash here, do you mind if I sleep in ya bed?"

I don't reply, and the chick looks between us both, her eyes darkening in anger. She leaves, running out the front door hurling angry words at me for no apparent reason.

"Come on brother, you killed my pash sesh."
Brennan looks at my crotch and laughs.
"You might have been pashing that chick for the night, but it doesn't look like ya dick was enjoying it much."
I sigh, hating to admit that my brother is right.
"She didn't even turn me on a little bit. But fuck…"
If a hot chick pashing me doesn't turn me on, I'm completely fucked.

I know what it means and it's bad.

"Fuck what? Are you still thinking you're completely into dudes?"
I shake my head, laughing. "No…I've been wanking to thoughts of a chick for like a month. I can't get her off my damn mind."
He rubs his hands together, elbowing me in the side. "Ooo…do tell brother?"
I feel my cheeks heat and my dick ache, just from thinking about telling Brennan about Elyse.

"Her name's Elyse…and she's forbidden damn fruit. I can't have her, no matter how much I want her."
"Why brother? Does she bat for the other team or something?"

Again I shake my head, gulping before I speak, "No, nothing like that I don't think, but I…um…I fucked her older sister…had a threesome with her older sister and Austin."

Brennan's jaw drops, and he chuckles.

"Oh damn, brother. I never knew…you're such a dirty son of a bitch."

He's practically shitting himself laughing and I jeer at him, "Talk about yourself."

He slaps my arm.

"I know…threesomes are the shizz, but a foursome is better."

It's my turn to gape. I know my brother's history—way too much about his sex life to be honest—but I didn't know he'd had a foursome. I'm actually kinda horrified but intrigued.

"You disgust me, Bren," I tell him laughing.

"I try. And don't tell me you haven't thought about a foursome."

"Of course I have, but the opportunity hasn't presented itself."

"Maybe one day, brother, but right now you need to get over yourself and get with this Elyse chick."

"Yeah," I reply heading to the kitchen to grab a beer.

I don't know what I'm going to do. I want Elyse more than anything but just the idea of being caught out with her—by Bella—scares the fucking shit out of me.

Ten | Couch Pashing

Elyse

A month or so later
May 2019

Once again I find myself home alone, and I'm trying to not shit my daks. Bella has gone home to Mum's to try and face her feelings about Travis. And sitting on the couch with the 'tv' blaring in the background I'm surrounded by my textbooks.

I'd told Bella I had shitloads of assignments to do, which is true but my head is spinning and I really just want to escape and not think about how uni is kicking my butt.

I'd always gotten good grades, acing my final year twelve exams so much so that I got joint Dux with Zack Rudensteine. I still can't believe our joint studying sessions turned into us losing our virginity to each other. He was such a dick after though. I don't know what I ever saw in him.

Yeah, he was gorgeous, smart, popular, basically every girl at Stawell high's crush but he hurt me so bad.

You know, the first cut is the deepest bullshit that annoying as fuck *'Sheryl Crow'* song tells us.

I've not been with another guy since Zack, resorting to using the bunny vibrator I'd found in Bella's room to get me off after I'd washed it near a hundred times.

Sometimes I feel guilty for not confiding in Bella more. I'd told her about sleeping with Zack and how much of a dick he was after but she had no idea about how I felt about him, how much him pushing me away had really hurt.

It still fucking hurts, but Zack has been on my mind a lot less recently, because of an ashen haired fucking guy who turned up on the doorstep months ago.

All I'd thought about since he came looking for Austin was kissing him on the very couch I'm sitting on, just like I'd caught him kissing Austin.

Fuck, now I'm fucking turned on

Laughing, I put a hand into my trackies and rub my clit through my knickers.

Just thinking of Kaden makes my whole body ache.

I don't even know him, but I want to so bad. I close my eyes, continuing to touch myself, getting close to release when I'm startled by knocking on the front door.

Pulling my hand out of my daks I stand up, tripping over my textbooks and stumbling to the door.

Opening it I'm completely shellshocked to find my fantasy on the doorstep again. Kaden is on my doorstep looking sexy as hell in trackies and a fleecy jumper. He smiles at me, and my fucking clit throbs when he speaks in his husky voice, "Hey Elyse."

I bite my lip and tell my brain to find some words, instead of just staring at him.

"Um, hi Kaden. What are you doing here?"

"I was just coming to see if you told Bella that I want to see Austin."

"Um, no sorry I didn't actually," I apologise, stepping aside, not sure if I should do what I'm about to.

I never thought I'd see him again, so the fact he's on my doorstep has to mean something.

"That's cool. I also just wanted an excuse to see you again."
I gulp, my stomach doing a complete flip flop with those words rolling off his tongue.
I know I'm supposed to be doing homework but fuck it I'm horny from thinking about him and he's here, so why not?
"Um, ok, do you wanna come in for a coffee?"
"Yeah, sounds wicked," he replies in his sexy husky voice.
I want to keep him talking just so I can hear it over and over again, fuel for my fantasies once he's gone.
He follows me inside, sitting down on the couch next to me when I brush the books aside.
"Looks like you were busy?"
"Nah, was supposed to be doing an assignment for animal husbandry but it's doing my fucking head in."
"Sounds thrilling," he says laughing and tipping his head back a little so I get a glimpse of his Adam's apple bobbing up and down as he speaks.
It makes me hot. I want to kiss it and lick up his neck to his lips.
"So not thrilling...boring as hell, so I'm kinda glad you turned up."
"Oh really? Only kinda?" he jeers at me.
"Yeah," I reply laughing.
"Well, Elyse, like I said I kinda wanted to see you again. I haven't stopped thinking about you."
"Um, yep, um, cool...you want a drink? Maybe not coffee?" I stammer a little standing up unsteadily on my feet to head to the kitchen.
Opening all the cupboards I can feel him staring at me when I stretch up on my tiptoes. My t-shirt hem lifts up, making me feel super aware of the heat that's rushing through my body.

In the last cupboard I find some vodka and taking it back to the couch I sit cross-legged on the floor taking a massive sip from the bottle before I pass it to him.
He takes a swig, and I again watch his Adam's apple as he swallows it.

I let out an *'eeek'* and Kaden laughs.

"You good, Elyse?"

"Yep, good. Just thinking."

"Oh really? Thinking about what?"

"Nothing." I gulp, taking another swig and swallowing hard, loving the burn in my throat for a moment.

"Right...so tell me about yourself, Elyse," Kaden says giving me a wink that stirs the pesky butterflies in my belly.

"Well, I'm...um...at Uni...to be a Vet."

"Nice, and you're from the country yeah?"

"Yeah, Stawell."

"Do you miss it?"

"Yeah, heaps. Being in the city is hard, but I like it and living with Bella is good."

"Yeah, I've lived in the city my whole life."

"That's cool, do you have any siblings?"

"A younger brother, yeah."

"Nice," I reply, "so um, do you have a job?"

"I'm an apprentice carpenter, but you don't wanna hear about that I'm sure." His tone is sad. I do want to know more about it, more about him, but I'm super aware of the alcohol starting to rush through my body and I'm so turned on.

"I'd love to hear more about you, but um...maybe not now...I um...I want to...um..."

He laughs. "You want to what Elyse?"

"Do you have a girlfriend?" I ask, hoping he says, *'no'* and also doesn't say , *'no, but I have a boyfriend'*.

"No, I don't have a girlfriend," he says laughing, "nor a boyfriend."

"Oh, um...cool," I stammer biting down on my lip.

"Why're you asking?"

"Because of this," I answer, standing up and kneeling on the couch at his knees and pressing my lips against his.

My heart is hammering in my chest and I fall against his body, deepening the kiss. He moans against my mouth and it makes my whole body throb. His hands find the hem of my t-shirt, slipping under it and he runs them down my back, gasping when he finds out I'm not wearing a bra.

Breathless a few minutes later I break the kiss, looking down at him.
"Um...sorry. I shouldn't have done that."
"Don't be sorry for that kiss Elyse. Fuck."
"I've thought about kissing you since I caught you out kissing Austin."
He chuckles, his chest meeting mine.
"Really?"
"Yeah, but I never thought it would actually happen and that it would be that good."
"Yeah, well I've thought about kissing you too. Not for that long, but yeah."
"So you're not gay?"
"No, I'm not gay, and Elyse?"
"Yeah?"
"Kiss me again, please."
I don't reply, instead I crash my lips back to his, biting his lips and hearing his moans that are going to be my new favourite sound.

Our kiss deepens with our tongues clashing and I tell my heart to calm down, tell my clit to stop throbbing.
We're both definitely turned on by our hot pash session. I can feel his hard dick pressing against my belly and I rock my pelvis over his hardness for a moment before I break the kiss.
"Damn, Elyse. Kissing you, fuck."
"Shut up, Kaden and kiss me." He obeys, kissing me so hard my breath catches in my chest. His kiss is everything I wanted and so fucking amazing.

My crush on Kaden has just gone up a notch and I'm not sure if that's a good thing or a bad thing.

Eleven | Guilt Termination

All I'd thought about the entire weekend was my pash session with
Elyse. I got so caught up in the moment, let my damn dick do the talking
and I feel so guilty.
I enjoyed it way too much, and now I can't stop thinking about her,
about wanting more.
Every damn second she's on my mind, my dick stirs and now I've kissed
her it's practically a tent in my daks twenty-four seven.
I've never had blue balls before, but fuck me I've got them now and
short of going over to her house again to take things further, I have to
resort to wanking.
And wanking is all I've done, all weekend. I've seriously lost count of
how many times I've come thinking of her over the weekend.

It's a warm morning when I head off to work, and I park the commodore
on the street outside my latest work site.
Glancing around to see if anyone's around I put the window down a
touch and cut the engine.
I shouldn't do what I'm going to, but my dick is a steel rod in my daks
right now and I can't get out of the car without dealing with it.
Sliding a hand into my jeans I grab it in a fist, starting to stroke myself
but it's so damn awkward and I feel like a damn pervert wanking in my
car.
Stopping I grab my bag from the passenger seat and get out of the car,
again glancing around to see if anyone else has arrived on site yet.
The house I'm currently working on is in lockup stage, but I don't have
keys.

Scooting around the back I find as usual though that the back sliding door into the laundry is unlocked. My dick is throbbing, so fucking painful.

No one else is here, and even though what I'm about to do is incredibly wrong, I've got to do it as I'm in agony.

Walking down the passage to the toilet I drop my bag and yank my daks to my feet as I sit down on the dunny fisting my dick.

I start stroking it thinking about Elyse and closing my eyes I imagine her mouth around me. I'm Imagining her sucking me; fuck I want that so bad.

I want to feel her pretty soft pink lips wrapped around my dick, and feel her tongue lick my tip until I fill her hot mouth with my salty cum.

I can't help the moans that are escaping my lips as I'm fisting my dick, pumping my hand harder and harder, her name on my lips, "Elyse, oh fuck, Elyse, fuck, fuck, fuck!"

I'm about to explode. I can feel my release building from deep within my balls, but I'm cut short when I hear a bellowing voice.

"Fuck is right Kaden! What the fuck are you doing?"

My eyes shoot open, and I'm mortified to find my boss standing in front of me, absolutely irate.

Standing up I awkwardly pull up my daks, shuffling forward a bit.

"I'm um...I'm sorry boss. I've um..."

"What Kaden? There's no excuse for that behaviour on a job site."

He's so serious, but I laugh. He'd just caught me with my daks down and seen my dick. "I've got a bad case of blue balls. It won't happen again, I'm sorry."

"You bet your arse it won't happen again Kaden. You're fired!"

"You can't be serious. I fucking apologised. I...I..."

"Dead serious. Grab your shit, and leave the site."

His expression is unreadable. I want to hurl words in anger at him, but it's not worth bothering.

I'd fucked up, and I'm still horny as all hell. I'm so annoyed with myself, but at the same time I'm glad to be walking back to my car so I don't have to deal with his hard arse anymore.

He was always a tool of a boss, and he can go fuck himself.

I didn't tell Elyse much about my job, because it's not me, not what I really want to do.

It's work but just a job and getting fired, although not great on the money front is exactly what I need. It's time to kick my butt into gear and apply to become a firefighter.

It has always been a dream, and it's time to make it a reality.

Twelve | Inferno Approval

I've been an anxious wreck since I submitted the online application to be a firefighter. Constantly checking my emails has become my new pastime, my phone a permanent attachment to my hand.
I'd also gone on a complete cleaning craze, making my apartment sparkle. It was no easy feat as how I'd left things recently had been disgusting and was evidence of my being a complete slob when work was getting me down.

Waiting on the email to find out if I'm taking the next step with firefighting is holding me back from taking steps to find a new job.
I'd saved a bit though so I can at least pay my rent and eat decent food until I do find some work.
Spooning the last couple of bites of my Cornflakes into my mouth I refresh my emails again and nearly choke when I see the email pop up in my inbox.
Opening it I read it slowly, the word *'Accepted'* sticking out making my eyes boggle. Surely I'm seeing that word, but it's there and the rest of the email outlines the next steps of taking the written selection test.
I'm completely flabbergasted as I honestly thought my licence suspension would have been an automatic blacklist against my name.
Putting my dishes in the sink I head to my bedroom to get dressed, dialling Brennan on the way.
He answers almost immediately.
"Hey Bro."
"Hey, Bren. You busy?"
"No, you sound peppy. Did you get laid?"
"Nah, something even better and we need to celebrate."

"Celebrate? You telling me you got in to be a fiery?"
"Yeah, past the initial application process. I'm absolutely stoked."
"That's ripper brother. I think you're right, we should go out with the blokes and get tanked."
"Yeah, so meet ya at Portside at four."
"No worries, bro," he replies hanging up.

I send off a couple texts inviting some other mates along.
I really want to send Austin one, but I can't.
I fucking miss him so bad.
Getting with Elyse has definitely helped get him off my mind a little but if I'm being completely honest with myself I've actually had dirty, really dirty thoughts about a foursome with him, Elyse and another guy.
It gets me all pent up with lust when I think about it.
I quickly dress in running gear heading out for a jog to clear my head, ready for later.

~~

Sitting at a table in Portside I'm surrounded by my brother and some high school mates and previous workmates.
Sipping on my beer I'm glancing around feeling a little out of it.
The alcohol is starting to course through my body, but it's a good buzz and takes my mind off things.
I'm definitely on the way to being tanked and looking across the room I swear Elyse is standing against the bar.
Brennan can obviously sense my unease.
"Bro, what's up? You look like you've seen a ghost."
"Nah, I thought I saw Elyse."
"Oh, really?"
"Yeah, but she wouldn't be here. It's far from a local for her and she doesn't drive."
"Yeah, maybe you should hook up anyway. Get ya dick wet."

I nod, shaking away the thoughts of Elyse that are making my dick hard.

I down the rest of my beer, scoping out the talent and spot a dark-haired girl dancing with her friends.

Our eyes lock, giving me a sense of déjà vu. She beckons me over and I saunter over to join in. She's feisty and runs her hands all over my body. It turns me on a little but only because she kinda reminds me of Elyse.

I shouldn't be thinking of her, I need to let go.

I tasted the forbidden fruit and it's going to kill me.

I need to focus on this new chick, who's now nibbling on my ear, swaying her hips against mine. I need to give in, get the thoughts of fucking Elyse out of my damn head. The new chick whispers in my ear when the music stops. "Kiss me, stud."

Her lips are a whisper from mine then, and I crash my lips to hers in a hungry kiss full of the lust from thinking about Elyse. This new chick moans against my mouth, and the kiss becomes frantic. It's not kissing Elyse, but it's good and pulling back I take her hand.

"You down to come back to mine?"

She nods and glances at her friends behind us who give her a thumbs up as I lead her away.

I nod to Brennan on my way out and he gives me a thumbs up.

I'll probably regret the hook up later, as usual, but at least for tonight I'll not get a bad case of blue balls.

And at least for tonight I can get my dick wet inside a willing chick.

It might make me forget about Elyse, but I honestly doubt that.

I'm going down into an inferno of lust for my almost raven-haired Elyse.

Thirteen | Guilty Escapades

Once back at mine I drag the new chick towards my bedroom.

And pushing her down on the bed I kiss her.

I don't want to talk, I just want to forget and feel. It's getting to me how much she looks like Elyse, except for the shorter hair and blue eyes they'd pass as doppelgängers.

The fact she looks like Elyse though is the only thing making my dick come to the party and I try to think of Elyse when kissing this chick.

She pulls back from the kiss, giving me a panicked look.

"What?" I snap, annoyed at her for breaking the moment between us.

"I um didn't catch your name. I'm Ally." I hear her words, but her name sounds like Ely to me, not Ally and I wonder if Elyse likes being called Ely.

"Your name?" Ally asks me again.

I don't want to tell her my name, so I spit out a lie, "Kyle, my names Kyle."

"I like that name," she says sickly sweet turning my gut a little.

Why did I ever think fucking a random chick was going to be a good idea?

"That's great Ely," I reply, pushing her down on the bed, "can we cut the talking and get to the fucking now?"

She mutters an 'mmm' and pulls me down for a kiss, fumbling with my jeans.

I break the kiss, yanking my jeans and boxers off before discarding my T-shirt. She gazes over my body, licking her lips appreciatively.

"Like what you see huh?" I tease, jutting my dick towards her still clothed body. She's not wearing much, a skimpy tight as fuck body-con red dress. I could rip it off her in a second.

"Definitely like," she replies with a giggle, sitting up and pulling the dress over her head. Underneath she only has a g-string on, and I don't hesitate to rip that, throwing it aside.

"I don't fuck bare," I tell her stretching over her to grab a condom out of my bedside drawer.

She nods at me, and I slide it over my hard dick.

I'm honestly surprised I'm still hard enough to fuck her.

"Shut up, Kyle," she giggles like a fucking hyena, again pulling me down for a kiss.

I can feel my dick is at the entrance of her pussy and I slip in, just the tip at first to test how tight she is. My eyes are closed, and as I slide my dick further in I think of Elyse, wondering if she's tight, if she's a virgin.

I don't care either way, I just want her.

Ally is panting underneath me now, as I pound my dick into her pussy.

It's just sex, honestly, I would have felt better if I'd just wanked but she's enjoying it.

I shove my pelvis against hers, breaking the kiss to concentrate on fucking her to get thoughts of fucking Elyse out of my mind.

It's only a minute later, when Ally screams out, "Kyle! I'm coming, fuck Kyle!"

I feel her shudder around my latex covered dick and pull out, ripping the condom off and throwing it on the floor.

I fist my cock, closing my eyes for a moment, stroking my cock up and down. The only way I'm going to get off is to think of Elyse. And with thoughts of her filling my mind, I come all over Ally's stomach.

I don't even open my eyes until I hear her voice.

"Damn Kyle, that was hot."

I look down at her and regret hits me, but I lay down next to her, kissing her and rolling over as I pull the sheets over us.

She doesn't appear to be making a move to leave, so hopefully being cold to her will give her the hint and if not in the morning I'll make some excuse to get her out of my house.

Drifting to sleep I'm cursing myself for once again letting my dick do the talking. I need to get my fucking act together because meaningless sex is doing nothing for me.

Fourteen | Daytime Rebuttal

Waking up the next day I feel dirty like my skin is covered in dirt from fucking yet another stranger. Getting up whilst she's still sleeping I quickly shower, wrapping a towel around my waist and drying my hair with another.

When I wander out of the bathroom she's stumbling out of my bedroom, now dressed in her red dress. She's lucky I didn't rip it or she would have been walking out into the cool June morning butt arse naked. I smile, laughing on the inside at that thought.

"Morning Kyle," she says giving me a once over with her eyes.

She's probably hoping the towel will drop to the floor, but it's knotted tight against my hips.

"So I was hoping we could do this again sometime?" she asks when I don't say anything in response to her morning greeting.

I scoff, laughing and taking a few steps closer to her. I lean in like I'm about to kiss her, and she takes a deep breath in, anticipating my kiss but I pull back.

"Sorry the sex wasn't that good. I was bi last night but I think I might actually be fully into dudes now," I tease and her eyes boggle at me. Her whole body tenses up, and she grunts in anger.

"You could have just said that last night, before taking me to bed."

"Takes two to fuck, Elly," I taunt her, making her scoff and leave in a huff.

I feel like shit, because not only do I regret my choices but I'm confused as hell. Heading back to my bedroom I yank the towel off and fall against my bed starkers.

I lie on my bed thinking of Elyse again. I can't work out why I want her so damn much. Yeah, she's gorgeous but I've had my fair share of gorgeous chicks and guys in my bed before.

What makes her so special?

I can't get her pretty dark brown eyes out of my mind, the way she locks them on me before she kisses me, and fuck her perfect lips that melt against mine when she's devouring me whole with a kiss.
I'd wanted to take things further the moment we first kissed the other week, but at the same time I'm glad we didn't.
It would have only made this undeniable attraction to her even more intense.
I've never felt this way about anyone, any chick or guy. My feelings for Austin are different. I think I'd always been in love with him and lusted after him after I fell for him. I'd never lusted after a chick, wanting anyone with such animalistic *'I want to fuck you like animal'* lust.
But with Elyse I've got a bad case of desire racing through my blood. And I need to be with her again, but I also need more.
I want to actually take her out and make her feel special. Falling straight into bed with Elyse isn't going to help me win her heart.

Fuck, do I want her heart as well as her body?

I've got no fucking idea, but I need to find out, starting by taking her out on a date and hoping she doesn't rebut my advances.

Fifteen | Missing It

Austin

Sitting at the dining table, I'm eating Vegemite toast when Dana comes into the kitchen wearing her signature silk boxer shorts and pink tank top. The first time I'd seen her wearing it in person after she sent me a pic of herself wearing it I practically creamed my daks on the spot.

She's alluring as all hell, and she knows it, most of the time.
She saunters across the room, kissing my cheek. "Morning, stud."
"Morning, gorgeous. You didn't wear that to bed last night?"
"No," she replies winking, "I just had a shower, and I wore nothing to bed last night in case you've forgotten."
"Oh, I haven't forgotten making love to you, sexy."
"Up for a morning quickie, right here on the kitchen table," she suggests leaning against the table with her crotch close to my face, so close I could dak her and lick her pussy right there.

I love this side of my fiancee, her confidence and provocative side.
"Oh, you bet I do," I tease dakking her and touching her clit. "Mmm, gorgeous, you're wet as fuck."
"I was thinking about you, stud," she taunts me back.
I push my chair back and pull her into my lap. She kisses me, taking my breath away.
Rocking her pelvis against mine, her arousal is coating the front of my boxers and it's making my cock ache with need.
"Mmm, Dana, fuck, gorgeous, " I moan breaking the kiss.
I lift her up then, sitting her down on the edge of the table.

Standing up then I yank my boxers off and step closer to Dana, kissing her again and wrapping my arms around her to pull her closer.

She lifts the tank top over her head, exposing her perfect rounded tits.

Running my hands down her body she shivers at my touch and it feels so intimate with our eyes locked on each other.

Reaching her mound, I tease her by running my hands over her thighs and between her legs, forcing her to spread her legs open.

My cock is rock hard and kissing her passionately, taking her breath away I slip into her entrance, just the tip at first.

Breaking the kiss, I look at her longingly. "I love you, Dana."

"I love you too, Austin," she replies softly, then laces her voice with lust, "now fuck me hard."

I don't reply, instead I shove my cock balls deep inside her sex.

She starts to moan her pleasure and I thrust in and out, harder and faster, my own pleasure increasing.

I'll never get tired of being with her, she completes me and the sex is always off the charts.

Whether that's partly because I know the chance of Dana getting pregnant is practically non-existent or whether it's because her dirty, naughty side comes out when we have sex I honestly don't know.

Letting out a loud moan, she giggles, wrapping her arms around my neck and pulling my lips to hers. Her kiss at first is a peck. "Do you want me to come, stud?" She teases, smirking at me.

"Oh you bet I do, gorgeous," I taunt back giving her another sweet kiss. "Then you know what to do."

And she's right. In the last months I've gotten to know every little thing that makes her moan and let go, every little thing that sends her over the edge.

So, I start by sucking each of her tits in my mouth, biting each nipple and making her push her hips against my body. The smacking sound of our bodies against each other as we try to get as close as possible is a heavenly as fuck sound.

After giving her tits sweet torture, I kiss her lips hard, sliding a finger between us to her clit and teasing her, still kissing her and parting her lips to tease her tongue with mine. She bites down on my lips, and I feel her sex starting to shudder around my cock.

Against my lips, she speaks, "I'm coming, Aust, fuck!"

And with the 'fuck' rolling off her tongue she breaks the kiss, screaming out my name as she explodes, ricocheting over the edge with me, my cum filling her.

I pull her into my arms, lifting her off the table and she wraps her legs around me.

Carrying her to bed I kiss her forehead, and once in the bedroom we lay side by side together. I feel so content, so in love with her but something is missing from my life and I know I need to tell her what's been on my mind of late.

"Dan, can I tell you something? I don't want you to get upset."

"Anything, Austin. I promise I won't get upset unless it's something bad about the wedding."

"No, it's not that, it's um..." I swallow hard, unsure of how to even broach the topic.

"What Austin? You can tell me anything. Nothing will change how I feel about you."

"I love you, so much Dana...but I...I...miss being with a guy to."

I look across at her, shifting so I'm lying on my side. She looks at me, sadness in her eyes and I curse myself for bringing it up.

I knew I shouldn't have bought it up, as it's clear its made her insecure side come out again, just like it did when we were first together.

"Dan, please say something," I say softly, brushing a hand against her cheek.

"Um...I don't know what to say...I'm...um...shocked."

"I'm sorry. I shouldn't have said anything. It's just been on my mind."

"Don't be sorry, I get it."

"Really? I just feel like I found a part of me and something is missing now. It's nothing to do with you though, gorgeous."

"It must be something to do with me. That I can't be enough for you."

"You'll always be enough for me, Dana, but I can't deny that part of me is missing if I completely shut out the thought of being with a guy ever again."

"I guess. Have you spoken to Kaden?"

"No, I can't face him. He's still in love with me, and it's so weird."

"Yeah, I get that. But maybe you should or I don't know."

"What Dan?"

"I don't know...maybe we could go out to a gay club or something."

I'm shocked at her words. They don't seem like something that would come out of my gorgeous but shy in public Dana's mouth, but she has a soft smile on her lips.

"You'd do that for me?"

"I'd do anything for you Austin."

"Thanks, gorgeous, and likewise," I reply kissing her and pulling her close, kissing her hair as well.

"Maybe I should contact Kaden or at the very least get back to boxing. I need to stop avoiding him."

"Yeah, you need to do what feels right."

I let out a little chuckle. "Being with you feels right, Dan. And being inside you is right."

She moans, kissing me and as I deepen the kiss, ready to show her pleasure again I think about feeling pleasure from a guy.

I definitely need to feel that again, but I'm not ready to contact Kaden yet.

Sixteen | Beginning Rendezvous

Thankfully Elyse didn't rebut my advance of actually asking her out on a date. But fuck I've been a nervous wreck, messaging her first and telling her I needed to ask her something over the phone. She called me back, and I spluttered out the words, *'Will you go on out on an actual date with me Elyse?'*

Her reply was practically instant like she'd been waiting for it and I felt a little guilty that it'd taken me so long to actually ask her out. Having already kissed her, it feels like we've already gone out, our relationship, no, our, fuck I don't know what to call what we have.

All I know is I want her, and I want this date to be special, so I'm taking her somewhere that's special to me.

I'd told her to wear something that screamed balmy early spring evenings and driving over to her place I'm practically salivating thinking about her possibly wearing a dress.

I know it's unlikely that she will, as she seems to always be in boyish clothes; shorts, jeans and a t-shirt. They always hide her figure and I'm desperate to see her curves underneath the baggy stuff she does wear. Kissing her on the couch a month or so ago I'd copped a good feel but it's been so long my mind is a little foggy.

Arriving at her house I tentatively walk up to her doorstep. Knocking on the door hard I swear my heart is fucking hammering in my chest.
I never have this reaction to taking a chick out.

What the fuck is wrong with me? Why does seeing Elyse make me feel like a damn teenager again?

After what seems like forever she opens the door, and as I suspected she's not wearing a dress, but her outfit is still just as sexy. She has on dark cropped jeans, a long-sleeved black t-shirt that sits off her shoulders and a black and red checked cap that she has on backwards and slightly askew.

My mouth gapes and my dick throbs just looking at the creamy skin of her exposed shoulders. Around her neck, she's also wearing some kind of choker and a thought flashes in my mind of choking her as I fuck her. God, I want to fuck her hard, but first I need to take her out and kiss her again.

Smiling at her I greet her, "Hey Elyse. You look gorgeous."

"Hey Kaden, and you look hot."

"Thanks," I reply, even though I'm sure she's dreaming.

I'm wearing white jeans, ripped at the knees and a pale pink button-down shirt, untucked.

Taking her hand I lead her to the car after she closes her front door behind her. She seems giddy, excited about going out with me and I'm glad as it quells the nervousness a little. I give her hand a squeeze and she smiles at me, a cock aching gorgeous smile.

I'm being all gentlemanly, opening her car door for her and she slides into the seat as I head around to the driver's side.

"So where are we going?" she asks as I slide into traffic, heading back out onto Bridge Road.

"It's a surprise, but we'll be outside." Again she gives me that smile, and it makes my heart race.

What I'm feeling for her is new to me, the heart racing thing is so scary. The traffic is thankfully light as we head through the city and with a chuckle I ask her, "Any guesses yet?"

"Docklands?"

"Nope, but you're close."

"St Kilda esplanade."

"A little warmer." I laugh, smirking at her to throw her off track.

"Luna Park."

"Now you've gone cold."

"Oh um, I don't know. St Kilda beach."

"No, but warmer," I reply chuckling again.

She huffs. "Tease. I'll just wait and see."

Passing Southbank and Crown casino I turn towards Port Melbourne beach. The sun is just beginning to set and parking the car on the esplanade I glance around, happy that there's only a few people around, even though it's a nice warm evening.

I get out, going around to the passenger side to help Elyse out. It feels weird to be such a gentleman when usually I'm a dick with a one-track mind but I'm loving it as Elyse can't stop smiling at me. It stirs up an odd sensation in my stomach.

Again I take her hand and we start walking down the pier towards the gazebo at the end to watch the sunset.

"It's such a nice night," she muses softly, looking at me still with that cheeky smile, "I'm surprised not many people are out."

"Yeah, but I'm glad it's quiet. Makes it more special."

"Yeah, so the beach huh?"

"Yeah, I love the beach. Makes me feel not so alone. An escape from the real world."

I lean against the railing of the gazebo, both of us silent as we watch the sun hit the horizon. It's so quiet I can hear the soft lull of Elyse's breathing and realising I'm still holding her hand I squeeze it again, finding it a little clammy.

I turn around so my arse is resting on the railing, and I pull Elyse close to me, our bodies pressed together.

Our eyes lock, and she laughs slightly.

"Elyse, are you ok?"

"Yeah, I'm just nervous. I've never been on a date before."

"Seriously? Never?"

"No, my boyfriend...well um...the guy I was with in high school we never went out officially."

"Well, I'm glad I could be your first date."

"Me too," she replies again with a smirk before she kisses me.

I like how she's so brazen. I might be thinking about kissing her, but she just does it without warning me and it takes my breath away.

I deepen the kiss, biting her lip and making her whimper in pleasure against my mouth. Her kisses are so frantic and tempting.

Her lips dancing with mine make my dick ache and I want so much more than a kiss, but feel like I should keep it in my daks for a bit longer.

The thought of pushing her too far and scaring her off is at the forefront of my mind and I can't bear the thought of not getting to spend more time with her.

I want to be with her, but I'm so scared of falling for her to. I don't want to fall in love again.

Breaking the kiss, I smile at her. "Damn Elyse, kissing you is something else."

"I know, right back at you. I don't have much to compare to though, but woah."

"I can't believe you've never been on another date. I'm sure guys would have been lining up around the block to go out with you."

She laughs, blushing. "I was a bit of a nerd, not exactly popular."

"I can't believe that Elyse. You're fucking stunning. The boys at your school must have been fucking blind."

"Yeah, maybe or they just weren't interested in the geeky tomboy after Zack dumped me."

"Tools then," I tell her, again kissing her hard. She accepts the kiss, teasing me with her tongue and I'm so beyond tempted to drag her back to the car and straight back to mine, but I won't.

Breaking the kiss, even though I don't want to and could kiss her for god knows how long I ask, "So, you good with fish and chips on the beach for dinner?"

"Sounds great," she resounds loudly as we head back down the pier, hand in hand.

This time I lace my fingers with hers and the cheeky smile on her face stirs up that feeling in my stomach again.

I've only ever felt that one other time and that was when I realised I liked Austin as more than just a buddy, when I wanted more than to just kiss him and now I'm feeling that for Elyse I'm scared fucking shitless.

Seventeen | Clothes Off

After our picnic dinner on the beach under the moonlight, things get a little heated. We start kissing, her body underneath mine and it's turning me on so bad I know I need more.

Brushing the hair back from her cheeks, that wasn't contained by the cap I ask her softly, "Elyse, please come back to mine?"

She nods. "Yes, but I can't stay over. Not yet."

"That's ok. I just want to kiss you somewhere more private."

We stand up, and I watch the blush rise up her cheeks as my words sink in.

Running back to the car I watch her, the way her gorgeous body moves makes me wonder if she plays any sports and if she's flexible in bed.

I want her toned legs wrapped around my back whilst I fuck her.

God, I want to fuck her, but I can't.

She's leaning against the car, and I unlock it so she can get in. She's laughing, crazy giggling and it's kinda sweet and makes her seem like an innocent sexy minx. I know she's not innocent but her sweet giggles make her seem so.

I gun it back home, making sure I cruise past the speed cameras as I can't afford to lose my licence again now it's a career requirement to have it. Even so, we make it back to mine in record time, and the moment we're out of the car she's kissing me, so brazenly and zealously. We stumble to my front door, lips still locked and thankfully I find it open when I turn the knob behind my back.

The thought that Brennan is over crosses my mind for a moment, but I'm taken with kissing Elyse and wanting to get her out of the boyish clothes that the thought of my brother catching us is fleeting.
I break the kiss for a moment, pulling back to grab her hand and lead her to my bedroom.
She looks around at my space, obviously shocked by the cleanliness of my room. I'd always kept my space clean, there was no way anyone could call me a slob and when it came to keeping my house clean I certainly wasn't like most men I knew.

"Your room is um...nice," she says glancing around, her eyes focusing on my bed and the white sheets and checkered doona cover.
"Thanks, I like keeping things clean." She gulps and looks at me with lust flaring in her eyes.
"Are you nervous?"
"Yeah, kinda I guess. I um..."
I don't reply, instead push her gently onto the bed, climbing onto it and laying over her to kiss her. The kiss quickly becomes frantic, the lust between us pulsing through our bodies right to my damn dick.
I run my hands up her side, feeling her shiver in pleasure at the touch and when she breaks the kiss, sitting up she takes off her t-shirt throwing it aside to the floor with a giggle.
Underneath she has on a strapless bra that has her tits spilling over the top and kissing her again I reach around and unhook the clasp.
The bra falls between us and I palm her tits in my hands, loving how her pretty pink nipples harden at the callous touch of my hands.
She moans against my lips, my hands edging further down her torso to the waistband of her jeans. She arches her hips up, but breaks the kiss and bites her lip.
"Lys, can I touch you, please?"
She gives me an odd look, and I'm worried that calling her a nickname has scared her. And even worse that I'm pushing her too far.

"Yes," she hisses, "please touch me, but can I touch you too?"

"Damn straight you can," I reply, chuckling as she arches her hips up to me. Undoing the button and zip, I yank them down, pulling them and her tight boyshort undies down.

Her pussy isn't bare but is neatly shaved into a landing strip, pointing straight down to where I want to touch her.

She watches me as I undress slowly, and when I throw my shirt on the floor her hands find my abs gliding down the ridge in the middle until she reaches the v of my muscles.

Her hands against my skin feel incredible and my dick jolts, tenting the front of my jeans. She lets out an excited shriek and again watches eagerly as I undo my jeans, yanking them off and kicking them to the floor as I lay over her again to kiss her.

I want to touch her, and kiss her everywhere, her skin against mine is electric.

Still kissing her I slide a finger between our bodies, flicking her clit and she moans, biting down on my lip before breaking the kiss.

"Fuck, Kaden, that feels good."

"Oh yeah, have you ever been finger fucked before, Lys?" I ask slipping another finger inside her pussy.

She shakes her head. "I don't think I've ever had an orgasm," she says blushing.

Chuckling I taunt her, "Well, fuck Lys. That changes right fucking now."

"Um, ok, can I touch you too?"

"Let me make you come first, and tell me what feels good."

"Ok, um…" she mutters, arching her hips up to mine and squirming in pleasure at the touch of my finger flicking her clit, the other slipping in and out of her soaked pussy.

"You're so fucking wet, Lys."

"Um, yeah…you um…turn me on, Kad."

I slide another finger inside her pussy, pressing them both against her g-spot.

"I love hearing my nickname on your lips. Call it out when you're going to come Lys, please." I pause a moment, bending over to kiss her hard as my fingers tease her.

She's squirming in pleasure and I can feel her pussy starting to clench around my fingers. Murmuring she breaks the kiss, pulling back and screaming out, "Kad, Kaden, fuck, fuck, I think I'm coming, fuck!"

Her pussy pulses against my fingers and she groans, her whole body shaking as she comes down from her release.

"Damn, Lys, that was hot," I tell her withdrawing my fingers and licking them clean.

"That was amazing, Kaden. Thank you."

"You don't have to thank me for making you come, Lys."

"Well, I am, and I want to return the favour, but first kiss me."

I love the demanding tone of her voice, her taking charge.

It's so fucking sexy.

Crashing my lips to hers, my dick jolts when she licks my lips, tasting herself on them. Every damn kiss with her makes me want to practically cream in my daks.

Pulling back I yank my jocks off and kick them aside.

Elyse licks her lips, her gaze on my dick appreciative. She murmurs, reaching out to touch my length.

Starting to stroke my dick, it grows further with her touch.

"Fuck Kaden, your cock is big."

I laugh. "I guess thanks. You're good at that," I inform her, nodding towards my dick in her hand.

"Um thanks," she replies blushing.

She continues stroking my dick, sitting up to fondle my balls at the same time.

Normally I'm not one for getting a hand job, but Elyse's touch feels beyond amazing. In minutes my dick is throbbing as I explode in release, ropes of cum covering her stomach and her hand.

Grabbing the sheet I wipe it away, licking and sucking on each of her fingers, before kissing her again.

We lie down together, side by side and I find myself kissing her forehead.

She murmurs softly. "This is nice, but I really should be getting home."

"Yeah, really nice. Just say a little longer, please Lys."

"Ok, but just for a little and only if we can pash for a bit."

Pulling her close I kiss her hard, pouring all the pent up lust into the kiss.

Being with Elyse makes me feel amazing, but I'm still so damn scared and confused.

I want her, all of her, but I've also never been one for commitment with one person, especially when feelings are involved.

And I'm scared that I'm starting to feel something for Elyse, and I'm certain she's feeling something for me, but I don't want to fall in love again.

Love hurts too damn much.

Eighteen | Beach Play

Elyse

After the night I nearly fell asleep at Kaden's I'd seen him practically every chance I could get. Sneaking around and not telling Bella I'm seeing him is so hard, but after confessing I had a crush on him and her warning me to be careful I know I can't tell her more, even though I want to get her advice.

It's the first nice warm day we've had in months, and Kaden has a weekend off which he hasn't in ages so we're heading to the beach.
St Kilda beach this time as it's better for swimming.
In the car, I have the window down, and the nice warm breeze is wafting in as we drive down the esplanade.
I shiver but it's from Kaden's gaze on me out of the corner of his eyes.
When he'd picked me up earlier, he'd gaped, admiring the simple white sundress I'm wearing over my red bikini.
I rarely wear a dress, usually only when I'm heading to the beach or if I have to attend a formal event.
I do like the freedom wearing a dress gives me sometimes, especially when going somewhere like the beach.
The wind is whipping my hair, and I curse myself for not putting it up.
I mutter a *'fuck'* under my breath which Kaden hears, and he asks,
"What's wrong Lys?"
"I'm annoyed at myself. Should have put my hair up."
He lets out his dirty chuckle, the one that makes my insides flip flop with longing.
"I like it down Lys. It looks sexy as fuck."

His words make me flush as red as my crimson bikini.

"Um, thanks."

"Lys," he says my new nickname with lust in his tone, pausing as he effortlessly pulls into a parking spot on the esplanade.

His gaze turns to look me up and down the moment the car stops.

"You're fucking gorgeous, you know that, surely."

"Thanks, Kad, you're pretty fucking hot yourself."

We get out of the car, and Kaden is around to my side before I can shut the door properly.

He pushes me against the side of the car, his lips a whisper from mine.

"I fucking love it when you call me Kad."

I don't have time to reply before his lips crash against mine in a hot kiss that takes my breath away, and sends that illicit rush straight through my body to a pool in my bikini bottoms.

I've never felt so turned on by another guy.

Just thinking of Kaden makes me so wet, so wet my clit throbs and as we kiss frantically in public that throbbing is intensified because it feels so naughty, so taboo and it's driving me wild.

Breaking the kiss, I taunt him, "I love it when you call me Lys."

I lean in and nibble on his ear a moment, making him moan.

"And Kad, you make me so wet," I whisper in his ear huskily.

"Fuck, Lys," he groans, kissing me again and sliding a hand up under my dress, his callous hand making me shiver with pleasure as he brushes it across my hips.

My pulse is quickening too and I feel like I'm going to come even though he's not touching my pussy.

Breaking the kiss, I'm panting for breath, stuttering when I speak,

"Kad...fuck...I...I...nearly came."

"You're fucking dirty, Lys. I love it."

I giggle, taking his hand and running towards the beach, dragging him behind me.

"Come on, let's go swimming."

We're both laughing as we strip from our clothes to our bathers and when I see that Kaden is wearing red budgie smugglers that match my red bikini I pull him close to me and sneakily slide my hand into the front of them, squeezing his cock.

"You look fucking hot in these, Kad."

"Yeah, and you look like a sexy delicious candy cane, Lys."

Taking my hand out of his bathers I playfully smack his abs.

"I'm not that pale!" I shriek at him.

"No, you're not, but you're definitely candy I want to eat."

I laugh at his silly teasing words, grabbing his hand again to drag him into the surf.

Glancing around I'm glad to see there aren't too many people around for a Saturday arvo.

Dropping his hand, I casually dive into the waves.

Coming up for air, he's next to me and grabs me around the waist but I squirm away, splashing him and diving back under the water to get away.

We keep playing around in the water, touching each other under the waves.

Pulling me close again Kaden slips a hand into my bikini bottoms and with his forehead against mine and a finger rubbing my clit he says huskily, "Lys I want to fuck you."

I kiss him, moaning against his lips as he rubs my clit more.

I feel like I'm going to come apart just from that naughty touch under the waves.

"Lys, please, can I fuck you? Can I be your first?"

I laugh grabbing his hand and pulling it out of my bikini bottoms to lick it.

The taste of saltwater mixed with my arousal is weirdly erotic.

"I'm not a virgin."

He chuckles. "Really?"

"Yeah lost it years ago, but haven't been with anyone since."

"Right. I thought because you hadn't had an orgasm you were."

"Nope, but you gave me my first orgasm and maybe you can give me my first orgasm from a fuck."

A mega smile curves the corner of his delectable lips.

"Oh, you bet I will be Lys. And it's going to happen right now."

"Here? Like, right now? In the water?"

"No. Over there, here," he says pointing towards the little beach huts lined up along the beach.

"Seriously?"

"Oh yeah," he replies chuckling, effortlessly grabbing me around the waist and throwing me over his shoulder.

He trudges out of the water, shaking his head to get the hair out of his face. And he stalks across the beach, not listening to my protests to put me down until we get to a blue, red and yellow hut.

"Do you own it?" I ask him.

"Fuck no, but this one doesn't have a lock like the others," he says, trailing his eyes along the nearby huts.

Pushing the door it opens effortlessly.

He enters first after quickly glancing around before pulling me inside.

Nineteen | Hut Dance

Pulling Elyse inside the beach hut I push her up against the wall, barely looking around before I'm crashing my lips against hers, and reaching around her back to untie the strings of her bikini top.

She moans against my mouth wrapping her arms around my back, her hands sliding into my bathers.

Palming my arse in her small hands she edges the fabric down my arse cheeks and they fall to my feet.

She breaks the kiss giggling and looking down at my dick that's sprung forward against her flat stomach.

Locking her eyes on mine she lifts the bikini top over her head, throwing it aside carelessly.

"Fuck, you're sexy Lys," I groan watching as she unties the strings at the side of the bikini bottoms, so slowly.

It's sweet torture and I'm licking my lips, salivating from thinking about seeing her pussy up close again. I can't quite believe I'm about to fuck her, about to sink my hard as dick inside her wet cunt.

Her bikini bottoms drop to her feet and my dick throbs when I catch sight of her now completely bare pussy.

"You waxed?"

"Yeah, I thought you might like it."

"You bet I fucking do," I groan, slipping a finger inside her pussy.

She's so turned on, her arousal is dripping down her thighs.

"God Lys, fuck you're wet."

"Mmm, please Kad, fuck me please."

Again I groan, loving her begging for my dick to be inside her.

Kissing her, my dick presses against her cunt, just the tip teasing her and my whole body is throbbing just thinking about coming apart inside her.

Still kissing me, devouring my mouth she jumps up to wrap her legs around my arse and I groan against her lips, my fantasy of feeling her toned legs wrapped around me coming true.

Breaking the kiss she locks eyes with me, panting for breath.

Her arms grip around my neck and she holds on tighter fisting my hair as I push my dick up into her hot cunt. And holy fucking hell does it feel good, so fucking good.

She starts to rock her hips, riding my dick like I'm a damn bull.

Moans and panting breaths are escaping her lips and spurring her on I tease, "God Lys. Where have you fucking been? You fuck me like an animal."

I pound into her harder, impaling her on my dick and lifting her into my arms as I step backward towards the bench seat that wraps around the other side of the hut.

Having slowed my thrusts into her, we're still connected but not moving and kissing her softly, I whisper against her lips, "I want to fuck you from behind Lys."

She gives me a worried look, but slides off my dick, bringing her feet to the floor before she turns around and bends down, placing her hands on the bench seat in front of her. Her arse is in the air, pert and fucking glorious.

Smacking a cheek I shove my dick back inside her dripping pussy and thrust in and out, balls deep.

Our bodies smack together and it's fucking euphoric. I haven't had sex this good in months, maybe in years if I'm being honest.

She turns her head to look at me, her eyes dilated with desire.

"Kaden, fuck that feels so aaa...amazing. I want to come on your cock."

"Not yet, sexy," I tease.

Bending down over her back, I touch her clit teasing it a moment before my hand grips her stomach to bring her back up against my chest.

She stretches up to kiss me and rocking my pelvis against her arse I fuck her harder, fucking her mouth with my tongue at the same time.

Again she's moaning against my lips, showing me how much she's enjoying every second of our fuck.

Breaking the kiss she begs, "Touch me again please Kad. I'm going to come so hard."

I obey her sexy request, reaching down to flick her clit and in mere seconds I feel her pussy clenching around my dick, feel her body start to tremble with her orgasm rushing through her body like a wave.

"Oh my god, oh my god, fuck, fuck! Kaden!" Her words are a scream as the peak of her orgasm hits and with a final thrust I crash down with her in a hard wave of release, filling her cunt with so much cum it's dripping down her thighs when I pull out.

She falls into my arms.

"Fuck Kaden, that was amazing. I...I...don't know what to say."

"Me either Elyse. I haven't fucked a girl and had it feel that good in ages." She gives me a confused look. "I'm bi, Lys."

"Right, I knew that. You told me." She laughs, but her eyes are still giving me the worried look.

"Is that not cool with you?"

"Um, I...um haven't thought about it. But that was seriously the hottest sex ever."

"You're telling me Lys. I don't think I've ever come so hard."

"Don't lie to me, Kaden. I'm not stupid," she says harshly crossing the small hut and putting her bikini back on.

I follow, putting my budgie smugglers back on.

"I never said you were Lys. And I'm not fucking lying."

"Whatever," she snaps pulling the hut door open and rushing out.

She runs over to where we left our belongings on the sand and quickly slips her dress on, grabbing her towel before she runs off down the beach.

I let her go.

I don't know what I could possibly say to her. I'm dumbfounded by the complete one-eighty in her behaviour.
She was right that it was the hottest sex ever, there is no way I can deny that.
But now I'm scared that fucking her has fucked up any chance I have of being with her, and it's scaring me that the thought of never having her in my arms again is like a bullet to the damn heart.
My heart is feeling something for her, but it shouldn't.
I can't have her, and only her.
That's just plain stupid, right?

Twenty | Panic Time

Elyse

Since running down the beach, away from Kaden after we fucked for the first time a few weeks ago I've thought of practically nothing else.

The few times I'd had sex with Zack had never felt that good, and I certainly wasn't lying to Kaden about never having an orgasm before.

But the truth is the fact he's given me two absolutely mind-blowing orgasms and nearly made me come even without touching me, scares the shit out of me.

In the moment when he tore the orgasm from my lips whilst he fucked me, the word *'love'* had tumbled in mind and almost threatened to escape my traitorous lips.

I can't feel that way about Kaden, as he sure as hell doesn't think that way about me.

I'm just a good fuck to him I'm sure.

But I still can't help but want him, and I definitely want to fuck him again, even though my head is telling me that will be a very bad idea for so many reasons.

The first one being that every damn moment I think of him, being with him my whole body throbs with need and my knickers become a damn swimming pool.

But I can't be with him for the other reason that's been plaguing me for the last week.

My period is late.

I'd wanted to tell Bella the other day, the night after Travis stayed over but I didn't want to hear her berating words.

She would have told me off for being so damn stupid that I let him fuck me bare, that I let him fuck me at all.

Still weeks later I can't get him off my mind, and with my rags missing in action even though I'm scared as fuck I need to tell him.

Bringing up his name on my phone, I text him.

Elyse: we need to talk
Kaden: go fuck yourself Elyse.

His reply hurts, a direct hit to my heart that shouldn't be feeling anything for him, but I can't deny it does and his hurtful words make me panic more.

Elyse: I'm serious Kaden...my rags are late
Kaden: are you fucking shitting me?
Elyse: no...nearly a week now
Kaden: go get a damn test...and come over after
Elyse: no...I'll send you a message

I want to add that I'm not going to see him or talk to him until he apologises but I don't, instead I grab my wallet and keys and head to the chemist to get a pregnancy test.

At the chemist, I'm staring at all the different pregnancy tests on the shelves completely stupefied.

There's so many different types, some funny shaped sticks and others flimsy strips of paper.

Again I wish I'd told Bella so she could have been here with me.

She'd know which one I should get, having obviously had to use one when she found out she was pregnant with my niece Nora.

I love being an Aunty but staring at the pregnancy tests makes me wonder about whether I could be a mum myself, and whether I want to be at all.

I especially don't want to be a mum at nineteen but I guess I'll have to cross that bridge if I'm pregnant.

Glancing around the store for a moment, I bite the bullet grabbing one of the digital Clearblue tests that says pregnant.

I won't be able to deny the words if they're right in front of my eyes.

Quickly I pay for it, heading out to go home.

On the tram on the way home, my stomach is in knots and cramping.

I'm feeling incredibly anxious and getting home I run straight to the bathroom, pulling down my knickers quickly with my leggings.

Ripping the packet open I don't even read the instructions before sitting on the dunny.

I'm about to take it but look down to my knickers at my feet to see that they're stained with blood; its started.

I've never felt so relieved and getting up from the dunny I undress completely to run a bath.

Sinking into the warm water a couple of minutes later feels so amazing for the cramps that are stabbing me from the inside.

I grab my phone from the clothes basket I'd left it on beside the bath and call Kaden, putting him on loudspeaker.

I'm surprised he answers and seems to be in a better mood than he was earlier.

"Hey, Elyse."

"Hey, Kaden." I gulp, not sure how to approach telling him he's off the hook.

"So, did you take a test?"

"Yeah, it was negative. Thank god."

"Thank fuck for that...and Lys?"

"Yeah, I'm sorry about earlier. I shouldn't have said that."

"It's ok. I shouldn't have run off after we fucked and not spoken to you."

"Yeah I haven't made much of an effort either, but things with this firefighter gig are fucking tough."

"Yeah, I can help take your mind off it."

"Not tonight Lys, I'm fucking wrecked and traffic is a bitch."

"Ok, all good. Text me."

"I will. Are we good?"

"Yeah, we're good."

"Sweet, have a good night Lys."

He hangs up and I put my phone down on the clothes basket again, pushing my body down under the water for a moment.

I'm glad things are better with Kaden again, as shutting him out hurt like hell.

Just hearing his voice again has made me horny as anything, and once again I'm scared that I'm going to fall for him.

Twenty-One | Intimate Touching

Since the pregnancy scare a few days ago, Elyse hasn't left my mind.
I've been in the thick of training, having to travel out to the northern
suburbs every day in peak hour traffic and the whole drive there and
back I think of her.

Coming home I eat something quickly and fall into bed thinking of her,
wishing my sheets still smelled like her.
She hasn't been avoiding me, but we've not spoken, just sent cheeky,
silly texts to each other.
It's kinda crazy that I saved one of the pics she'd sent me and put it as
my lock screen.
It's so damn cute though, her luscious chocolate hair half up on the top
of her head, her tongue sticking out cheekily and her dark hazel eyes
looking away from the camera.
Every time I look at it, at her, my dick aches and my lips tingle.
If I don't see her again soon, I swear I'm going to combust and my dick
and hand are both going to fall off from constantly jerking off to
thoughts of her, thoughts of fucking her in the beach hut.

It fucking hurt that she thought my words were lies, but they aren't.
No chick has ever made me come that hard in my fucking life. And I
desperately want to fuck her again, this time with a franger on my dick
because even though fucking her bare was beyond amazing I can't take
that risk again.

My phone pings in my pocket as I cross the threshold, feeling like
someone has sucked all the oxygen out of my body.
It'd been a really hard day at training, fighting a fake apartment blaze.

All I want to do is crash on my bed, and think of fucking Elyse.
Actually fucking her would be so much better and fishing my phone out I see a message from her on my screen that makes my heart race with anticipation.

Elyse: Kad, I miss you. Can I come over for some fun?

I quickly reply.

Kaden: miss you too, sexy minx. Come over in twenty. Just got home.
Elyse: ok xx

Heading to my bedroom, I strip off my daks and suspenders, the navy T-shirt I wear underneath and throw them into the laundry basket before stepping into the open shower in the ensuite bathroom.
Standing under the spray of warm water I wash the soot away, slicking my hair back against my head.
Thoughts of Elyse are tumbling in my head, especially the kisses at the end of her text.
She's never sent me anything of the sort before and it makes that odd feeling stir in my stomach.
The way she gets to me is fucking scary.

God, I'm a fucking nutcase. I can't...I can't be with her. I'm not enough.

My dick is painfully hard when I turn off the shower after standing under the water for way too long.
Grabbing a towel I hear the doorbell ring, and quickly drying off I pull some shorts out of the laundry basket, yanking them on as I stumble to the front door.

Opening it to find Elyse on my doorstep, even though I'm expecting her my mouth falls to the ground taking in the sight of her.

Her chocolate hair is down, immaculately brushed so it's shiny and she's wearing baggy Adidas trackies with cuffed ankles, essentially boy trackies as they hang low in the crotch.

She's paired them with a slightly baggy puma t-shirt, and I can just see the outline of her tits under it.

As her eyes gaze over my body, my dick is tenting the front of the shorts even more now.

I can see her nipples harden through the thin fabric of her t-shirt and I wonder again if she's braless.

"Hey Lys," I greet her with a smirk, "come in and please tell me you're not wearing a bra?"

She laughs, crossing the threshold and following me inside as I step back and then close the door behind her.

"I'm wearing a bralette," she replies giggling and lifting the hem of her T-shirt up, "See?" she teases showing me too much tempting skin.

I avert my gaze for a moment, knowing looking at her gorgeous body is going to make my dick damn near explode.

But I can't stop my eyes from darting back to look at her, and I catch a glimpse of her tit, the nipple poking out the side of the lacy cup of the bralette.

"Fuck Lys, you do realise that you're practically falling out of that. You can hardly call that thing a...a what?"

She lifts her top up again, tucking her hard pink nipple back into the lace.

"A bralette," she tells me blushing.

"Yeah that," I reply laughing when her gaze locks on my dick that is definitely saying ,'hello' at the front of my shorts.

"Um, your cock is hard, Kad."

"You don't say...you made it hard you minx."

"Sorry."

"No, you're not," I jeer at her and step closer to her, battling with myself at getting closer to her again.

I'm sure there's consequences for being with her, wanting her so much.

I haven't really told anyone about us, about how much I want her and I wonder if she's told Bella.

If she has, I'm surprised I've not heard from her with a warning about staying away from her baby sister.

"Kaden, are you ok? You seem weird, distant. Is it because of the baby scare?"

"Yeah, kinda," I tell her sitting down on the couch to try and resist the urge to kiss her breathless.

"Well, you're off the hook, remember. My period started."

"I know, but that doesn't mean I'm not scared Lys."

"What do you mean? Scared?"

"Have you told anyone about us? That we fucked?"

"No, no one."

"Not even Bella?"

"Definitely not Bella. Have you?"

"I've kinda mentioned you to Bren, but I haven't told him we fucked. You're my dirty secret Lys." I wink at her, and the crimson blush creeps up her cheeks. Her whole body would be flushed; she can't keep her desire hidden.

I lean forward, closer to her on the couch to push her back down against it.

"God Lys, I want you so fucking bad."

"I want you to," she murmurs reaching up to fist my wet hair in her fingers, bringing my face closer to hers so our lips are just a whisper apart.

"Kiss me, Kad," she moans, her eyes dark with desire and begging me. Softly I crash my lips to hers, and just like that the kiss is frantic, full of the pent up lust that is pulsing through our bodies.

The want and need to be together after it's been weeks apart.

I shouldn't feel this way, I've never felt this way.

I want all of her, again and again, never wanting to break this kiss but wanting to fuck her, to fuck her so hard another explosive orgasm comes bellowing out of her pretty pink lips that fit with mine like they meant to be on mine forever.

Fuck! Forever...no...no...not forever

Blood is rushing through my body; Lys's tongue teasing mine in an erotic dance and that's the only reason I'm thinking these stupid thoughts.

All the blood is obviously rushing to my dick and my brain is going haywire from the lack of blood. That's the only explanation for such crazy thoughts.

Breaking the kiss, feeling suddenly breathless, I blurt out my words, "I want to fuck you."

"We can't Kaden. I'm still bleeding."

"Oh, shit...well...I could fuck you in the arse instead."

A look of shock and wonderment crosses her face. But her words almost make my dick shrivel up in protest.

"I don't think so. I'm not feeling up to anything like that, but maybe we could just pash some more?" Her words are pleading, and even if I can't fuck her until she screams right now I can still make her come so hard she'll see stars.

"Fine but only if I can play with your arse whilst we pash?"

She gapes at me. "Why? I don't think that will feel good."

I chuckle, shoving my hand into the back of her trackies when her hips involuntarily thrust up against my crotch.

"Trust me Lys it will feel good and I'm going to fuck you in the arse at some point so it's prep."

"Um, ok...I guess, but please be gentle."

"Of course," I reply, kissing her as I slip my hand into her knickers.

I can feel her tensing her body up, worried about the intimate touch in her virgin hole.

Pulling back I brush the hair from her face with my other hand.

"Relax Lys. Just kiss me and relax your body. Let me in and I promise it will feel good...so good."

"Ok," she replies breathlessly kissing me again, this time melting against me, taking my lips with hers and biting down on them when my finger makes contact with her arse.

As we continue kissing frantically I touch her arse, circling and swirling my finger over it gently. The contact makes her moan against my lips, and it's making my dick scream for attention, but this is about her.

Tearing her lips from mine, her pelvis arches up as I slip my finger inside her arse hole, massaging it with my finger, slowly, teasingly, in and out.

"Oh my god, Kad, fuck...don't stop," she screams out, lifting her head a little off the couch to look at me.

I can't wipe the fucking grin off my face. Seeing her in pleasure is fucking infectious. Giggling she puts her hands on my sides and daks me, grabbing my dick in her hands and stroking it. And god does it feel good to have her hands on me again.

Teasing each other is fucking amazing, her hands on me are absolute bliss.

"Tell me Lys? Does it feel good?"

"It feels a...a...a...amazing!"

"Then come for me Lys. Come with me."

She moans, her body shaking and I can feel her arse muscles clenching as well. Lifting up her T-shirt with my other hand I watch the pleasure starting to rock through her body, her eyes darting between my dick and my face.

"Kaden, Kaden, fuck, god I'm coming!"

Her body convulses with a shattering orgasm, just as ropes of cum spurt out of my dick onto her stomach.

She's panting for breath, and taking my hand out of her pants I wipe the cum from off her stomach. And lay over her to kiss her forehead softly.

"Damn Lys, that was hot. Watching you come is my new addiction."

She doesn't reply, just lets out a moan, and pulls my face to hers for a hungry kiss.

A guy could certainly get used to her kisses, to making her come and that's damn fucking scary.

I'm fucking addicted to Elyse.

And that's so fucking bad.

Twenty-Two | Dirty Research

Elyse

Sitting in the packed lecture theatre at uni the next day thoughts of Kaden fill my mind. I can't concentrate on anything but thinking about him touching my arse last night and making me come so hard I saw stars.

Fucking stars in my eyes.

I'd always thought that shit was myth worthy romance novel crap, but no, it absolutely fucking happened and now I'm sitting here, bored out of my freaking brains in my Animal Management course feeling the all too familiar ache in my knickers.

Since my iPad is in front of me on the little desk I open it up to Safari and type *'anal sex'* into google.

I glance across at my friend Maia when her eyes focus on my search.

She leans into my side.

"Why are you looking up anal sex Elyse?"

"I um...my um...friend...touched my arse last night."

She screws her face up in disgust. "Eww seriously?"

I laugh softly. "Yeah whilst we were pashing on his couch."

Maia scoffs. "So weird."

"It was at first, but it actually felt good and I..." I lower my voice and lean into her Maia's ear to whisper, "I came really hard."

"Shit...so anal really?" Maia practically bellows.

My face flushes, sure the whole lecture theatre just heard her loud question.

Glaring at her I reply, "Don't say it so loud, but yeah I'm thinking about it. I want to make Kaden happy."

She gives me dagger eyes, again scoffing like she thinks I'm a complete idiot.

"He must be some guy if you want to do that to make him happy. I thought only gays did it that way."

"He's bi," I reply laughing.

"Oh right," she replies, standing up as the lecture has ended.

I wait until everyone has left, closing my iPad cover and shoving it in my bag.

Mentally I'm kicking myself for looking up something so intimate in class, but I can't think about much else and want to rush straight over to Kaden's to tell him what I've been thinking about all night, but I know he's super busy with training and needs some space.

Most nights I message him, thinking of him as I lie in bed and he's clearly tired as his replies usually come first thing in the morning when I'm still sleeping.

Walking out of the lecture theatre the corridors are abuzz with people rushing to and from classes, and with my head down a little I bump into a familiar figure who drops his books all over the floor.

Picking them up and handing them back to him we stand up together.

His eyes lock on mine.

"Oh my god, Ely is that you?"

Sheepishly I reply, "Hey Zack, what are you doing here?"

He lets out a sweet chuckle. "I go here, Elyse. We both got dux remember? And I got into medicine remember?"

I nod. "Yep, so um, yep I gotta go."

Of course I remember the last couple of years, studying with Zack, losing my virginity to Zack and crying on Lillie's shoulder when Zack decided I wasn't worth hanging out with anymore.

He'd fucked me and dumped me, and was still popular as hell, and smart enough to equal me for dux of Stawell high.

It still makes me so angry thinking about it.

Shrugging and pushing my bag up onto my shoulder more I walk off.

I can hear his feet pounding the floor as he runs after me and I stop, my back against the wall when he reaches me touching my shoulder.

It doesn't send the same rush through my body that it used to, but the look he's giving me strikes me with a strange longing, that familiarity hitting me hard in the chest.

"Ely, would you go out for a coffee with me?" he asks pleadingly, giving me puppy dog eyes.

My mind wanders to Kaden for a minute, and I bite down on my lip when I reply, "Um, I've um…" I cut my words short, not sure whether to label Kaden as my boyfriend.

"Got a boyfriend?" Zack asks, his smile dropping from his lips.

"Well um, no not exactly but…"

He laughs then. "It's just coffee Ely…after class on Thursday?"

"Ok," I agree, smiling, "but just as friends."

"Friends," he replies smiling back and walking away.

I curse under my breath, as confused thoughts start running through my head from my dirty research but also bumping into Zack of all people.

Seeing him definitely brings up past feelings, but also past pain and I don't know whether even seeing him as friends is a good idea.

Like he said though, it's just coffee.

Coffee never hurt anyone, right?

Twenty-Three | Friendly Advice

Elyse

As soon as I get home I drop my bag down and flop down on my bed to FaceTime Lillie. Her smiling face pops up on my screen almost immediately.

"Hey, Ely. What's up bestie?"

"Hey, Lil. You'll never guess who I saw today?"

She smiles, laughing. "I don't know. The man in the moon."

I laugh at her silly childhood song reference, singing the words in my head from the song we made up together about the man in the moon, that we forced Austin (her older brother) to write music for.

"No you dufus. I ran into Zack."

"Oh my, is he still cute?"

"Um, yeah I guess Lil. But he um…"

"He what? Did he kiss you?"

"No, he asked me out for coffee."

"That's good, isn't it? Don't you still like him?"

"Um, no…I don't know. I'm really confused."

"Why Ely?"

"Because of Kaden."

"Who's Kaden? Tell me Ely!" she shrieks excitedly.

"He's a friend. And knows Austin."

"Oh really? He knows my brother?"

"Yeah well he did but he's so awesome Lillie, and being with him is so amazing."

"So go out with them both?" she suggests laughing and sticking her tongue out at me.

I'm shocked, wondering if I'm actually talking to my sweet innocent best friend or if some other crazy person has taken over her body.

If I couldn't see her face on my screen I'd honestly think that was the case.

"Who are you? And what have you done with Lil?"

Lillie laughs. "It's still me Ely, but I'm just saying I don't think it would hurt to go out with Zack. Maybe he's changed."

"Yeah maybe. Anyway, Lil, I gotta go and make something to eat."

"Is Bella home? Can I say hi?"

"Nah, she's not here. Probably at Travis's."

"Ok, well say, 'hi' from me."

"I will. Good seeing ya face, ugly."

"You too, uglier. But I'll be down soon."

"I know. Can't wait to see you in the flesh. Bye bestie."

I wave at her and she smiles back, waving as she says, "Bye bestie."

After Lillie hangs up, her face disappearing from my screen I get up and head to the kitchen to make some dinner, all the while thoughts about dating two guys fill my head.

It makes me feel like I'm a hussy.

But maybe it might be fun. And getting the milk out for cereal I make a mental note to get myself on birth control.

Twenty-Four | Yucky Coffee
Elyse

Thursday came around so quick my head is spinning with anxiety.
I'd not seen Kaden for over a week, and I'm missing him.
We'd texted each other, but it wasn't the same as seeing him of course and I was on edge, with my hand down my knickers a lot more than I care to admit.

Getting dressed in jeans and a t-shirt I glare at myself in the bathroom mirror, wondering if I should bother putting on makeup, if I should make an effort for a date with Zack.

He's just a friend Elyse remember. You don't wear makeup around Kaden and well you know how he looks at you.

Shrugging I sigh, deciding to forgo makeup and opting to just put my hair up.
Passing Bella's room, I think about telling her I'm going to see Zack, but she's asleep and I don't want to wake her, so instead I grab my bag and head to class.

Anxiousness plagues me the whole time I'm in class before the coffee date. And I can't concentrate again on animal management.
I'll have to get my head in the game at some point for it or I'm sure to fail the subject because I've got no way of managing my damn feelings.
The anxiousness doesn't let up, even right up to when I meet Zack outside the lecture theatre after the class ends.

Walking out the uni building with Zack by my side, the tension is thick and it's making my anxiety reach boiling point.
Why the hell I agreed to this, I have no idea.
It's making me feel really edgy.
He's glaring at me as we walk to the Gloria Jeans around the corner from Uni. His hand brushes against mine and it makes me jolt back in shock.
I don't want him close.
It's clear he's still attracted to me, just from the way he looks at me out of the corner of his eyes like he's trying to not make his staring obvious.

Reaching the coffee shop he steps back as I push the door open, and his fingers brush across the small of my back.
Again I want to retreat at his touch. It certainly doesn't have the same effect on me as Kaden's touch.
We quickly order at the counter, taking a seat and the whole time Zack keeps touching me. But I feel nothing, no butterflies in the stomach, no tingles, absolutely zilch.
It makes me wonder if I ever had feelings for him.
"So Ely, how have you been?" he asks, acting nervous which is odd for him. He'd always been super confident, even though he was geeky smart, he was never shy.
"I've been fine Zack," I tell him , chuckling because I feel stupid making small talk, "You?"
"I've been good. Seeing you though, it made me realise how much I've missed you."
He smiles, his eyes lighting up and it turns my gut.
"You've missed me?"
"Yeah, Ely. I've not been with another girl since you."
I scoff—loud—waving my arms and nearly whacking the waitress in the face when she brings our coffee's to the table.
I smile at her, apologising under my breath when she puts my Vanilla Latte down in front of me and Zach's Mocha in front of him.

She nods and walks away, giving us an odd look like she can lip read our conversation.

"Bullshit. As if Zack. You dropped me after we had sex like I meant nothing to you."

He drops his head down, hiding his eyes. "I was scared, Ely."

Again I scoff, not believing a word that's coming out of his mouth.

"Right...scared. How do you think I felt Zack? I was sixteen."

Again he looks forlorn, the odd sparkle from earlier gone from his eyes.

He takes a long sip of his Mocha, before looking at me.

"Yeah, I know. I'm sorry, but I've not stopped thinking about you."

I take a long sip of my latte, completely lost for words.

I don't feel anything for him, but it's sad to see him hurting.

"I um...yeah," I reply, gulping down a bit more coffee.

He's silent, just staring at me as we continue drinking our coffee's.

Once I've finished I try to get some words out, but I don't know what to say so I'm glad when he puts his cup down and stands up to head out.

Together we walk out to the tram stop.

It's awkward standing there, looking at each other speechless. He's probably thinking something completely different to me.

I honestly just want him to fuck off, and I'm hoping I never have to see him again.

He turns to look at me, his hand brushing my arm.

"Ely..." he muses softly, leaning a little closer.

I panic, about to push him away when his lips press to mine in a soft kiss. I don't register for a moment, not completely repulsed but he tastes of cigarettes and coffee, and pulling back I try not to gag.

His lips have curved into a slight smile at the corner.

"Go out with me again, Ely, please?"

My gut churns with his question because I don't want to go out with him again.

"I'll um think about it," I blurt out.
"Fine," he snaps, then laughs, "don't be a stranger though sexy."
I cringe at the nickname, not liking the sound of it from his lips, instead of Kaden's.
I'm glad that the tram pulls up then so I don't have to spend another minute in awkward silence or risk having him kissing me again. And boarding the tram I wave at him.
As the tram rattles away my thoughts wander to times gone by with Zack, how I felt about him in the past. I don't have regrets, but I'm definitely not feeling the same towards him as I once did, all because of Kaden.
Just thinking of him is making the butterflies flit in my belly, and the all too familiar rush of warmth is hitting my knickers.
I don't think I've just got a crush on Kaden anymore.
I'm falling for him.
And I want more than anything to tell Bella, but I don't want to worry her as she's got a lot on her mind.
But I've never felt like this, and I know that's something that my sister would definitely understand.

Twenty-Five | Coffee Again

Elyse

After another lecture, my head is spinning with new information and pounding from a headache right behind my eyes.

Needing a coffee, and some strong painkillers I head into the Uni cafe.

The coffee isn't the greatest but I need the caffeine stat, and can't be bothered heading around to Gloria Jeans.

Having ordered a double shot strong latte, I'm waiting in line for my order when someone stumbles, bumping into my shoulder. Rubbing it, I jerk my head to the side coming face to face with Zack again.

I'm shocked seeing him, as I've been making a conscious effort to avoid him for the last month.

Things with Kaden had been going steady, not that I'd seen him as much as I'd wanted to with him always giving me some lame excuse about being too tired or having to go to boxing, and even one which I called bullshit on, seeing his family.

Zack is glaring at me, in that annoying way, his signature look.

"Hey Ely, I'm sorry about the other week," he says with a sickly sweet smile.

"It's fine. You don't have to be sorry," I tell him, my eyes not meeting his but glaring at the barista whose eyes meet mine over the coffee machine.

"Yeah, I do. I shouldn't have kissed you," he declares seeming apologetic, but I'm not sure if he's being sincere. He'd made his feelings pretty clear.

"Um yeah, but...um," I stammer, feeling like a complete idiot.

My name is called and grabbing my coffee I sip it turning away from Zack to sit down at a table. He follows after grabbing his coffee and sits down across from me on the picnic-style table.

His eyes lock on me, making my head look up at him, albeit reluctantly but his stare is so damn intense.

"I really do miss you, Ely. I was honestly telling you the truth that I haven't been with anyone."

He seems really sincere this time, with these words and my heart goes out to him, our past friendship tugging at me.

"I know, I haven't either...well until recently."

I take another sip of coffee, gulping it down.

"So you do have a boyfriend?" he asks with a hint of sadness in his tone.

"No, well, um...I'm kinda seeing someone. I...um."

I'm mumbling because I don't know what to call Kaden. I want him to be my boyfriend, but since Lillie is the only one I've told about him I really don't think I can give him that label, and I'm sure if I mentioned it to him he'd run to the fucking outback quicker than a damn emu.

"What Ely? Tell me, please. As a friend," Zack says pleadingly resting his hand on mine on the table.

It's a super sweet gesture, reminding me of the old Zack.

The Zack who studied with me in my room, laughing and smiling at me when we got a little to close.

The Zack who didn't throw me aside after he'd fucked me. And I liked that Zack, so I lean a little closer to him, talking in a hushed voice,

"We've only been out like twice officially, kinda...but I um...slept with him and I'm really confused. I really like him, but he's bi and I don't know what he really wants from me."

Zack is clearly shocked, his mouth dropping open. "You seriously slept with him after your second date?"

"Yeah...I know I shouldn't have but I've never felt like this before."

He scoffs, "Harsh Ely. But I get it."
He has that forlorn look on his face again like I'm actually breaking his heart and I feel like such a bitch.
"Really? I'm sorry to dump this on you. It's just really confusing and I don't have anyone to talk to."
His eyebrow raises at me questioningly. "What about Bella? Surely she has some advice."
"Yeah, she probably does, but I'm too embarrassed to talk to her."
He nods even though I'm sure he doesn't understand. "Fair enough. So nothing is going to happen with us then?"
I shake my head at him, trying to smile to let him down easy.
"I'm sorry Zack, I don't think so. I really like Kaden. I think I need to give him a chance."
"Ok, but friends yeah?" he asks, smiling again.
"Friends," I reply, downing the rest of my coffee and getting up.
I round the table and pull him into a hug. He squeezes me and pulling back I laugh.
It definitely feels platonic, and when I pull back to see his quirky smile on his cute face I know my friend from my past before we fucked is back in my life.

Walking out I ask him, "So does this friendship mean I can call you Za-za again?"
He laughs hard, clutching his stomach and winking at me.
"Only in private, Ely-el."
"Ok," I laugh, smiling when we part ways and he kisses me on the cheek.
"See you soon, Za-za," I tease, watching him start to walk away.
"Definitely, Ely-el, you can count on it," he calls back to me, turning his head to see me flip him the bird.
I definitely don't have feelings for Zack Rudensteine anymore, but having an old friend back in my life feels good.

Caz May

Twenty-Six | Beach Shower

For late August it's quite warm, and feeling restless and aching all over nothing feels better than stretching out for a swim in the ocean.

As always these days, Elyse is on my mind, even more so as memories of our first date at the beach crash into my mind as I lay on my back in the waves.

We'd gone out on another to my fave restaurant and she'd ordered steak, devouring it like a trooper. That turned me on so bad, as I love a girl who can eat a decent meal.

I'd wanted to take her back to mine for dessert, meaning I wanted to taste her for dessert, but she got all shy and it was a shot to my dick to calm the fuck down.

It had me so confused, because everything between us after the baby scare was going well, and then she shut down like she didn't want me anymore.

It shouldn't hurt but it does.

Even her messages seem more platonic and friendly, making me wonder if I'm reading too much into her feelings for me.

After spending way too long in the warm sea, I get out, wandering up the beach and looking at all the chicks already getting out their bikinis as though it's summer.

I can only think of Elyse, in her crimson red bikini. Just the thought of her in that makes me crack a fat as I head to the outdoor shower on the shoreline.

Closing my eyes, I tip my head back under the spray of water, thinking of how dirty and risqué it would be to fuck Elyse in this very spot under the stars one night when I feel someone step up next to me.

I tell myself I'm dreaming, that I don't suddenly feel a kiss on my lips.
A kiss so hot, my dick throbs.
I'm about to moan, about to call out 'Lys' but I'm too scared to open my eyes and stop this kiss in case it's just some fucked up very vivid daydream.
The kiss is broken by the initiator and I feel a hand grip my dick, sliding into the front of my board shorts.
My eyes shoot open, now knowing this is no daydream and it's definitely not Elyse's hand in my daks.
Looking the stranger up and down I push her away, completely gobsmacked.
"You gay or something?" she snaps at me, her nostrils flaring.
"No, I'm not gay," I snap at her, annoyed, "But I kinda have a chick I'm doing so could you rack off."
I glare at her scornfully and she turns to leave me to shower without another word.
It feels like everyone on the damn beach is staring at me, and I can't stand it anymore.
Thankfully, thanks to the stranger my dick has deflated from it's Elyse induced hard-on, but still, I feel the glares, so I decide to head home for a night on the couch.

Before heading home, I grab some greasy fish and chips to eat. And some beers to down.
Maybe getting tanked will block out some thoughts of Elyse for a while, but I doubt it.

The moment I step inside the front door, I kick my thongs off and flop down on the couch to eat.
Flicking on the TV, I scroll through Netflix deciding on watching the 'Big Bang theory' for a laugh. It'd always been a go-to show when I needed to get myself out of a funk.

After watching a couple of episodes I've downed a few beers, and I'm feeling the edge of a buzz hitting me. I'm sure that's what makes me grab my phone from the kitchen to message Elyse.

I'm downing another beer, leaning back on the kitchen bench when I type.

Kaden: you busy Lys? ;)
Elyse: yeah it's Bella's last night here. She's moving out tomorrow
Kaden: oh yeah, didn't think that was happening so soon
Elyse: yeah it's snuck up on us for sure.
Kaden: yeah...maybe I can come over tomorrow night then.

I type those words—then delete them—before typing them again and pressing send. Elyse replies almost instantly, and my fucking dick jolts in my daks.

Elyse: i'd be down for that
Kaden: sweet Lys. I'll message you tomorrow.

I go back to the couch, scoffing down the rest of the fish and chips.

My head wanders to thoughts of her, of being alone with her, without the chance of being caught and thinking about her, of course, gives me a massive hard-on.

I wonder if she'll suck me off this time.

Sticking my hand into the front of my daks, I fist my dick, stroking it rhythmically, thinking about her mouth on me and thinking about giving her an Aussie kiss.

I'm not sure when I last gave a girl one, but it doesn't fucking matter.

I cream my daks then, my dick spasming with my release as I moan Elyse's name.

God, I want to fucking taste her so bad.

Twenty-Seven | Dirty Kisses

Like an idiot, I'm searching through my wardrobe for what to wear to
Elyse's. I'm probably not going to be wearing the outfit for long, but part
of me wants to blow her away and make her sexy boyshort knickers
damp with arousal when she sees me.
She'll probably be wearing something that'll knock me for a six.
I'd really fucked up at training today, failing the damn beep test because
I was too in my head thinking about tonight.
Thankfully though, I have another chance to nail it next week. I can't
afford to fuck this opportunity up. It's tough as hell, fiery hell, but I want
to be a Firefighter more than anything.
Deciding on some black knit drawstring shorts and a skin-tight white
tank I dress quickly, slicking my hair back but forgoing gel, so I can feel
Elyse's hands running through my hair.
I haven't told her that is basically crack for my dick. It's weird, but I find
it hella good and strangely erotic.
I also splash on some aftershave, Calvin Klein One; My go to fave.

Quickly I text Elyse, dashing out the door to the Commodore.

Kaden: cant wait to see you tonight Lys

Her reply comes as I slip into the driver's seat, and it makes my dick
throb already.

Elyse: cant wait to touch you and maybe taste you x
Kaden: tasting sounds fun...

God I can't fucking wait to taste her and have her finally taste my cum

Stupidly I gun it to Elyse's, hoping I didn't pass any speed cameras or I've done my career in a flash of light. I park outside, my heart hammering in my fucking chest just thinking about seeing Lys which scares me.
I don't want to feel, I don't want to get bogged down in emotional shit again. It hurts too fucking much but Elyse just gets to me and rapping on her front door I breathe in deep, telling my damn heart to calm down.

She opens the door a moment later and I feel my dick jolt in my shorts. She's standing against the doorframe, smirking at me and her outfit is begging me to tear it off her sexy body. Her short pyjama shorts practically show her pussy; they're so high up her toned creamy thighs.

God, she's fucking stunning.

As if that's not enough, she's wearing a skintight tank top with a scoop neck that makes her tits pop up into perfect mounds, her cleavage fucking delectable.
I don't even say, *'hello'* to fucking mesmerised by her, with her body practically on show and her chocolate locks down, cupping her pert arse. It's fucking stupid but I'm jealous of her hair getting to touch her arse all damn day.

Giving me a cheeky smirk, she steps away from the door to invite me in. "Hey, Kad. You look hot." She licks her lips, her gaze falling to my cock that's practically pointing straight at her; it's so damn hard.
Once I've walked in she closes the door, flicking the lock closed and giving me the same cheeky smirk with an accompanying giggle she steps closer.
Placing her hands on my waist her fingers brush against my v muscle. My skin heats at her touch, and I groan before kissing her.

She whimpers against my mouth, pleasure rushing through both of us when we push our bodies closer together.
My clothes suddenly feel so restricting and I want to tear them off, as well as hers until I have her naked in my arms.
Seeing her in clothes is enough to make my cock as hard as steel, so seeing her naked is sure to make me self combust, and tonight the promise of tasting each other is in the air.

Breaking the kiss I'm about to open my mouth to ask if we should head to her bedroom when she plunges my daks—trackies and boxers—to the floor without warning.
Her eyes are dark with lust and seeing my cock so incredibly hard she hisses in appreciation, biting down on her lip a moment.
The way her eyes shine with lust turns me on more, my cock throbbing and ready for her to wrap her lips around it.
"Lys, please...please..suck me."
Her cheeks flush, and she drops to her knees in front of me.
My heart races and I lift my tank off, throwing it aside.

Inhaling a deep breath I grab her hair, and guide her onto my cock.
She whimpers when I push her head down further onto my length.
I know my cock is big, but Elyse swallows it down, taking it into her mouth like a damn icy pole. Her tongue starts licking it, teasing me with swirling motions in and out of the tip.

Pulling off for a moment she looks up at me, panting a little.
"That feels amazing, you sexy minx. Can I come in your mouth now, Lys?"
She nods, moaning as she takes my cock back into her mouth.
Teasingly she takes it in and out, just to the tip and every time she licks it all over.

It's driving me crazy, I'm on the damn brink and again fisting her hair I push her down to take my entire length in her mouth.

My cock throbs, spasming hard as I shoot my load down her throat.

She gasps, and I see her swallow hard before she pulls off and stands up, looking at me with a cheshire cat smile.

"Wow, Lys. You give good head, sexy minx."

"Um, thanks, I've only done it like once...and I bit his cock so hard he screamed."

"You can bite me anytime," I tease, winking at her, "but right now, you need to show me where your bedroom is so I can spread your thighs wide and taste your pretty pussy."

Her cheeks flush and she shivers in delight, taking my hand and practically running down a hallway opposite us.

The moment she enters her bedroom she starts to strip off her clothes, tossing them aside carelessly. And in barely a minute she's standing in front of me only wearing a g-string, if you could even call the scrap of lace covering her pussy a g-string.

"God, Lys, you're fucking hot. Lie back on the bed, and spread your legs."

She obeys, with a sexy smirk on her face the entire time.

Her knees hang over the edge of the bed and her legs are scissored open.

Kneeling down in between her thighs, I lean closer to her pussy and inhale her arousal. And she smells fucking glorious, musky but sweet. She's sitting up, so she can see me, and giving her a wink I lick her clit through the lace.

She lets out a moan, an *'oh'* when my tongue slides up and down her slit. Tasting her through the lace is mouthwatering and I need more.

"Sexy minx, can I take these off?" I ask, hooking my fingers in the elastic at the sides.

"Yes, yes, please," she pants in anticipation.

Lifting her arse of the bed I glide the g-string down her legs and it drops to the floor at her feet. She takes a deep breath, preparing herself, and before she exhales I bite her clit, slipping a finger inside her dripping pussy.

She's so turned on, it makes my cock throb, thinking of sliding inside her, but tonight is about tasting pleasure only.

Pulling my finger out I replace it with my tongue, lapping up her delicious musky cream. Her hips are writhing, moans escaping her lips as I devour her pussy.

I've given plenty of chicks Aussies but there's something about Elyse showing her pleasure that makes me want to never come up for air.

I continue sucking and licking her clit, and inserting my tongue deep within her pussy.

I know she's close when she grips the sheets in her fist, clenching her whole body and letting a squeal escape her lips.

"Oh my god, Kaden!" she screams out as I bite her clit again, flicking my tongue against it.

Her hips shake and panting she bellows, "Fuck, oh my god fuck, I'm coming. I'm coming."

And her release spills out, onto my face. I lap it all up, standing up and leaning over to pin her down on the bed.

Crashing my lips to hers, I kiss her so hard, letting her taste herself on my tongue. Her moans against my lips when she licks them are wild and make my cock twitch.

Breaking the kiss she looks at me with hooded eyes.

"That was so amazing, Kad. How are you so good at oral sex?"

I laugh. "Practice, sexy minx."

"You must have had a lot of practice."

"Some, but that doesn't matter. I only wanna make you feel good, Lys."

She giggles sweetly. "I feel better than good, Kad."

"Me too," I reply kissing her again, softly and then deeper when she moans against my lips.

Pashing her is just as arousing as tasting her or fucking her and I know thats damn scary because kisses only turn me on this much when feelings are involved.

Even though I know I'm completely fucked and it's a beyond moronic idea I break the kiss and ask her, "Lys, can I stay the night? I wanna wake up next to you."

She doesn't reply, just wraps her lean legs around my arse and kisses me, completely taking my breath away.

Yep, feelings. I think i'm going to fall, but I can't.

Twenty-Eight | Moving Bestie

Elyse

Rolling over in bed realising I'm naked I murmur, looking at Kaden.

Thoughts of the night before hit me.

Actually tasting each other was so hot and then pashing like crazy, touching each other before we fell asleep wrapped in each others arms was just divine.

His eyes flutter open and focusing on me he smiles.

"Morning, sexy minx. Did I taste your sweet pussy last night?"

"Yeah, foxy you did, and I sucked your cock."

"Foxy huh? And yeah you did suck my cock. Fancy doing it again?"

Smirking I reach down to grab his hard morning cock in my grip.

"I'd love to foxy, but Lillie is moving in today and we have to get up."

"Damn, Lys. Just pash me for a minute then?"

"Fine, but only cause you're irresistible," I taunt rolling over so I'm on top of him when he lays on his back.

Cupping my cheeks he pulls me down for a kiss, licking my lips and taking my tongue with his.

His cock is so hard and it's teasing me, at my entrance. It feels so amazing, and still kissing him I rock my hips, my pussy sliding up and down along his length, without it slipping inside me.

He breaks the kiss moaning. "Damn, sexy minx. That feels good, keep going."

Sitting up I continue rocking my hips, riding his cock but not letting it enter me.

"Lys, seriously, you're gonna make me come," he bellows, reaching up to grab my tits in his palms. He flicks my nipples between his fingers sending a rush of electricity through my body and straight to my aching core. Feeling my whole body ache, my pussy is spasming, my release building and I crash over the edge.

"Fuck! Fuck!"

I open my eyes, not realising I'd closed them and find Kaden jerking off as he watches me.

"God, Lys, watching you come is a fucking delight."

I giggle and he shoots his load with a loud moan onto my stomach.

He pulls me down for a kiss, murmuring against my lips, making the kiss deeper.

Breaking it I pull back and he chuckles.

"You're fucking voracious, Lys."

"Talk about yourself, Kad," I tease, climbing off the bed and heading to the bathroom. "I'm gonna have a shower, help yourself to anything in the kitchen."

He sits up in the bed, his hands behind his head.

"Thanks, sexy minx." He winks at me, his gaze following my arse as I saunter out of the room.

In the shower I hear him in the kitchen, opening the cupboards to get breakfast. I quickly shower, concentrating on my lower body to wash away the evidence of our night and morning of pleasure.

I still can't get over how amazing it was to have him give me an Aussie kiss and to suck him off as well.

Just thinking about it is making me wet again.

Getting out of the shower, I wrap a towel around my body, knotting it at the top as I head out to my bedroom.

Passing the kitchen I find Kaden sitting on a breakfast stool, sipping a coffee. He's dressed again in his clothes from last night, having picked them up off the floor. He winks at me, putting his coffee down on the bench.

"Do you have to get dressed, sexy minx?"

"Yeah, Lillie will be here really soon."

"Ok," he says sipping his coffee again.

I run into my bedroom, quickly getting dressed in some jeans and a shelf bra tank top.

Going out to make a coffee for myself Kaden grabs me around the waist.

"I should probably head off before your friend arrives."

"Yeah, I guess," I say softly, not liking his tone.

He breaks contact, heading towards the door and unlocking it. I open it , stepping closer to Kaden and wrapping my hands around his neck.

"Thanks for a great night, sexy minx," he teases before kissing me, hard and closed mouth.

I feel like I've done something wrong, but don't say anything when he breaks the kiss.

"I'll text you later," he says turning to walk away, as none other than my red headed bestie comes stumbling up the footpath carrying about four bags of god knows what.

Kaden is at his car, and toots the horn as he drives away.

I wave to him before turning my attention to Lillie, grabbing one of the bags off of her.

She follows me inside, dropping the rest of her bags on the floor.

"Hey Bestie," she shrieks excitedly when I close the door.

"Hey to you too, Lil. Isn't your mum coming in to say, 'hello?'"

"Nah, I told her to go. And that I'll call her later."

"Oh ok...cool, so ready to see your new digs?"

"Yeah, but first Ely spill. Was that Kaden I saw kissing you?"

"Yeah, that's Kaden."

"Is he your boyfriend now?" she asks eagerly, giggling like crazy.

"I um...I guess. We haven't really talked about it."

Again she laughs, following me down the hallway to her new bedroom, one of the bags slung over her shoulder.

We plonk down on the bed, and she blushes.

"So have you done anything with him?"

"Like sex?" I ask, laughing at my innocent best friend who can't help her blush when anything remotely sexual is mentioned.

"Yeah that. Have you done it with him?"

"Oh yeah, Lil…a-maz-ing!" I squeal.

She laughs. "I don't want to know the details, Ely. You know I haven't even kissed a guy."

I poke her in the stomach, playfully taunting her. "Well, we might have to change that Lil…you're a uni girl now. It's time to grow up."

"Yeah, no thanks Ely," she says before laughing.

She's still blushing and it's so cute. I'm definitely going to get my best friend to come out of her shell.

I love her to bits but she needs to grow up, and become a damn woman. She's always been the baby of the family, Amanda and Austin both being super protective of her.

If Austin wasn't engaged, she would have been moving in with him, but I'm glad she's going to be living with me and me only.

It's our childhood dream coming true. And I'm definitely looking forward to a whole lot of bestie fun, starting with teasing her.

"Suit yourself, Lillie! You're missing out you prude!"

She laughs so hard, not taking my words to heart and I tease her again.

"Lillie the prude!"

She slaps me on the arm. "Stop, bitch and help me unpack."

"Fine, Lil. But agree to think about going out with me to get drunk?"

"I don't know, Ely."

"Come on Lil. It will be fun. You can wear something super cute and we can check out cute boys."

"Ok…but tomorrow. I want an early night."

"Ok, fine," I snap, heading out of the room to grab the rest of her bags.

I'm already thinking of all the fun we're going to have together.

Twenty-Nine | Bloody Hearts

Travis

Getting home from training I call out to Bella, "Honey, I'm home."
I expect to hear her laughter coming from upstairs, her heading down to greet me with hugs and kisses like usual, but the house is unusually quiet.
Rushing through the house, and straight up the stairs to our bedroom I can hear muffled sobs coming from the ensuite.
My heart crashes to the floor, my eyes scanning the bed which shows a red pool of blood on Bella's side of the bed.
There's no way that is happening again.
It cant be.
I cant lose another child.
But my fear is confirmed when I walk through the open wardrobe to the ensuite.
Déjà Vu hits me hard in the chest, my heart stopping for a moment when I stare at Bella sitting on the red stained bathmat.
She's crying wretched tears, clutching her stomach and looking up at me her breath hitches in her chest, my name coming out from between her lips in a scream.
I'm completely lost for words, tears falling down my own cheeks, muffled sobs catching in my throat.
I sit down next to her wrapping my arms around her and pulling her close.
For a moment she sobs into my chest, and I kiss her forehead comfortingly.

I'm still completely lost for words, still quietly sobbing, the pain overwhelming me.

We'd only just recently seen our baby as a blip on the screen, a steady heartbeat and now at only eight weeks our bliss is cut short.

Bella looks up at me. "It hurts Travis, it really fucking hurts," she says through her sobs.

"I know, honey. I know," I tell her softly feeling completely overwhelmed with emotions, so much so that I'm sniffing back the wretched tears that are pouring down my cheeks.

Seeing the woman I adore, and love with my whole fucking heart in so much pain is breaking me. She murmurs softly, looking at me with a slight smile, before she kisses me softly.

Kissing her back, I pour all my emotion into the kiss, telling her without words how much I love her.

Breaking the kiss I caress her cheek. "We'll have another baby, honey. Keep positive, yeah?"

"I know," she says softly, before raising her voice, "I love you Travis Banes."

"I love you too, Bella. You know no matter what, it's always only you, yeah?"

"Yeah, it's always only you too, no matter what."

"Music to my ears, honey. Are you in pain?"

"A little. Just feel empty, but I think I'll be ok."

"You will be, Bella. We'll get through this."

I kiss her forehead again and she smiles sweetly at me.

"Yeah," she says, shifting a little in my arms.

"How about I run you a nice warm bath?"

"That sounds lovely."

Standing up I lean over the bathtub, turning the hot water tap on and putting in the plug. Once the water starts filling I turn the cold on and help Bella stand up.

"Hold, your arms up, honey," I direct her.

Her body is weak, but she does what I've asked, and bending down I lift her nightie off her body.

Helping her step out of her knickers, I kiss her belly softly, murmuring my words, "Bye, little one, fly high."

Bella lets out a pained whimper and I wrap her in a tight embrace again, kissing her hair. When she pulls back I give her another soft kiss against her lips before helping her climb into the bath.

She lies back, closing her eyes and brushing her hair back from her cheeks I ask her, "Want me to stay with you?"

"No, I'll be ok. But could you get Nor up from her nap."

"Of course, honey. Call out if you need me," I tell her walking out and heading to our daughters room.

She's sitting up in her cot, playing with her bear and picking her up I hug her tight. She'd really taken to me in the last months, and I was loving having a stepdaughter but I'm longing for a child of my own.

I just hope our chance hasn't passed by.

My heart is shattered, and I know Bella's is too, but I have a plan formulating in my mind of how to put it back together, to show her that hearts may bleed, but they can also heal from love.

Thirty | Ignition Sparks
Elyse

Sitting on the couch, surrounded by textbooks I'm bored out of my fucking brains, and trying to not think about Kaden. It's been a good couple of weeks since I'd seen him, as I didn't want him coming over when Lillie was home and also he's been so busy with his final weeks of training that we've barely even texted each other.

About to throw in the towel for the day, my phone pings from somewhere near me, buried underneath all the books.

I shuffle through them, closing them until I find it and a text from Kaden is on the screen.

Kaden: Shit day Lys. I'm buggered. But fuck I miss you sexy minx

My core throbs thinking back to the first time he'd called me sexy minx and he'd given me an Aussie kiss. I want to feel that pleasure again, and also I want to actually fuck him again.

I'd gotten the birth control injection, so I'm good for three months and I so want to have his cock fill me again, without worrying about the consequences.

Sighing I reply to his message, hoping he doesn't say no.

Elyse: Want me to meet you at yours? Lil is home tonight.
Kaden: Yeah, that would be sweet. I won't be much company but
Elyse: Doesn't matter I want to see you. Make you feel better.
Kaden: Sweet...you know where the key is. I'll be there asap. Don't touch your pussy until I'm there.

There's dirty promise in those words, that makes my pussy clench with need. I'm going to fuck Kaden again tonight and tell him how I feel. I can't hold back the words anymore.

Elyse: No worries 

Quickly dressing in some shorts and a singlet top with a g-string and crop bralette on underneath I grab my keys and wallet and head over to Kaden's. The whole way over on the tram I'm on edge wishing I could just touch myself to relieve the ache between my legs but I promised him I'd wait.

Finally reaching the stop closest to his house, I jump off the tram and sprint down the street to his apartment block. I let myself in using the key he hides under the rock in the communal garden at the front of the apartment.

Again I'm taken aback by how clean his space his, and oddly it kinda turns me on more. Putting my keys and wallet down on the hall table I head into the lounge room opposite. And I strip to my underwear, leaving my clothes in a pile by the couch.
I'm not sure how long he's going to be, so I dash to the kitchen and grab a beer out of the fridge before I go back into the lounge room to sit on the couch with the beer in hand.
Stretching out on the couch, I slowly sip it, taking a hard gulp when I hear the sound of Kaden's key turning in the lock.
He comes in, looking tired, but hot as fuck, with soot in his hair and on his face; with his training suit on.
"Hey Lys," he purrs in his husky voice that makes my core throb.
I'm already wet from thinking about him coming back and stripping me before fucking me on the couch.

"Hey Kad...you look sexy," I tell him, standing up as he comes over to the couch. He looks down at it like he's not sure if he should sit down or not. "Come on Lys. I look like shit."

"No, you don't," I say stepping closer to him and kissing his lips, softly and then harder. He moans against my lips and pulls back.

"Damn Lys...don't...let me get cleaned up first."

"Fine but can I help you get out of your sexy uniform, foxy?" I say grabbing his dick through the constricting fabric of his fire suit.

He groans at the contact, even though with his fire suit on he'd barely be able to feel the touch.

He doesn't say anything, just glares at me with hooded eyes, so I undress him, slowly stripping him of his fire suit.

He takes in a sharp breath when I dak him so he's only in boxers and his navy t-shirt that clings to his exquisite abs.

Bending down, crouching on my knees I grip the v muscles of his hips, licking over his cock through the fabric of his boxers.

Again he groans and I tease him, licking along the top of the boxers, before dakking him.

His cock springs out and I'm about to suck him when he says, "Please Lys...I just want to have a shower."

I stand up leisurely, taking his body in.

When I meet his eyes, he chuckles, making my stomach flip flop.

"Wait in bed for me, naked," he teasingly whispers in my ear before he turns away heading to the bathroom.

I watch his lush arse as he walks away.

Yep, I'm a fucking goner. I want all of Kaden because he's got all of me.

Thirty-One | Flaming Hot

Elyse

Giggling to myself I take the empty beer bottle to the kitchen, throwing it in the bin and I head down the hallway to his bedroom.

I can hear the shower running and soft moans coming from the ensuite.

Quickly I strip from my barely there underwear, but I don't get in bed, instead I head into the ensuite.

His glorious, tantalising body looks fucking edible in the open shower with water cascading down the ridge in his back. Watching him getting clean is turning me on so bad.

His dick is hard and he's stroking it and moaning deeply.

Walking into the bathroom further, stepping in the shower I enfold my arms around his waist.

"Want some help with that?" I ask grabbing his hard cock in a fist.

He doesn't reply, just groans in that super sexy way turning around before kissing me.

It's a dirty kiss, flaming hot and it makes my lips tingle.

Breaking it I slide down his body to the shower floor, licking down his abs and across the v muscle of his hips before taking his length into my mouth.

Slowly I tease him , licking and sucking him. He moans when I kiss the tip, swirling my tongue in and tasting the precum that hits my tongue.

He fists my hair, pulling me off his cock and grabs my arse to make me stand up.

Once I'm standing up again he's kissing me fiercely, lifting me up with his hands underneath my thighs.

I can't read the look on his face.

It's like lust but something else I can't work out.

Still gripping my thighs, he takes a step back, his back crashing against the tiles. He hisses before kissing me and lifting my arse to then lower me on his cock. He breaks the kiss, locking his eyes on mine when he bounces my body up and down on his cock.

It feels absolutely amazing, even more so than the first time we fucked. I can't help but moan in pleasure, calling out, "Fuck, fuck that feels good."

"Oh yeah," Kaden groans, dropping my legs down so I'm standing up again. He lines up his cock with my pelvis, pushing inside me sideways and I lift my leg up, bracing it against the shower wall to steady myself. He pumps his cock in and out, hard and fast at first, then slower. With some thrusts he stops his movement, holding himself inside me and it makes me feel full and content.

Feelings crash into my mind, and when he starts pumping inside me again I can feel my climax building, can feel his cock starting to throb inside me.

He kisses me hard again, groaning against my mouth when his cock starts to spasm with his impending release.

"Oh fuck, Lys, I'm going to come." He starts to pull out, but I push my pelvis down on him harder, impaling myself on him as my climax rocks through my body.

I nearly confess how I feel, the words I love you on the tip of my tongue, but he shuts me up with a kiss when we come together in ecstasy.

Yep, I'm in love with him. You fucking idiot, Elyse, you can't love him.

Pulling out, he chuckles, smiling at me and kissing me harder and deeper like he can't get enough or is telling me something without words. When breaking the kiss, he turns off the shower and brushes my wet hair from my cheeks.

"You're so fucking beautiful Lys. That was fucking incredible."

"You don't say, and you're so fucking gorgeous, Kad. I think I'm in l…"

"Don't Lys, Please don't," he begs, pressing a finger to my lips as we get out of the shower, wrapping ourselves up in towels we head back to the bedroom.

There's an odd tension between us now that's eating me up. I'm sure he feels the same as me, but he's scared to feel that for a girl.

I'm never going to be good enough, but I want to be.

We have flaming hot sex, and for now that's all I can expect from Kaden and hope that in time he'll fall for me.

Thirty-Two | Girly Night

Lillie

Living with Elyse for the past few months had been fun for sure. But with her at Uni and being at Kaden's all the time, we had barely seen each other much.

I'm missing my bestie, so I've planned a fun, girly night knowing that she can't go to Kaden's because he's in the country somewhere doing the final weeks of his firefighter training.

Not seeing him has made her a sour puss, so as her bestie it's also my duty to get my best friend out of her funk.

In the lounge room, I've pushed the couch out of the way and covered the floor with pillows and blankets.

On the coffee table, I have raspberry cordial, chicken twisties and chicos. All of Elyse's favourites and our go to sleepover treats as kids.

It has been forever since we've had a sleepover, but I can still remember staying up late in our lounge room playing 'Bubsy' on the Super Nintendo and watching silly girly romance movies.

My fave was 'Sleepover' but I always giggled excessively at the end when the characters kissed.

Watching stuff like that always made me feel a little tingly all over, but especially in my knickers.

I knew that was naughty, but I kinda enjoyed it.

I've never told Elyse about that. She'd probably think I'm crazy, especially because I've never kissed a guy.

I've thought that guys are cute before but I've never had a crush on anyone like Elyse has.

I'm sitting down on the pile of pillows when Elyse comes home.
She kicks off her thongs at the door, smiling at me. "Hey Lil, what's all this for?"
"Just thought it would be fun to have a sleepover like old times."
"Aww, Lil, that's so cute. Let me just get in some pyjamas."
"Ok, the pizza isn't here yet, so take your time."
She lets out an excited giggle heading to her bedroom.

Ten minutes later, after the pizza has arrived, Elyse comes back into the lounge room in cute Mickey Mouse pyjamas. I laugh, considering that I'm wearing a Mickey Mouse nightie.
Sometimes it doesn't make sense that Elyse and I are best friends, we are practically chalk and cheese. But the little things we have in common, from when we were toddlers make our friendship.
One of these is our mutual love for Mickey Mouse and pretty much everything Disney.
Sitting down beside me she grabs a piece of pizza out, biting into the meatlovers pizza with a wide mouth.
Swallowing it down quickly, she gulps, asking me, "So bestie, what Disney movie is on the agenda?"
"Not Disney, but 'Sleepover,'" I inform her with a laugh.
"No! Lillie! You always blush when they kiss at the end."
I swat her arm. "I know, but I always thought he was cute, and well you know...it's a good kiss."
She laughs at me, hard. "Lillie, that is so not a good movie kiss."
"Well, I don't know. Can we just watch it?" I ask, taking a piece of pizza and biting into it, turning away from her to hide my blush.
She touches my arm softly. "Lil, I'm sorry. But could we watch something else? Maybe something a bit more adult."

Glaring at her I feel the blush rise up my cheeks more when I reply, "Like what? Fifty Shades?"

"Well, that's a hot movie, but no..."

"Oh, um...yep," I quickly retort, eating more pizza.

"Lil, you can't handle a hallmark movie, let alone fifty shades of grey."

"Stop Ely. Just because you've done it, and k..k..kissed...more than one guy, it doesn't mean you can be a bitch to me."

"Sorry Lil, but it's not like you haven't had the chance to kiss someone. Jack liked you so much in high school."

"Yeah, but...just the thought of kissing someone scares me."

Squirming on the spot I can feel her intense gaze on me.

"Why Lil?"

I honestly can't believe I'm about to tell her this, about to confess that I'm a super weirdo.

"Because whenever I think about it, or watch a movie with a kiss I get all tingly in my knickers."

Elyse laughs sweetly. "Oh, Lillie! That means you're turned on girl."

"It's really weird though, Ely. Have you felt it?"

"Of course," she trills, her voice raising before she laughs.

"Do you feel it with Kaden?"

She blushes then. "Oh yeah, big time. Whenever I think about him I get wet."

"Wet? Like that peed yourself feeling that happens?"

"Yeah that one, Lillie...have you felt it around any guys?"

"No, as if Ely!"

"Ok, whatever Lil. Let's just watch the movie."

I turn the movie on but look over at Elyse, smiling.

"Thanks for talking to me about it Ely. I love you."

"Aww, Lil. That's ok. I'm always here, and I like talking to you about this stuff. I love you too."

We both laugh, and hug each other giggling.

Thirty-Three | Naughty Screen-time
Elyse

After watching a couple of movies we decide to hit the hay and once
Lillie has gone to bed I flop down on my bed, opening my MacBook to
FaceTime Kaden.
A huge smile cracks my face when he answers and his face appears on
my screen.
He hasn't shaved for a few days, stubble across his chin and his hair is
unruly on his head too.
He looks fucking gorgeous and I so wish he was in my bed giving me an
Aussie with that stubble on his chin, not away for some country training
back home in Stawell of all places.

"Hey Kad. Wish you were here…" I tell him.
"Me too Lys."
"I'm naked under the sheets," I tell him, giggling and blushing.
He gives me a dirty, hot as smirk. "Oh really? Show me."

I drop the sheet from my body, pushing it aside and tilting the computer
screen down so the camera takes in my crotch as well as the rest of my
body.
"Mmm Lys…touch yourself for me," Kaden moans, panning his phone
down to his cock as he gets it out of his daks.
We watch each other playing with ourselves, panting and moaning.
Kaden's face comes back onto my screen after a few minutes.
"Taste yourself on ya fingers Lys…tell me what it tastes like," he taunts,
panning between his face and his hard cock as he strokes it furiously.

I retract my fingers from my pussy, bringing them to my lips and lick them, teasing him. "Like honey...foxy."

He moves his phone again, and I hear him moan.

"Mmm...fuck..." He comes all over his hand.

Sliding my fingers over my clit I explode in ecstasy watching Kaden looking at me, biting his lip.

"I love watching you come, sexy minx."

I'm about to reply when Lillie knocks on my door, her soft voice saying my name.

I pout. "Shit Kad...Lil wants something...I gotta go."

I blow him a kiss, and he puckers his lips to catch it.

"Ok Lys, text me."

Ending the call, I yell out to Lillie, "One sec Lil."

Quickly I pull on my pyjama shorts and top rushing to the door and opening it up a little, leaning against it.

Lillie gives me a worried look.

"You ok? I heard you screaming."

"Um, yep I'm fine...just a nightmare. I'm fine," I tell her, stifling a laugh.

"Oh right. Were you talking to someone?" Lillie asks, tilting her head and giving me dagger eyes.

I hate lying to her but I have to.

"Nope, you must have been hearing things."

She nods, laughing like she doesn't believe me for a second.

"Ok Ely, goodnight."

She heads back to bed and getting back into bed myself I laugh texting Kaden.

Elyse: Lil heard my screams. Told her was having a nightmare
Kaden: lol I take it your bestie is way too innocent for her own good?
Elyse: oh yeah. She blushes when I say the word kiss, but I love her

*Kaden: yeah...anyway...I'm buggered. I'll come over tomorrow night
when I get home. Cool?*
Elyse: sounds great...xxxx

He doesn't reply after that, and I'm worried that sending him kisses was
a bad idea, but I'd done it.

Lying back down on my pillow, I also wonder if having him come over
when Lillie is home is a good idea.
The walls are super thin and if she heard me screaming and moaning
from touching myself, then she's going to get an ear full when Kaden is
actually in my bed.
But hey, it's about time my sweet innocent best friend is corrupted.

Thirty-Four | Zip Up

Watching Elyse ride my cock is a sight to fucking behold, the moans and screams of pleasure coming out of her mouth are super hot, but also super loud.

Knowing her innocent best friend is sleeping just in the next room I shove my fingers into Elyse's mouth and she sucks on them whilst still rocking up and down on my hardness.

Her perky tits are bouncing in the same rhythm as her pelvis, and god it's fucking hot.

Taking my fingers from between her lips she moans loudly pushing her body down onto mine.

My fingers then brush against her clit and I swear I've released some wild sex crazed animal into the bed with the moan that comes out of her mouth when her orgasm shatters her.

The way she grips my cock when she comes apart makes it throb inside her and I fill up the franger covering me when we come down from the high together with screams we can't hold in.

I hope to God that her best friend is asleep or blocking her ears because we certainly forgot to be quiet.

Elyse climbs off my lap, laying down next to me. I pull her close, feeling a weird rush of emotions hit me.

Giving me a sexy smirk, that makes me want to take her again she asks, "Kad, can you stay the night?"

"Lys...I...I...don't think I should."

She pouts at me. "Why?"

It's so fucking sexy and makes my cock stir again.

"Because..." I mutter, taking her lips to mine in a searing kiss.

She breaks it a couple of moments later, not letting me deepen the kiss. "Because is not a reason, foxy," she taunts me, pouting again.

"No, but if I stay over sexy minx, I won't be able to keep my hands off you and your innocent best friend has already heard you screaming like a banshee once tonight."

"I don't scream when I come. You do!" she teases, slapping my abs playfully.

"Can't help it when my cocks inside you, sexy minx."

"So, are you staying or not? I kinda like lying here naked with you."

"Fine, but don't blame me if I can't stop touching you and kissing you."

She doesn't reply, but kisses me instead, hard and oddly passionate, taking my breath away.

Fuck it feels good, so fucking good, sending a jolt of hot lust through me, but also it stirs up a feeling in my guts that I've never felt before and it scares the fucking shit out of me.

I can't feel that again, because heartbreak hurts too damn much. Breaking the kiss I pull her closer, wanting to feel her bare skin against mine. Softly I press a kiss to her forehead, closing my eyes after I watch her drift to sleep beside me.

~~

Rolling over I see my phone vibrating on the bedside table. Rubbing my bleary eyes I stare at the clock seeing it's just gone one am. Picking up the phone there's a text from Brennan.

Brennan: bro where you at? I'm pounding on ya fucking door, man
Kaden: At Elyse's. Let yourself in. Key is there.
Brennan: nah bro it isn't. And I need somewhere to crash.
Kaden: go home Bren
Brennan: can't...dad on a rampage. Give me addy, I'm coming there.
Kaden: Fine...12 cope lane Richmond

I put my phone down, getting out of the bed carefully to not wake Elyse up. She murmurs in her sleep, rolling over and the sheet falls to her waist, exposing her bare tits.

My body jolts with longing just looking at her. I shouldn't be feeling this way, for any chick, but especially not Elyse.

She hasn't told Bella about us, and that makes me feel so incredibly guilty. I don't like being her dirty little secret.

Wandering out to the kitchen, after pulling on my boxers I grab a drink of water and sit on the couch to wait for Bren to turn up.

For some reason I'm feeling super nervous about him coming here, like letting him into Elyse's house makes things between her and I real.

I shake the nervousness aside when I hear him knocking on the front door.

Opening it to him, he looks a right mess. His eyes are bloodshot, and his clothes reek of alcohol.

"Hey bro. Ya girl gots sweet digs." He's slurring his words, and can't meet my eyes when I usher him inside.

"Hi, Bren. You look like shit."

"Feel great bro, but need to sleep."

"Well, you'll have to sleep on the couch."

He glares at it, before rushing over and diving face first into the cushions.

"Mmm, nice couch."

I pull the throw up over him, and he shivers even though it's not at all cold.

"Bren?"

He rolls over, clutching the throw tightly against his chest like a baby holding a comforter. I think for a moment he's going to bite it.

"Yeah, Kad?"

"We'll be leaving in the morning before the girls get up."

"What? Some other chick lives here?"

"Yeah, Elyse's best friend Lillie. And don't get any ideas. She's not your type."

"Ok, fine. I'll keep my daks zipped," he promises with a wink.

When he lies back down on the couch, after pulling his T-shirt off I head back to Elyse's room, crawling back into bed with her.

She's awake and looks at me oddly.

"Where were you?"

"Just getting a drink, sexy minx."

"Oh ok," she replies as though she doesn't believe me.

I don't reply or let her say anything else, instead, I kiss her hard, rolling my hips so our bodies are crashing against each other. Entangling our legs together my body jolts with the rush of electricity that races through me.

Fuck, she does something to me and fuck it's good, but fuck.

Thirty-Five | Sweet Redhead

Brennan

Hitting something hard I'm jolted awake with a start.
When my eyes open I'm flat on my back on a hard wooden floor,
without any fucking clue of my damn whereabouts.
Rubbing at my eyes I try to piece together the night before in my head,
but I'm coming up blank.
My gut and head feel like I've been punched repeatedly, and it's my
telltale comedown from a sweet night.
Stretching my hands above my head I take the surroundings in, about to
get up to take a leak when a shadow falls across my body.

Sitting up my face is practically in lick-able distance of a chicks pussy in a
leotard.
I'm about to lick it through the fabric when the owner steps back,
shrieking in horror. I've never had a reaction like that before, so
obviously my night didn't consist of bedding this beauty.

She's looking down at me sitting on the floor, her curly red hair falling
about her shoulders in soft waves. Her grey eyes have a sparkle about
them, and when she glares down at the visible tent in my daks her thin
lips curve up in a slight smile.

"Who are you? And what are you doing in my house?" she screeches at
me.

Her words are a question, but damn does her voice sound like honey, so sweet and melodic. I swear my fucking dick throbs hearing it, so much so I'll do anything to hear her speak again.

Standing up I stumble falling against the coffee table.

"I'm Brennan," I tell her, staring straight into her pretty grey eyes.

I've only just met her, and I'm already feeling like I'm drowning in her.

Red hair, grey eyes, and wearing a leotard that shows off a tight, hot as fuck body.

Yes, my fucking dick is having a party in my damn daks.

"And you're here on my couch, because why?"

"Just crashing, princess."

"My name is not princess," she berates me, folding her arms across her chest when my gaze locks on her tits just a little too long.

"Well, what is it then?" I taunt, stepping closer to her, so close I'd barely have to move to kiss her.

She takes a deep breath in, clearly affected by my proximity and gulping she mutters her name, "Lillie."

I say it back, "Lillie." And just her sweet name on my lips makes my body hum.

In my head, I hear my brother telling me to keep my dick in my daks, and I step back from Lillie, smiling at her.

She's blushing from head to toe, practically matching her pale pink leotard. Her lip is between her teeth, and she's absolutely fucking mesmerising.

The tension between us is electric. I can tell she's feeling the same as I am and I'm also sure if I parted her toned thighs to expose the crotch of her leotard, there'd be a wet patch showing me she's turned on.

"Um, so...I...um...have to...get to ballet," she mutters, turning away when my brother and Elyse saunter in the room wrapped around each other and kissing each other. It makes me fucking sick watching my older brother hooking up.

Probably because seeing him all loved up makes me insanely jealous. I've not had a serious girlfriend since high school. And as much as I love sinking my dick into any willing chick on a night out, I'm kinda ready for something more.

Lillie looks at me, then at them, clearing her throat. "Um, Ely. I've gotta go. See you later."

Elyse breaks her hold on my brother, and calls out from the kitchen to Lillie, "No worries Lil."

Kaden stalks over to me, his nostrils flaring and his eyes shooting damn daggers at me.

"Tell me you fucking didn't?"

"Didn't what?"

"Anything, Brennan. Tell me you didn't make a move on Lillie?"

"Damn brother, calm ya fucking tits. Anyone would think she was ya girl instead."

"She's Lys's best friend, you wanker. And definitely not your type."

I'm about to say, 'gorgeous and sassy' is most definitely my fucking type, but I bite my lip and nod.

"Noted brother, so lay off."

Elyse comes over from the kitchen with a couple mugs of coffee, handing one to Kaden before she reaches out a hand to me, to shake.

"Hey, you must be Brennan?"

"Yeah, and obviously you're Elyse. My brother here doesn't shut up about you."

"Oh really?" She laughs, giving Kaden a wink. It makes my gut turn.

"Yep, I think he's pussy whipped."

"Shut it Bren, or I'll whip ya arse."

Elyse laughs, holding up her coffee towards me.

"Do you want coffee?"

"Nah, I could do with a shower though, if that's sweet?"

"Yeah, sure, down the hallway, first door on the left."

"Thanks," I reply, shuffling away.

In the bathroom I drop my boxers to the floor, getting into the rather lavish open shower and washing the night away
I think about Lillie, wondering what her sexy dancer's body would like under her leotard.
Fuck I want her, but something other than my brother's words of warning, tells me Lillie is most definitely not my type of chick. And damn does that make me want her more.

Thirty-Six | Little Crush

Lillie

Standing against the bar in the ballet studio I can't concentrate.
All I can see is his deep muddy brown eyes on me, undressing me from my leotard.

Lifting my leg up to stretch my crotch feels damp and I shriek audibly in shock, putting my leg down for fear of embarrassing myself.
I've never had that reaction to any guy before, and it's scary.
It feels exciting, warm and stirs up butterflies in my belly.
My whole lower body aches, but it's not painful. He hadn't even touched me, but his eyes on me are etched into my mind.
The ballet studio feels stifling when people come rushing in, including my extremely uptight teacher, Mrs Babcock.
Sashaying up to her to try and hide my damp crotch I tell her I'm unwell, and she lets me go home, much to my surprise.

After rushing back home, I'm glad to find Elyse home alone now, sitting on the couch in her pjs eating ice cream and watching some comedy on TV.

Dropping my bag, I shiver before sitting down next to her.
She doesn't turn her head, but says, "Hey, Lil. How was ballet?"
"I...um...left early."
"Why?"
"I'm um...feeling off."
She pauses the TV then and turns her gaze to me. I cross my legs, so she can't see the wet patch.

"Really? Did you eat something bad? Cause I feel fine."

"No, it's nothing like that."

"Then what Lil? You can tell me."

"It's about Brennan."

She giggles then, bouncing up and down on the couch excitedly.

"Ooo...Do tell me! Did he kiss you? I know he told Kaden he didn't but did he?"

"No, but how he looked at me Lys, it made me feel all tingly in my hoo-ha."

"Lil! You know what that means, remember?" she taunts me, poking me and making my legs uncross.

Her eyes dart to my crotch and I quickly try to cover up to no use.

She sees the wet patch on my leotard between my legs.

"Damn Lil! You are turned on."

"Stop Ely. It's embarrassing enough that I actually wanted to kiss him, without this complication."

She laughs at me, actually belly laughs. "Ooo....Lil has a crush!" she taunts, laughing.

I laugh then too because my best friend is right. "I think I do."

Elyse gives me a serious look then, which has me worried.

"Be careful Lil. I don't know much about Kaden's younger brother but I say go for it."

"Um, yeah, maybe," I reply blushing and standing up.

"I'm going to go have a shower. I feel dirty."

"Ok, Lil," she replies, laughing and turning the TV show back on.

I don't think I'm ready to have a crush on someone, especially someone as gorgeous as Brennan.

Thirty-Seven | Baby Drop-off
Bella

Everything in the last few months has been an absolute whirlwind and I'm upset with myself that I haven't taken more time to see Anni. I've missed my friend so much, and damn well hate myself for the fact that it's taken a tragic, sad event in my life to make me go see her.

Clutching Nora against my hip, I knock on the penthouse door and smile wide when Anni opens it with one of the twins against her hip and the other sitting on the floor with a death grip on her leg.

They aren't identical and I know Ryder is my godson, but I honestly can't tell her two blonde baby boys apart.

"Hey Bel, come in. I've got my hands full."

"Hey Anni, that's ok. I'll just drop Nora off and be out of your hair."

"Are you sure?"

"Yeah thanks, all good."

She asks me, "Are you sure Bel? Seems like something is bothering you." She takes an awkward step back.

"No...well, um yes."

"Come in and tell me. Nor can play with the boys whilst we chat."

"Ok, I guess," I reply following her inside and putting Nora down next to the child still clinging to Anni's leg.

She puts the one she's carrying down, kissing his forehead and sweetly talking to him, "Reid, be a good boy for mummy and go play blocks with Nora and Ryder, please?"

He claps excitedly and taps his brother on the shoulder.

Ryder lets go of Anni's leg and she sighs in relief.

I follow her to the kitchen, listening to her as she talks whilst walking, "Thank god you came over now. Ryder has been a sook all day. Wouldn't leave me alone."

"That sucks. Must be the clingy baby stage," I say, my voice stumbling on the word 'baby'.

"So Bel, tell me what's been going on? It feels like forever since I've seen you. And now you're living the dream with Travis."

"Um yeah, it's good but we...um...I." I'm muttering, but actually thinking about it again has tears stinging my eyes.

Anni puts a hand on my arm comfortingly.

"What Bel? Tell me, please. Did something bad happen with Travis?"

"No, well kinda...I had a miscarriage."

"Oh Bel, I'm so sorry."

"Yeah I was about eight weeks along and we'd just seen the heartbeat." She stops making our coffees and pulls me into a tight hug.

"Oh Bel, that's so sad."

"Yeah, it hurt so bad, but seeing how much Travis broke down got to me the most."

Tears are streaking my cheeks now.

"Yeah, he's a softie just like his best mate. But you guys getting away, just the two of you will be amazing."

"Yeah, exactly. Speaking of Jairus, where is he at the moment? They don't train on Thursdays and it's a bye week."

Anni sighs. "I don't know. He's been getting these suspicious messages on his phone. Like 'I can't wait to see you' and 'I miss you.'"

She looks really worried, and it hurts to see her upset and worried about him cheating on her.

It takes me back to high school when she first got with Austin and he flirted with Faye White. She'd cried for a week, even though Austin apologised.

"Well, I'm sure it's fine. Maybe it's just a friend. Jairus would never cheat on you."

'I hope not,"she replies, swallowing hard, and wiping an arm across her cheeks,"are you going to be ok?"

My heart swells with love for my her, my caring, always sweet friend.

Even when she's worried about something herself, she always thinks of others.

I smile at her, taking the coffee she holds out to me.

"Yeah, we just need to get away and have some us time."

"Ok, don't worry about anything. Nora will be fine. I'm kinda excited to have a little girl around for a few days."

Taking a sip of coffee, I smile again. "Thanks, Anni, I love you."

"I love you too, Bel. Go have some fun with your man. And don't forget to take some pics and come home to tell me all the details."

"Oh, I will, just not the dirty ones."

She laughs. "Yeah, I don't need to know what Travis is like in bed, but no doubt it's dirty and hot." She winks at me, and I try not to laugh as I finish my coffee.

"So, everything for Nora is in her bag. And I'll let you know when we arrive. Are you honestly sure it's ok to have her here? I can take her to Austin's if you want."

"No, it's fine. Great actually. As I said, it will be nice to have a little girl around for a few days," she replies, heading to the door.

"Ok, thanks Anni. Chat soon," I tell her, hugging her again before I bend down to scoop Nora up for a hug goodbye to.

I kiss my baby girl's forehead, telling her, "Be good for Aunty Anni, Nor."

She giggles excitedly, pressing a kiss to my cheek that makes me smile.

Anni takes her from my arms, holding her against her hip and they both wave at me as I leave the penthouse, ready to go meet Travis for our getaway to Fiji.

Thirty-Eight | Old Friend

Jairus

Pulling into a carpark outside the strip of shops on Bridge Road, I'm a little nervous about seeing her again.

Exchanging messages was one thing, but meeting up is a whole other thing.

She'd said it's only as friends, but still, my gut is in knots that she's going to try something, especially since her baby daddy is still completely out of the picture from what she's told me.

Walking into the coffee shop, she's already seated with her little girl sitting on the bench seat next to her, munching on a biscuit.

She's a spitting image of her pretty mum, a mass of curly dark, almost black hair on her head. She must have gotten the curls from her dad, because Sara's hair is dead straight.

She spots me, and stands up, pulling me into a hug.

"Hey, Jai. Thanks for coming."

"Hey Sar, and no worries. You look good."

"Thanks, so do you," she replies sitting down when I go to order my coffee.

I sit on the chair opposite, gulping as I'm not sure what to say.

She ruffles her mini me's hair when she glares at me and says in a meek voice, "Is he my daddy?"

"No, sweetie. Jairus is not your daddy."

"Oh, ok."

"Sorry, Jai. She keeps asking about her dad."

"That's ok. What's your name, sweetie?" I ask the little girl and she looks up at me smiling with her cute little dimples showing.

"Kinney," she replies proudly.

"That's a pretty name."

"Thanks," she replies giggling and taking a bite of her biscuit again.

My coffee is bought to the table and I take a big sip, even though it's freakishly hot. Sara is glaring at me, and it's hella awkward.

"So, I'm um...sorry for everything that happened with us. I never meant to hurt you."

"I know, Jai and I'm sorry for everything too. I should've been more supportive."

"It's fine Sar, really."

"Are you happy now?" she asks, biting down on her lip worriedly.

At one point that would have turned me on, but even though she's still beautiful she's not my Annika, the amazing stunning mother of my boys.

"Insanely, Sar. And I'm sorry things haven't worked out for you and Brad, but you deserve to be happy. The right guy will come along."

She chuckles softly. "I always hoped that was you."

I take another big gulp of my coffee. My heart breaks for her.

"I was never the right guy for you, Sar. But there's someone who is."

"Yeah, I know. Thanks again for everything. Especially the cash. I know that sounds petty but it's going to help so much."

"No worries. I'm always here," I reply, standing up.

"I appreciate that, Jai. And please tell Annika I say, 'hello'. I honestly don't mean any hard feelings and would love it if we could remain friends."

"I'd like that to, Sar. Keep safe, we'll chat soon."

I lean down kissing her on the cheek and head home, feeling a little guilty, but knowing that I have to tell Anni everything.

Keeping things from her is not the right thing to do and even though I've done nothing wrong, except catching up with an ex, I hate hiding anything from my wife.

Thirty-Nine | Makeup Sex

Annika

Finally, I got the twins and Nora down for a nap, but I'm still feeling anxious as Jai still isn't home and it's near five pm.

It's not like him to not tell me where he's going or when he'll be home, and I can't help but worry.

I'm about to call him when I hear the click of his key card on the door lock, and he saunters into the penthouse like nothing has happened.

I've been pacing the room for the last half hour and I stop dead, hands on my hips and glaring at my husband.

My blood is boiling with anger and before he can even say, 'hello' I bellow at him, "Where the hell have you been, Jairus? I've been worried sick."

His gaze is sheepish, not his confident self and my mind flashes to the messages I'd seen on his phone.

He walks across to the kitchen, opening the fridge and staring into it as though it's an abyss that is going to swallow him whole to get him out of the situation he's put himself in.

Following him, I lean against the bench.

"Well, Jairus?" I chastise, balling my fists in anger that he still hasn't replied.

He grabs out a beer, shutting the fridge with his arse before pulling up a stool.

"Seriously, sweetheart. Calm ya tits. I was just catching up with a friend."

"Right, sure. Why not tell me then?"

He takes the top off the beer, gulping some down.

"I don't know. Didn't think about it."

"You should have told me, Jai. I've been worried about you all arvo, thinking you had a car accident or something."

"I'm sorry. I'll tell you next time. I don't see what the big deal is."

"The big deal is that you should tell me things. You shouldn't lie to me."

"What the fuck are you talking about? I didn't lie, Annika. I didn't tell you I was seeing an old friend but I never lied."

I scoff when he takes another sip of beer.

"Yes, you're lying right now. I saw the messages on your phone."

"What messages?" he asks shrugging his shoulders.

"You know the messages I mean. The ones to some other chick."

Again he scoffs. "Fine, for fuck's sake...they were to Sara. I was with Sara this arvo."

"Your ex, Sara? Are you...are you sleeping with her?"

"God, no, sweetheart. How could you even think that?"

"I don't know, Jai. You didn't tell me. I just presumed the worst."

He stands up, putting his near-empty beer bottle on the bench before coming around to my side of the bench and grabbing me around the waist to pull me against his body.

His face is close to mine when he speaks slowly, "I saw Sara as a friend because she's in a bad place at the moment. There is nothing going on between us and it never will."

"How can I believe that? When you deliberately hid the truth from me?"

"Have I ever lied to you?"

"No, but..."

"There's no but about it Anni. I love you more than anything, and I only want to be with you, forever."

His eyes show he's sincere, and I can feel his hard dick pressing against my belly.

I laugh at the thought that fighting is turning him on.

"I'm sorry. It was stupid of me to think you'd cheat on me. But please don't lie to or not tell me things again."

"Of course sweetheart," he promises with sincerity in his tone, kissing my lips softly.

"Wanna know a secret?"

"Yeah," I tease, knowing he's going to say exactly what I'm thinking.

"Fighting with you sweetheart...turns me on."

"I can tell."

"Yeah," he chuckles, his strong taut muscles shaking when he leans into me. "So how about some hot makeup sex?"

I kiss him hard in reply, pulling back just a little to lick his lips and whisper against them, "Maybe in the spa. Nora and the twins are asleep."

"Ooo, yeah, sweetheart. I love fucking you the spa and watching you come extra hard with the water jets teasing your sexy body."

My clit throbs just thinking about it, and kissing Jairus hard he grabs me around the waist and I jump up against his body, climbing him like a damn tree and wrapping my legs around his arse.

He carries me towards the bathroom, our lips locked together and our tongues dancing in a fight of their own.

In the bathroom he puts me down, bending down to turn the water on in the spa bath before he turns to look at me with lust flashing in his gorgeous olive green eyes. They make me melt every damn time I look at him and locking my blue eyes on his I start to strip from my clothes, loving his appreciative gaze.

"God, Anni, you're so fucking beautiful."

"Mmm, you're fucking handsome, baby. Your birthday suit is your best outfit." My words are a tease, and reaching forward I dak him, shorts and tight white jocks in one swift movement.

His hard dick springs forward and I grab it as he lifts his t-shirt off.

He gives me a smirk. "Sweetheart, you still have too much on."

His gaze wanders my body and stepping closer to him grabbing his dick harder in my grasp I tease him, "Oh really? Mind helping me."

He chuckles softly, hooking his fingers in my boyshort knickers and sliding them over my arse, letting them drop to the floor.

His hands roam my body, running them up my back to unhook my bra clasp.

I take a step back, letting it fall down my arms to the floor and again Jai's gaze wanders over my body.

I still feel a little self-conscious of my post-baby body, especially the fact that I've not really waxed or shaved my bikini area since just before the twins were born.

"Damn, sweetheart, that's better," he says, winking at me, before his voice falls, "Is something wrong?"

I feel a little stupid for the words I'm about to say, "I haven't waxed."

He laughs loudly. "Do you honestly think I give a shit, sweetheart?"

"I don't know. I just..." He doesn't let me finish speaking, instead, snakes an arm around my waist and pulls me against his erection.

"I don't give a flying fuck Annika. You're the most beautiful woman on the fucking planet, and nothing, especially not waxing because you've had two sweet boys recently will change that."

There are no words to say, so I kiss him hard, pouring all my love into the kiss.

Breaking the kiss, he turns the bath tap off and climbs into the spa bath, stretching out his long legs. I climb in the other side, and slide up in the warm water to straddle him. Wrapping my legs around his arse I kiss him again, rocking my pelvis against his erection. His dick slides into my wet core, and he breaks the kiss gasping.

"Damn, Annika, you're so wet, sweetheart."

I giggle. "Fighting with you turns me on, baby."

He then lets out a deep chuckle and I wrap my arms around his neck, pulling him closer for a heated kiss. Parting his lips with my tongue I slip my tongue into his mouth to tease him and feel his dick throb inside me.

Continuing to bounce up and down on his dick, the water is splashing around us and it's definitely erotic.

He breaks the kiss, laughing. "I think it's time to turn the jets on sweetheart."

"Do it , baby," I taunt, and he presses the button, making bubbles erupt from the jets behind my back and underneath us.

The sensation from the bubbles, along with our pelvises rocking together makes my climax build quickly.

"Jai, I'm gonna come."

"Let go, sweetheart," he teases, "I'm gonna come with you."

Impaling myself hard down on his dick, I feel it throb inside me and I tremble, my orgasm rocking through me as Jairus comes inside me.

"Damn, sweetheart," he says with a chuckle.

I slide off of his lap, laying back against the bath.

The jet of water pulses against my clit and I shiver in delight again when another rush of pleasure hits me.

"Fuck," I cry out, closing my eyes and biting my lip as I come down from my second blissful release.

Jairus chuckles when the jets turn off. "God Anni, that was sexy as fuck. Get over here."

I'm about to shuffle over to sit closer to him, when I hear the unmistakable cry of Reid coming from their bedroom.

"Stay in the bath, sweetheart. I'll go check Reid. I think you should turn the jets back on."

He winks at me as he gets out, wrapping a towel tightly around his waist as he heads out of the bathroom to attend to our son.

Turning the jets back on, I lie back, feeling the bubbles vibrate against my body. They make all the tension rush away, all the worry seem insignificant when I again feel my body pulsate with pleasure.

Forty | Mine Forever

Travis

Bounding out of bed, I caress Bella's cheek with my hand and kiss her forehead. Sleepily she murmurs, her mesmerising brown eyes fluttering open to look at me.

"Morning," she purrs at me, "why are you up?"

"Can't sleep, but it's early, so go back to sleep and..." I cut my words off, not wanting to let anything slip about my surprise for her.

I'm feeling fucking giddy, and can't wait for four pm to hit.

I'm hoping everything goes without a hitch, from the lavish Fijian brunch this morning, to the formalities of the afternoon, as well as the evening spent together; just us.

Quickly I shower, splashing on the aftershave I know Bella likes when I get out and sitting down I pen her the first note.

Bella,
You're my sunshine. And when you wake up basked in the sunshine on this beautiful morning meet me at the restaurant. The best is yet to come, honey.

Heading down to the resort restaurant I bump into the manager on the way.

"Good morning, Mr Travis. Is everything set for today?"

"Yeah, I think so. I'm expecting Bella around eleven am for brunch, and at that time the dress needs to be put in the room. I'll send her for hair and makeup in the meantime as well, and meet on the beach at four pm."

"Sounds wonderful Mr Travis. I hope it all goes to plan. Please ask me if you need anything. And good luck to you."

I chuckle softly. "Thank you, but hopefully I don't need luck."

"Yes, yes, no doubt Miss Bella loves you, so much."

I nod, heading into the restaurant and straight to the back table facing the beach and elaborate pool.

It's been set with two place settings, and wine glasses, with a bottle of champagne on ice to toast with.

In the middle is a single white lily and it smells divine. Checking my watch I see it's just gone nine am and the second hand is ticking ever so slowly.

I'm not expecting brunch until eleven, as we generally sleep in late on weekends, or at least Bella does when I get up to attend to Nora.

Some mornings, she gets up earlier and comes to a game to watch me play, and that makes my heart swell. Having her support means so much.

Sitting down at the table, I check my shorts pocket for the ring box.

It's still there, and just touching it makes my heart pound.

I never thought I'd fall in love again after Meaghan, let alone actually want to marry someone else, but I can't imagine my life without Bella in it and I want nothing more than to call her my wife; to make her Mrs Bella Banes.

A waitress walks past and I order a coffee; which comes quickly to the table. I've only taken a few sips when I hear Bella's voice as she enters the restaurant and asks where to meet me.

She's directed to the table and I stand up giving her a soft kiss.

"You're early, honey."

"Sorry, I woke up and saw your note, so I came straight here after I got ready."

Smiling at her I nod; taking in her gorgeous appearance. She's dressed perfectly for a sunny Fijian day in a short blue sundress that grazes the top of her thighs, almost showing me a glimpse of her pussy underneath. I can tell she's wearing her white string bikini, as the bow's at the side jut out at her hips.

The dress is a halter neck, just like the bikini top and it holds her perfect tits up. She looks absolutely stunning.

"Sit down, honey. I'll get the brunch sorted."

I pull out the chair for her, being all gentlemanly and she laughs at my uncharacteristic behaviour.

"I can be a gentleman, sometimes." I wink and again she laughs, her face showing a wide smile which after the last couple of weeks is a welcome sight.

I'd planned this trip super quick after the miscarriage, quickly getting her to the doctor to get the all-clear to try again. She was reluctant of course, but the doctor calmed her worries and said it would be beneficial to try again as soon as possible as she'd be more fertile.

We'd not had sex since though, and I was more than ready to make love to her again. Just the thought that the next time we'd make love would be as husband and wife is enough to make my cock throb in my daks.

The waiters bring out our food about ten minutes later, and all I've done is stare at Bella.

"Captain, are you ok? You're acting weird."

"Yep, I'm fine. Just thinking."

"Really? And what are you thinking about?"

"You really wanna know?" I taunt, winking at her.

"Of course, Captain. Maybe I'm thinking the same thing."

"I'm thinking about making love to you on that king-size bed tonight."

She lets out her sexy whimper biting down on her lip. She looks so damn sexy doing that; I feel like forgoing brunch and taking her back to the cabin right now.

"I love the sound of that, captain," she teases, her foot under the table edging up my leg and teasing my aching cock, "But first food. It looks so good."

The food does look super good; rice dishes, sweet potato and bread which smells like coconut. Breaking some off, I devour it licking my lips and Bella does the same, letting out an appreciative hum as she swallows it.

"I love coconut," she beams, taking some more and stuffing it into her mouth.

"Eat up, honey. I have a surprise for you after we finish."

"Oh really, Captain," she says with a wink.

"Yes, really," I tease.

My heart is hammering in my chest, and I decide to change up the plan for the surprise. I'm sure she knows what the surprise is, but I still feel nervous and hope that she'll say yes.

After stuffing ourselves for twenty minutes I stand up taking her hand in mine.

"Come and take a walk with me."

She doesn't say anything, just stands up and presses a soft kiss to my lips.

We head outside to the expansive gardens, holding hands.

My palms are sweaty, my whole body warm and I'm nervous but excited. Bella pulls away from me, standing in front of the waterfall in the gardens.

Her back is turned, and she looks stunning against the fernery.

I drop to my knee, and say her name, softly, "Bella."

It's a whisper, but she turns around, gaping at me and smiling sweetly.

"Travis," she muses softly, "is this?"

I take the ring box from my pocket and hold it up to her.

"Yes, it is Bella. You're my everything. You opened my heart to love again and I can't imagine living life without you. I want to love you and make love to every day of my life. Will you marry me?"

"Yes, yes, of course, I will. Oh my god, yes!" she squeals in delight.

Standing up I put the ring on her finger and she pulls me close for a hard, searing passionate kiss that seals her answer against my lips.

"So, are you ready for the next part of your surprise?" I ask chuckling against her lips.

She laughs, poking me in the abs. "Seriously, captain?"

"Yeah, so pampering time. And I'll meet you back in the room when you're done."

"Ok, sounds wonderful. Thank you, Travis. I love you so much."

"I love you too, Bella. You deserve it. I'll see you soon," I tell her as she walks away and I can't resist smacking her curvy arse cheekily.

She giggles and blows me a kiss.

Heading back to the cabin, just as I requested, her dress is hanging up over the window and it looks stunning with the sunlight shining into the room through the lace.

It's sheer floral lace at the top, mainly over where her tits will be and it's soft and billowy chiffon that flows out into a short train.

I can't wait to see her wearing it and walking down the aisle to marry me.

My stomach is in giddy knots just thinking about it happening in mere hours.

On the bed is her bouquet, a mix of lilies, gardenia, some purple iris and ferns. I sit down to write her another note to leave with the bouquet.

Leaving it on the bed, I quickly dress, donning my grey slacks, and white shirt. I leave it unbuttoned a little and roll up the sleeves, before heading into the bathroom.

Quickly I brush my teeth and splash on a little more aftershave. The nerves are bubbling in my stomach when I head out to make sure everything is ready on the beach.

Bella

After my pampering session, I'm feeling on top of the world, partly because I've not had my hair done in forever, but mostly because of Travis proposing. It was certainly unexpected and the ring is so stunning I can barely stop looking at it.

It's a solitaire diamond, at least two carats set in a claw on a yellow gold band. It must have cost a fortune, but I know Travis spares no expense when it comes to making me happy.

Sometimes it makes me feel guilty, how much money he spends on me, and on Nora. I know he's rich, and we have more money than we'll ever need, but I still don't like him spending excessive amounts on me.

Heading back into the cabin, I expect to find him relaxing on the bed, but he's nowhere to be found.

My eyes drop to the bouquet of flowers on the bed, and the handwritten note beside it.

Reading his words makes my heart swell with love, it hammering in my chest.

Bella,

Today I asked you to marry me. And thank my lucky stars you said yes. But my beautiful Bella, my sunshine, I don't want to wait another day to make you my wife. Life is all about moments and memories, so please meet me on the beach under the gardenia arch. I can't wait to see you looking absolutely stunning wearing this dress I chose for you. Don't worry about shoes. We're having a barefoot wedding, honey.

Always Only you,

Love Travis Michael Banes (your hubby 😘)

It's then, with tears in my eyes that I look at the dress. It's absolutely stunning, completely breathtaking and something I definitely would have chosen for myself.

It's scary, but amazing how well Travis knows me and it shows how much he honestly loves me.

Taking the dress off the hanger, I touch the soft chiffon fabric between my fingers. It feels incredible and carefully I unzip it to put it on.

Pulling off my dress, I undo my bikini top at my neck and take that off too. Thankfully the dress has bra cups built into the lace, so I don't need a bra.

I wonder if Travis noticed this detail; knowing him he probably did and is probably hoping I'll not wear a bra.

Cheekily I slide my bikini bottoms down my legs, deciding to go commando to feel the soft chiffon against my skin, but also to tease Travis later.

Stepping into the dress, I slide it over my hips and up over my bust, zipping it up carefully. Shuffling to the bathroom, I admire myself in the mirror, tears threatening to spill down my cheeks and ruin my makeup. I'd only gone for a light dusting of foundation powder and blush with mascara on my top lashes, and lip gloss over my lips.

Still, I felt glorious and knew that Travis would find my look captivating. He'd always comment on how dazzling I looked when I wore the bare minimum of makeup and nothing had ever made me feel more beautiful.

Taking a deep breath in, I walk out of the bathroom and grab the bouquet off the bed. Heading out to the beach I feel like I'm walking on air, my dress swishing in the light breeze.

Approaching the beach, on the shoreline I see the arch; Travis standing under it in bare feet and a casual crisp white shirt rolled up to his elbows, paired with grey slacks that clearly hug his arse.

He's shifting on his feet, rubbing his hands together in nervousness.

His hair is a little dishevelled from the breeze, and he hasn't shaved which always makes him look delectable.

I stop a moment, standing where the grass meets the beach and music, 'Diamonds' starts to play. Travis looks down the aisle at me, a wide cheeky grin on his face.

Tentatively I take steps, getting closer to him and the celebrant under the arch. When I reach him, he kisses my forehead.

"Bella, you look phenomenal."

"You look suave and utterly handsome."

"Ready to get married?"

I nod, leaning forward to kiss him softly on the cheek.

The ceremony is quick; we promised to love each other always before we exchanged rings.

Travis slid a matching diamond-encrusted band onto my finger, saying, 'I do' with the sweetest smile on his face. It made my heart pound and the butterflies flit in my stomach as I slide a plain yellow gold band onto his finger, telling him, "I do, with every piece of my heart."

The celebrant smiles, announcing, "I now pronounce you, man and wife. You may kiss the bride."

"About time," Travis says, laughing before crashing his lips to mine in a heated kiss that makes me drop the bouquet on the sand.

He dips me low, swooping me back up into his arms into a tight embrace. He whispers in my ear, "I love you Bella, my wife."

"I love you Travis, my husband."

He takes my hand in his and together we walk back down the beach to our cabin.

Reaching the door, he scoops me up bridal style into his arms and carries me across the threshold.

Throwing me softly against the bed, he smirks at me.

Starting to undress, I watch him, smirking at him, knowing that when he takes off my wedding dress I'll be bare to him, ready to make love to him, my husband.

Forty-One | Always One

Travis

Kissing Bella passionately, I bunch up the soft chiffon, sliding a hand up her thigh. She shivers underneath me, her lips still pressed against mine and when my fingers roam higher I find her pussy is bare, not a scrap of underwear present on her body.

Breaking the kiss, I chuckle. "Seems like my wife is dirty as fuck."
"Only for you husband," she replies sitting up on the edge of the bed.
She undoes the zip of her dress and helping her bunch it from underneath her arse I pull it over her head, throwing it aside.
She's naked, bare before me and all mine.
Just looking at her naked body turns me on, makes my cock so hard and I want to fuck her so hard but also want to make sweet, slow love to her.
"Travis?" she purrs my name, jolting me back to reality from just staring at her stunning body.
"Yeah, honey?"
"Quit staring and kiss me."
I obey, chuckling when I kiss her lips, deepening the kiss with my tongue for a moment, before breaking the kiss and trailing kisses down to her perfect tits.

They'd always been a favourite body part on any sheila, but fuck Bella's are gorgeous, perfect pink buds that stand to attention with the flick of my tongue across them.
"Fuck, Travis, that feels so good," she moans, arching her hips up to mine.

So easily I could slide straight inside her pussy, but I want to taste her first and have her screaming my name as she experiences her first orgasm of our wedding night.

My kisses start to trail down over her belly, and teasingly I lick her hips, making them rise up as my kisses head lower, straight to her honey pot. And fuck, she's already deliciously wet.

She gasps when I kiss her clit, biting it before delving my tongue deep inside her pussy. And fuck me, does she taste good, great, heavenly.

Moans and her sexy whimper are escaping her lips and her hips are bucking up to my face, fucking my mouth.

I can't get enough, wanting her to release, to squirt all over the stubble on my chin.

"Bella, my beautiful wife, come for me."

She lets out her whimper, arching her hips up and her pussy clenches around my tongue, her release building.

"Fuck!" She screams out, moaning louder than ever when I bite her clit again, soothing it with a gentle kiss as her release hits, her pussy trembling and pulsating with her squirting orgasm.

Standing up I look over her body sprawled out in front of me on the bed. She's still panting when she hooks her leg around mine to bring my body crashing to hers.

"That was amazing, husband," she taunts.

"Oh yes, it was, wife but you're going to come again...with my cock buried inside you."

"Mmm," she moans, fisting my hair and bringing my lips down to hers. She whimpers tasting herself on my lips and tongue, and it makes my cock rock hard.

It teases her entrance and when she breaks the kiss, she locks her eyes with mine, and says softly and seductively, "Make love to me, captain."

Kissing her forehead, I spear my cock into her, deep, and slowly start thrusting in and out, filling her and then leaving her practically empty. Every time I slide back in, her pussy grips my cock tight and it throbs inside her.

She kisses me suddenly, biting my lip before pulling back and looking at me with her dark eyes.

"Travis, please can I ride your cock?"

"Oh yeah, honey," I bellow, grabbing her hips and lifting her into my arms with my cock still buried balls deep inside her pussy.

Her arms wrap around my back and she rocks her pelvis against mine, just the tip of my cock slipping out and back in again.

Slowing the rhythm I kiss her, turning around to sit on the bed, pulling her down with me. Her legs are still wrapped around me, and she pulls me closer with them, bouncing up and down on my cock, moaning and panting.

Her tits are in line with my lips and again I kiss them, making her whimper in pleasure, throwing her head back in ecstasy.

"Travis, fuck, Travis, oh my god...fuck!"

I lie back, my head propped up on my hands to watch my cock slipping in and out of her slick pussy as she rides me.

It's a fucking gorgeous sight, seeing our bodies becoming one.

She arches her body back, impaling her pussy on my cock, and she stills a moment, revelling in how amazing it feels to be as close as possible.

And then she lies down on top of me, kissing me and slowly rocking her pelvis on my cock.

I match her thrusts and tease her by deepening the kiss with tongue.

I seriously want to fuck her—no make love to her—all damn night, but she breaks the kiss with a loud whimper and she starts trembling again. Pumping her hips up and down on me I feel her release around my cock

and I pump my own release into her, filling her as I moan, "Bella, fuck...I love you!"
She shakes, her orgasm a rush and collapsing against my chest she says softly, "God, Travis, that was beyond amazing."

Pulling her body off mine, grabbing her by the hips I lay down next to her, bringing her close and entangling our legs together.
"Yeah , so amazing. I think we should stay in this bed for the rest of the weekend."
"Sounds like a dirty plan. We can fuck all day and make love all night."
I groan, her suggestion already turning me on again.

Kissing her I slide a finger across her clit, and whisper against her lips, "That starts now, and every night until forever."
She pulls back from my tender kiss, her hands finding my hair.
"Forever in your arms is the only place I want to be, Travis. I love you more than you could ever know."

Again I give her a soft tender kiss, conveying with the touch of my lips to hers, my hands on her beautiful body that she is mine, and I'll love her as long as my heart is beating.

Forty-Two | Baby Daddy

Austin

Getting home from the gym, I'm absolutely buggered. Dana isn't home from work yet, so grabbing a Ruski from the fridge I sit down on the couch. Cracking it open, I gulp it down, jumping up on the couch when my phone vibrates in my back pocket.

I'm shocked to see Bella's name flashing on my screen.

"Hey Bel," I say enthusiastically answering the call.

"Hi , Austin." Her tone is melancholic and makes my heart fall to the floor.

"Bella, is something wrong?"

"Yes, it's Nora. I um...need to talk to you, urgently."

"Is she ok?"

"Well, no, but Austin please I need to see you. Tell you something." She breaks down into tears.

"Where are you?"

"At...the...hospital."

"What? Which one?"

"The...royal...children's..." she says through sobs.

"I'm coming there now," I blurt out, dropping my unfinished Ruski and running to the door.

"Bella? Are you there?"

"Yeah, yeah, I'm here. Can you meet at my house?"

"Yeah, sure. Text me the address. I'll be there soon."

"Thanks, I'm so sorry Austin."

"Don't be sorry Bella. Is Travis with you? Jaxon?"

"Yeah, but I'll um...tell you more when I see you."

"Ok, I'll see you soon," I reply hanging up.

Hastily I go to get changed quickly, grabbing my ute keys as I rush out the door. Bella's text comes through as I get in the ute and I punch the coordinates into the GPS.

My heart is hammering in my chest, worry plaguing my mind. It's clear something serious has happened, but why Bella needs to tell me so urgently and in private is damn scary.

Before heading off I quickly text Dana, hoping she can answer at work and isn't busy with a client. She'd only just started working part-time at a psychology clinic on the desk whilst in her final year of study and often was busy helping book in clients or sitting in on appointments to gain experience.

Austin: Dan, I'm going to Bella's. She has some urgent news to tell me. Will fill you in when I get home. Love you.
Dana: No worries stud. Hope everything is ok. Love you more

Satisfied with her quick response I head out the gates, driving a little to fast to Bella's.

I have a feeling she's going to tell me something about Nora that I already know; the answer to the question that has plagued me since Nora's birth.

Bella's daughter has dark strawberry blonde hair, and that is unlikely to happen with dark brown and blonde genes mixing together.

I may have been a little daft when it came to science, but biology and especially genetics I'd actually been good at.

My heart is pounding in my chest because even though I'm prepared for that news, I'm worried it will crush Dana; that she will feel like she doesn't deserve to be with me, not able to give me the gift of a child.

I'm also worried because Bella's sobbing breakdown seemed more intense than a mere paternity issue, and she said something was wrong with Nora.

I can't bear to think about it, swallowing hard to calm my nerves when I pull up outside her house.

It's now or never.

Still, my heart is hammering in my chest, as I walk up the path to the front door of Bella's house. Rapping my knuckles on the door I take a deep breath in, exhaling it when Bella opens the door, in tears. Stepping inside I wrap her into a hug, letting her cry into my shoulder for a few minutes, before pulling back.

Taking a moment I glance around her house and I'm gobsmacked by how spectacular and immaculate it is. I feel a pang of jealousy hit me but brush it aside when Bella heads across the open living room towards some white leather couches. I follow and sit down on the two-seater one beside her.

"So...um...Austin," she starts, gulping and turning away from my intense gaze, "We had to take Nora to the hospital last night, as she took a turn for the worse."

"Sorry? Turn for the worst? Was she sick?"

"Yes, she'd been on and off unwell for months but we found out when she lost consciousness and was..." She gulps, holding back her sobs.

"Bel, take your time, I'm here," I soothe her, touching her arm lightly.

Even though I'm not attracted to her anymore, the tension between us is still thick.

"Well, um...we took her to the hospital and after some tests, the results came back that she has Leukaemia."

My mouth falls open, shock reverberating through my whole body.

"Cancer? But she's...she's barely even one. I...I...I can't believe it, Bel."

"I know Austin. My heart is shattered, but um...that's not all, Aust."

"What else could there be, Bella? Are you sick too? Or Travis?"

"No, but um...god I can't believe I'm telling you this."

"Telling me what, Bel?"

She takes a deep breath in, exhaling it as she blurts out, "Nora is your daughter."

Again I gape in shock. "What? You're shitting me, yeah?"

"No, Austin I'm not. I kinda knew already, but you were so happy with Dana and I didn't want to make things difficult."

"Well, fuck Bella, I don't know what to say."

"I'm sorry Austin. I should've told you when she was born, but I've...I've been in denial."

"You don't say. How did you even find out? Like what's made you certain?"

"Some of the tests were blood tests, and Jaxon's blood type and mine mean there is no way he can be her daughter."

"So, right...and mine does? Do I need to confirm that?"

"Well, yeah, you're the only other guy I slept with, so it's obvious but yeah, you'll have to get a blood test."

"Ok, um, well this is certainly a shock, but I kinda knew too. She has my hair."

"And your eyes."

"Yeah," I say softly standing up, my breath catching in my chest. I need to tell Dana, but I'm scared she's going to break down.

"Austin, I'm really sorry."

"It's ok Bella. I just don't know how I'm going to tell Dana."

She stands up then, grabbing my hand. "Are you trying for a baby or something?"

"No, we aren't. Dan can't have kids."

"Oh, Austin! I...I...I'm so sorry. That's so sad."

"Yeah, she told me before we slept together."

"You really love her, don't you?"

"Yeah, I do."

"It shows. So, I'll let you know about the blood tests, and any appointments for Nora."

"Ok, and please Bel, I want to be a part of her life. I already feel like I've missed out on so much."

She leads me to the door. "I know Austin, and I'm incredibly sorry for that. I just hope she pulls through."

"Me too, Bella. I'll talk to you soon," I say at the door, giving her a quick hug and kissing her on the cheek before I leave.

The minute I get into the ute, the tears cascade down my cheeks, all the emotions hitting me hard in the chest.

I have a daughter, with someone other than my fiancee, and my daughter is dying.

I start the ute, turning out into traffic, but not paying attention and a car nearly rear-ends me, honking their horn hard from behind me.

I flip them the bird out the window and accelerate to drive faster.

I've never known pain like this before, and all I want to do is close my eyes to block it out; that or make love to my beautiful fiancee, knowing that we'll never have to face the pain of losing a child together.

Forty-Three | Dirty Proposition

Dana

After Austin got home from Bella's, and dropped the paternity
bombshell on me, sobbing against my naked chest in tears I knew I had
to do something to get him out of the funk he's been in.

It's clear he's hurt; upset that Bella didn't find out about Nora being his
sooner and with Nora's diagnosis it's overwhelming him.
It feels to me like the pain of knowing I'll never be able to have kids, the
loss you feel and have to come to terms with.

Making love to Austin last night though, it was also clear it wasn't just
this news that had him scattered and not focusing on being with me.
The conversation we'd had a couple of months ago, about him missing
being with a guy had been on my mind since then and I know there is
only one thing I can do to make Austin feel better.

I've never been to the boxing gym without Austin, so walking in and
having every eye in the place turn to stare at me makes me blush.
I want to turn on my heel and rush out the door, whilst telling myself
this is a ridiculous idea.

Spotting Kaden across the room he smiles at me, beckoning me over
with a cheeky grin.
I don't know why I'm feeling super nervous but I am.
Reaching him, he greets me, "Hey, Dana. Is Austin with you?"
"No, I came without him because I need to talk to you about him."

"Oh, shit. Has something bad happened? I haven't spoken to him in forever. I fucking miss him."

"Yeah, well he just found out that Nora is his daughter."

"Nora?"

"Yeah, Bella's kid."

"Oh right, but fuck, that's crazy."

"I know. He hasn't been himself lately and now this," I say, feeling tears sting my eyes, my heart breaking for Austin all over again.

"How so?"

"He misses being with a guy and hasn't been in contact with any of his friends lately."

"That's fucked Dana," he says annoyed, "he shut me out and then tells you that. It doesn't make sense."

"I know, I'm sorry, but I just thought I'd try to help."

"I appreciate that, so much. I definitely miss him."

"I'll let him know and get him to contact you."

"Thanks, Dana. I've gotta go change, but I'll catch ya soon."

I smile at him, stretching up to kiss him on the cheek before we part ways.

Heading home, I'm thinking about telling Austin, wondering if he'll be angry at me for going behind his back to Kaden.

I don't honestly know what else I could have done and something has been on my mind for weeks since Austin first mentioned about being with a guy.

I'm just not ready to tell him that yet.

Getting home, twenty minutes later, I find Austin in the kitchen cooking dinner and it smells divine.

He's shirtless and wearing Adidas trackies hanging low on his hips.

He's humming something and dancing around the kitchen whilst he cooks.

Stepping up behind him, I grab him around the waist.

"Smells delicious, stud," I tease inhaling the smell of his freshly showered skin and the bacon and garlic cooking.

He turns around in my embrace, kissing my forehead.

"Hey, gorgeous. You're home late."

I kiss his lips softly and quickly.

"I went to see Kaden," I blurt out, not able to meet his eyes.

"You what?"

"Went to see Kaden, and tell him that you miss him."

"Why Dan? You should've told me. It's none of your business."

I pull back from the embrace.

"I'm sorry Austin, but it is my business. You're my fiancé and I hate seeing you so miserable because you miss him."

"I don't fucking miss him, Dan. I miss being with a guy in general."

"I get that, but you shouldn't have shut Kaden out of your life, just because you're scared to be friends with him."

"Of course I'm scared Dan. I'm scared I'll fucking cheat on you."

"I trust you Austin, but I know you miss Kaden and being with a guy."

He looks at the floor, sighing deeply before he looks up at me with odd lust blazing in his eyes.

"I do miss him so much, and really want to be with him again Dan, but I can't do that to you. I won't cheat on you Dana, I love you."

"I know, but you can't let go of a part of yourself Aust. I feel like I'm not enough for you."

He pulls me into a hug again, stepping back to the stove and turning it off behind his back.

Brushing my hair off my cheeks, he muses softly, "You're more than enough Dana. I chose you because I love you and I will choose you again, over anyone including Kaden or any other guy."

I pull back, starting to pace the room because the anxiety is rising in my chest.

Part of me knows what I'm about to say is right for Austin, but I don't know if I'm prepared for what I'm about to suggest.

Stopping my pacing, I shake my head, muttering, "No, no."

"No what Dan?"

"I can't let you not be yourself. Do you really still want to be with a guy again? Maybe even Kaden?"

"Of course I do Dana, but if you don't want me to, I'm not going to."

"I didn't say that. I...I...was wondering if..." I gulp.

My heart is hammering, the words on the tip of my tongue.

"Dan, what are you trying to say? You're confusing me."

"Um...have...no...would you ever have a threesome?"

He gapes at me and then laughs.

"I have...before we got together with Kaden actually and Bella."

"Oh shit...um...really?"

"Yeah, it was before she found out she was having Nora. Why are you asking that?"

"Because maybe we could have one?"

He smiles wide, chuckling softly as thoughts clearly tick over in his head.

"You would do that for me?"

"Yeah, of course, I will, Austin. I want to make you happy."

"Shit, Dan, I'd love that, but who with?"

My cheeks flush, thoughts tumbling in my head of how Kaden looked at the boxing ring; all sweaty and panting.

"Kaden maybe. I think he's kinda hot."

"Oh...um...yeah I guess."

"Contact him, Austin. Apologise for being a dick, and set it up. I'm in."

"Alright, gorgeous," he says winking at me, "right now though I think we should fuck right here in the kitchen so I can show you how much I love you before we finish cooking dinner."

I don't reply, just moan before kissing him hard.

My insides feel giddy with the thought of having a threesome, two guys paying attention to me and I'm excited by all the pleasure such a dirty proposition entails.

Forty-Four | Healing Discussion

Austin

Heading into the hospital to hear more about Nora's illness and how my blood test results are going to impact her treatment is making my heart pound hard in my chest.

The overwhelming smell of bleach hits my nostrils and gagging I try to hold back a cough, but I can't and coughing like mad makes me feel a little faint.

Spotting Bella in the waiting room, I power walk to her and pull her into a hug.

"Hey Bel," I say a little breathless.

"Hey Austin, are you ok? You look a little pale."

"Yeah, yeah, I'm fine. Just got a big whiff of bleach."

"Oh ok, do you need to sit down a minute?"

"Nah, all good. Let's go in."

I nod at Travis, who takes her hand with his, bringing it up to his lips to kiss.

I follow them, not sure what to say to him. He's possessive of her, but it doesn't seem menacing.

He clearly loves her and I'm glad she's got someone like him looking out for her.

Knocking on the doctor's office door, we wait until we hear him call us inside. He stands from his desk and ushers us to sit down in the chairs in front of his desk.

Travis sits on one side of Bella, his hand resting on her thigh comfortingly and I sit on the other, taking her other hand in mine.

"Welcome," he says oddly, "I'm glad you could all make it today to discuss Nora's case and your results Mr Belvinz."

"Thanks, doctor, we're glad you could fit us in on such short notice after having to reschedule," Travis says, looking at Bella out of the corner of his eye.

"It's no problem, Mr Banes," the doctor says calmly before looking at me.

"So firstly, Mr Belvinz, your blood test and DNA results indicate that you're most definitely Nora's biological father."

"Um, yeah, that's great," I reply, gulping and looking at Bella, squeezing her hand in mine.

She smiles at me before asking the doctor, "So can he help with her treatment?"

"Yes, but at this stage, we're not looking to head down the treatment path of a bone marrow transplant."

"Why is that?" I ask, my heart hammering in my chest.

Finding out about Nora being my daughter was enough of a shock, but having to face the fact that she's just a year old and has cancer is so horrible I can't even comprehend it.

"Nora is young, and we believe she will respond very well to chemotherapy. If that doesn't work or a relapse occurs after remission is established through Chemo then a bone marrow transplant would be considered."

"And would Austin be a match for that? Or me?" Bella asks, her voice trembling.

"Yes, Ms Mishal. Mr Belvinz is a suitable match in that case, as may any future siblings of Nora with Mr Belvinz."

"Oh, um...that won't be happening." She laughs slightly and Travis smirks.

"They aren't together doctor. Bella is my...partner," Travis says, stumbling on the word partner and Bella sniggers under her breath.

They're hiding something, but it's not important right now.
"So doctor, what is the process now?"
"We need to make sure Nora is well enough to begin chemo, so she will be on an intensive course of antibiotics and we will begin chemo early in the new year."
"Sounds good."
"Just try to enjoy Christmas, together as a family and I will be in contact to see how Nora is responding to the antibiotics and when her first chemo is scheduled."
"Thank you," Bella replies as we all stand up.

We each shake the doctor's hand and walk out of his office.
I give Bella a hug goodbye, telling her I'll message her soon and I head out of the hospital.

Once outside I suck in some fresh air and wipe the tears from my eyes as I head to the ute.
I don't know what to think, but I kinda wish I could take Nora's pain away by experiencing it myself.
It's not fair that my little girl has to endure so much so early in her life.
All I can hope is that she's resilient and healing comes.

Forty-Five | Three's Company

Austin

Receiving Kaden's text message a couple of weeks ago, after my conversation with Dana still came as a shock. And that was partly due to the fact that I'd been expecting it, but I'd also been thinking about the possibility of a threesome between him, myself & Dana.

I'd put it straight out there that I'd missed him and hearing he missed me as well gave me the damn feels and hurt like a damn punch to the chest.
I'd wanted to ask straight up about the threesome but thought it might be best to reconnect as friends first before we ended up in bed together, naked and fucking.

Just the thought of fucking him has my cock aching in my daks, as I head to the boxing gym for the first time in months.
I'd been going to a normal gym so I wasn't out of shape, but I was a little pudgy as boxing was different to a normal workout. And I certainly missed it, but I missed Kaden more.
I'm pissed off with myself for shutting him out of my life when I got with Dana, but the last couple of weeks had made me realise how much I missed having a guy best mate to talk to.

Of course, I love Anni to pieces, she will always be my bestie and I've definitely loved talking to her about the Nora news, as her female perspective made me see it more from Bella's point of view, but there's nothing like a guy best mate to get tanked with or give shit to.

So, I'm sucking it up, and heading back to boxing.

Walking in, the familiar smells of sweat and leather hit my nose and I inhale, closing my eyes for a moment. I feel someone step beside me, patting me on the back.
My eyes shoot open when a familiar chuckle reverberates around me.
Coach is standing beside me, an arm around my shoulders.
"Welcome back Austin. We've missed you around here, son."
"Hey, coach. I've missed it here too. Have you seen Kaden today?"
"Yeah, he just finished up training. Should be in the change rooms."
"Thanks, coach. I'll go catch him, and get into some low key stuff later."
"No worries, son. I'm sure Kaden will be glad to see ya."
I nod, heading to the change rooms.

Walking in, I find Kaden is the only guy in the room and his back is towards me, whilst he shoves his clothes into his locker.
I watch him for a moment, my cock aching as he strips from first his t-shirt and then his shorts.
His bare arse comes into immediate view, showing me he was commando underneath the short as fuck shorts.
I curse myself that it turns me on seeing him naked again.
I love Dana, but seeing Kaden looking as hot as ever definitely still has an effect on my cock.

Clearing my throat, he turns around, covering up his junk awkwardly with his hands.
I saunter into the room, teasing him, "Hey Kaden. You don't need to hide ya hot hard cock from me."
He drops his hand, and I glare at his cock which is semi-hard from my presence in the room.

"Hey, Austin. What are you doing here? I thought we were catching up for some frothy's next week."

"I wanted to see you, and ask you something in person."

"Ok, um, ask away I guess."

He's nervous and it's fucking sexy.

My whole body is screaming at me, and I want to kiss him and touch him, but I can't, yet.

"How would you like to have a threesome with me again?"

He gapes at me, gulping hard. "Um, yeah, that would be fucking ripper. Would it be with Dana?"

"Yeah, she told me how she came to see you and it was all her idea."

"Well, I'm down," he bellows, reaching out to bro hug me in a sideways hug.

"Thanks for not crashing your junk against me bro. I'm finding it hard to keep my cock in my daks right now."

"Damn straight. You still turn me on, Aust."

"Likewise, Kad. So when you free?"

"Next Friday night?"

"Sweet, I'll send ya deets to our new digs."

"Awesome, I'm gonna go shower thinking about when we fucked for the first time."

He walks away, wiggling his damn arse at me and heading out I laugh, waving to coach as I walk out the door.

I need to get home and wank hard or fuck Dana whilst I think about our upcoming threesome.

~~

I've been on edge all week, thinking about the threesome, but Dana has been even more on edge.

She's pacing the room now, wearing tight leggings and a crop top bra in neon pink.

As always she looks fucking gorgeous.

Putting my hands on her shoulders, I stop her pacing.

"Dana, calm down gorgeous."

"I'm nervous, Austin. I've never done anything like this before."

"I know, but trust me. It's all about pleasure, and you don't have to do anything you're not comfortable with."

"I'm not sure what I'm not comfortable with."

"Well, think for a minute…do you want Kaden to kiss you?"

"No, not really. I just want to kiss you."

"Ok, and what about him giving you an Aussie or fucking you?"

She sighs, huffing out a strained breath.

"Maybe an Aussie but I only want you to fuck me."

"Ok, then it's settled. Kaden won't kiss or fuck you, but give you an Aussie. Are you cool with me kissing him?"

"Yeah, I'm cool with you doing whatever you need to."

"What about sucking him?"

She blushes and giggles. "I'll see. Sucking another guy other than you sounds kinda exciting."

"Damn gorgeous, hearing you say that is turning me on already."

She doesn't reply, instead kisses me, pushing her hands into the back of my Flash sleep shorts.

Cupping my arse cheeks she pulls my body against hers, my cock pressing against the entrance of her pussy in her tight leggings.

"God, Dana, I love you. Thank you so much for this," I say, my forehead against hers when I pull back from the kiss.

"I'd do anything for you, Austin."

"Likewise, gorgeous," I reply with a smile.

We break apart when the doorbell rings. Grabbing her hand we walk to the door together.

"Ready, gorgeous?"

"Ready, stud," she replies with a teasing tone, as I open the door to Kaden.

He's wearing the same outfit that he was at boxing the other day, and I lick my lips when I usher him inside.

"Hey, Kad. You look hot."

"So do you, Aust," he tells me, looking me up and down, before his gaze shifts to Dana next to me, "And Dana, damn girl, you look gorgeous."

"Thanks," she replies meekly, "you look pretty hot."

"Thanks," he says sweetly, leaning down to kiss her cheek softly.

She blushes and her shyness coming out stirs my cock in my daks.

Walking towards the bedroom together, Kaden asks, "So what's our limits?"

We sit down together on the edge of our king size bed, me in the middle. I turn to Kaden.

"I'm open to anything, but no kissing or fucking Dan for you."

"Right, so Dana, are you good with me tasting your pussy and sharing it with Austin?"

"Yes," she hisses between her lips.

Kaden chuckles softly, locking eyes with me.

"Damn Austin, you've got a dirty gorgeous fiancee."

"I know, so how about we all get naked?" I suggest, grabbing the hem of his t-shirt.

He lifts it over his head and we both stand up together, dropping our daks to the floor with our eyes locked on each other. And even though I know Dana is behind me, I can't help myself; grabbing Kaden around the waist and pulling him close, crashing my lips to his in a heated kiss. Frantically I pash Kaden, stroking his cock to attention between us.

I'm so lost in his kiss I don't realise at first that Dana is behind me, now naked and stroking my cock with her dainty hands.

Breaking the kiss with Kaden, I tip my head back and kiss Dana, loving how different their kisses feel against my lips.

"God, Aust, watching you pash someone else turns me on," Kaden bellows, letting out a moan.
Breaking my kiss with Dana, I wink at him.
"Kissing you turns me on, Kad, but I think it's time to give my girl some pleasure."
"Oh fuck yeah," he says moaning.

Dana shifts away from me, lying back on the bed.
I watch Kaden as he falls to his knees between her legs, his mouth dipping to her pussy.
He licks her folds and moans, eating her pussy and loving every second.

Climbing onto the bed, I run my hands over Dana's body, loving watching her writhing in pleasure from Kaden's tongue deep within her pussy.
Once at her face, I line my cock up with her mouth, pushing the tip between her lips.
"Suck me, gorgeous," I demand, slipping my hard cock further into her mouth.
She takes it all, licking me and taking me in out as Kaden's pace increases.
I can feel her deep moans over my cock as her pleasure intensifies and I want to explode down her throat but also want to prolong the pleasure and have her come on my cock too.
Kaden bites down on her clit when I pull my cock out of her mouth and she screams out a loud *'Fuck'* as her first orgasm pulses through her body.

Kaden stands up, grabbing me around the waist and kissing me hard.
I moan, licking his lips to taste Dana on them.

Breaking the kiss we fall against the bed, and I look at Dana beside me.

"Dan, can I fuck you now?"

She nods and climbs on my lap, reserve cowgirl.

Slipping my cock inside her pussy I start thrusting up into her and Kaden just watches, hissing when Dana grabs his cock fisting it and stroking it.

I'm still thrusting into her wet pussy when she lies back against me and Kaden falls against us both. Firstly she kisses me, and I match the rhythm of my tongue with my cock.

She moans against my mouth and my cock throbs inside her. I want to come so bad, but the pleasure is so unbelievable I wish I could go all night.

I'm shocked when Dana breaks our kiss, and grabs Kaden's cheeks in her palms, kissing him hard.

I hear him moan, as their kiss grows deeper and Dana sits up a bit to be closer to him.

It turns me on so bad, my cock feels so close to release.

"Dan, fuck, keep doing that and I'll come."

She laughs breaking her kiss with Kaden.

"Not yet, stud," she teases climbing off my lap and crawling onto all fours.

"Fuck me, doggy please, stud," she begs, winking at us both.

I obey, sliding into her from behind and when I feel Kaden line his body up behind me, his cock slipping into my arse as I fuck Dana, I nearly come apart in that very moment.

I lean back to kiss him, pounding my cock into Dana's pussy hard and fast whilst Kaden rocks his cock inside my arse.

"Kad, fuck, fuck that's so good. God, I'm going to come so hard."

"Mmm, Aust," he moans, giving me a quick kiss, and pounding into me harder.

"Make ya girl come."

"Damn straight," I bellow, "I think we're all going to come together."

With a final thrust, we all scream out, "Fuck!"

Our bodies one as the wave of our orgasms rocks through us and we pull apart collapsing on the bed next to each other.

Dana is trembling from her orgasm, and I kiss her softly.

"I love you, Dana. Thank you for this."

"I love you too Austin. And it was amazing. But I'm sorry I kissed Kaden."

"Don't be sorry about that Dan. It was hot."

Kaden laughs next to me, propping his head up on his elbow and looking at both of us.

"Yeah Dana, kissing you was damn hot. Austin's a lucky bugger to call you his fiancee."

"Thanks, Kaden."

She cuddles against me, and I smile as Kaden kisses me again, softly and sweetly. He leans close to whisper in my ear, "I loved it, Aust. I hope we can have some us time again soon."

I don't reply, instead, I pull Dana closer, entangling our legs together, one of mine with hers and one with Kaden's. And I kiss him again, feeling confused, but happier than I have in months.

Forty-Six | Open Up

Dana

Lying in bed together after the most pleasurable sex I've ever had, courtesy of my fiancé and his gorgeous friend, I try to calm my breathing.

My eyes are closed, and my legs are entangled with Austins.
I feel content, the rush of the sex still has me on a high.

Next to me, even though Austin's body is entangled with mine I can hear him kissing Kaden, moaning contently and it's kinda turning me on again.
After the last hour, and now as Austin is clearly happy kissing Kaden I know I need to tell my fiancé what's been plaguing my mind for weeks.

Opening my eyes, I watch them pashing for a minute, reaching down to touch myself.
I can't help but moan and I whisper into the air, "Oh Aust."
His voice breaks through my haze, "Yeah Dan?"
I take my hand from between my legs, and hold it up to his face.
"Nothing, I was um...just enjoying myself whilst you guys were pashing."
"Oh really? Does us pashing turn you on, gorgeous?"
"Yeah, it does," I reply, feeling my cheeks heat.
"Damn, Dana that's hot girl," Kaden taunts me, winking at Austin when he continues, "Aust, touch her whilst you pash me."
"Oh yeah Kad, you're such a dirty fucker."

Austin reaches down to flick his callous fingers over my clit.
It feels so much better than my own fingers, and when he slides two inside me, his thumb still rubbing circles over my clit he kisses Kaden, and moans against his lips.

Austin's touch and the sounds they're making whilst kissing makes my whole body hum.
I've honestly never felt so much pleasure in my life.
Kaden breaks their kiss, and I look down to see him stroking Austin's dick in his big hands.
Austin moans in pleasure and presses his fingers up inside me.
"Feel good, Dan?" he asks, turning his head to mine and kissing me.
"Yes," I whisper against his lips, bucking my hips up as my climax starts to build.
He bites my lip pulling back, his orgasm shooting out of his dick all over Kaden.
"Damn, Austin. Watching you come makes me so hard," Kaden says with a sexy tone in his voice, "make ya girl come for me."

Austin looks at me, smirking and Kaden fists his own dick, stroking it whilst he watches Austin making me writhe in pleasure.
My clit starts throbbing and I start to tremble feeling my release starting to hit.
With a loud "Oh fuck! Austin!" I come, my whole body spasming from a hard release.
In the same moment, Kaden screams out, "Fuck!" his release spurting out all over Austin's stomach.

We all look at each other then, sitting up and Austin gives me a sweet loving kiss.
"I love you, Dana."

I'm about to reply when his eyes dart to Kaden, and he winks at him.
"And Kad, I don't know man...the way you make me feel; I need it more than air."
"Yeah, back at you, gorgeous. No guy makes me feel like you do."
It's now or never, I need to put my offer out there.
"Austin, can I ask you something?"
"Yeah, anything gorgeous."
"How would you feel about an open relationship?"

He gapes at me, looking to Kaden who's just as shocked by my question.
"Well, um I don't know. What would be the terms? It's a big ask, Dan."
"It's for you, not me."
"How so?"
"I know you enjoy being with both girls and guys, so you'd be free to hook up with each other or if you want to hook up with another guy."
"Um yeah, that sounds sweet, but what about you gorgeous, what do you get out of this?"
"You Austin, because you're free to hook up with Kaden or someone else if you tell me, but you can't be with another girl, only me."
"Dana, that sounds so fucking awesome. But only if you're sure?"
"I'm sure. I love you Austin, and I'd do anything to make you happy."
"Thanks, Dana. I love you so fucking much," he replies huskily taking a deep breath in, before he kisses me hard.

"So the only stipulation is you have to tell me before you hook up, ok?"
"Ok, gorgeous."
"I trust you'll be safe."
"Always," he replies, kissing me again, "So, Dan, are you cool if Kaden and I have some alone time now?"
"Of course. Have fun. I'll see you this arvo after I've done some errands."
"Sweet, gorgeous."

I get out of bed, turning to look at them already pashing and touching each other.

Going to shower, I know I've made the right decision.

I have my gorgeous happy fiancé back because I've given him the opportunity to open up to the pleasure he needs in his life.

Forty-Seven | Birthday Love

Elyse

I'd not seen Kaden much in the last few weeks, partly because exams were kicking my arse and partly because he was acting a little odd.
He'd told me he'd reconciled with Austin and was happy to be friends with him again, but that made me feel uneasy and thoroughly confused about what I want from him.

He'd text me, and told me to dress up because he was taking me out on a date for my birthday.
We hadn't been on a date since before we first slept together, and I'm damn excited.
It makes me feel like we're actually in a relationship, even though according to Kaden we aren't.

To tease him, and hopefully make him realise how I feel about him, that I want to be his girlfriend I decide on actually wearing a dress.
It's a plain white slip dress with spaghetti straps, and it's tight over my tits.
I've only put a triangle crop bra underneath it, so my tits are practically free under the dress.
I also decided on wearing a lacy white g-string, so hopefully, we're going to be inside as I don't want the world to see my arse.
Leaving my hair down, I brush it sleek and apply a lick of black eyeliner and mascara to my eyes, making them pop.
The only other makeup I put on is a thin coat of strawberry lipgloss.

My cheeks are already flushed from thinking about Kaden seeing me in this dress and telling him I'm wearing a g-string underneath.

I've never had birthday sex before unless you count pleasuring myself with the vibrator I bought myself a few years back as a present to myself; so I'm excited, so much so my clit is throbbing and the g-string is already damp in the crotch.

Grabbing my phone, keys, and wallet I head outside to wait for him on the kerb.
I'm kicking the grass with my thongs, feeling nervously excited.
My heart skips when his red commodore pulls up on the kerb in front of me.
I get in and lean over the console to kiss him.

"Hey sexy minx," he greets me, his eyes wandering over my outfit, "You wore a dress, huh?"
"Only for you foxy, and..." I wink at him, giggling as I open my legs wide.
"And what sexy minx?"
"I'm wearing a g-string under it."
"No way, are you serious?"
"Find out," I taunt, hitching the dress up across my hips.
His eyes drop to my pussy, and he groans, reaching across to touch me through the soft lace.
"Damn sexy minx. You make me want to pull you over onto my lap for a bit of fun."
Locking my eyes on his, I smirk and wink at him.
"Do it."
"Seriously? Birthday car sex?"
I giggle, lifting my arse off the seat and sliding my g-string down my legs.
Kicking it and my thongs off I climb over the console and Kaden slides his seat back, reclining the back a little.

Once in his lap, I rock my bare pussy over the bulge in his jeans.
"Get your cock out, foxy. I want to have birthday sex with you."
"Mmm, sexy minx," he moans, grabbing my cheeks to pull me down for
a kiss.
Against my lips, he murmurs, "Sexy minx, please let me fuck you now."
I laugh against his lips, licking them before I pull back and shift a little so
he can reach between us to undo his jeans.

He cheekily lifts up my dress a little, looking at my bare pussy that's
practically dripping onto his jeans; I'm so turned on.
He runs a finger up my slit to my clit, flicking it before taking his finger
between his lips and licking it.
"Mmm, yummy," he taunts smirking at me.
I grab his cock in my fist, freeing it from the confines of his Y-front
boxers, and without giving him any warning I slide over him, pushing his
hardness inside my wet hole.
"Oh fuck," I murmur, rocking my pelvis side to side on his cock.
"Fuck sexy minx, you feel so good. Kiss me."

Leaning over him I crash my lips to his in a heated kiss, continuing to
bounce my pelvis up and down on his cock.
The kiss becomes frantic, our tongues meeting in the same rhythm as
our bodies and I can feel his cock throbbing inside my pussy as his climax
builds.

"Lys, I'm gonna come. Hop off yeah?"
I shake my head at him. "Come inside me Kad. I'm on the shot
remember?"
"Oh right. God, fuck, you feel good riding me. Tell me sexy minx that
you're close too?"
"So...close..." I reply breathlessly, pushing down harder onto his cock,
making it deeper than ever.

I start to tremble, feeling my clit throb with my impending release. Kaden's cock is throbbing inside me, our bodies in tune with each other and I sigh, screaming out, "Fuck!" as I fall off the edge of my release; Kaden's throbbing release spurting inside me and making my whole body shake as I come down from my wave of pleasure.

"Damn Lys. You're something else."

"Back at you Kad," I reply kissing him softly.

My heart is pounding looking down at him with his limp cock still inside me.

I sigh before climbing off his lap and back over the console.

"So since we've skipped straight to the dessert portion of the night, do you still want dinner?"

"Yeah, of course. But um...Kaden?"

He starts the engine again, putting his seat upright again.

"Yeah Lys?"

"How do you feel about me? Am I your girlfriend?"

"I don't want to label what we have Lys. I really like being with you. Is that ok with you?"

"Well, no...not really. I want to be your girlfriend, Kaden. I'm falling in love with you."

"I told you Lys, I can't do love. I thought you were cool with just being together?"

"I'm not Kaden. It's not fair. I deserve better than that, even if the sex is amazing."

"Yeah, well I'm sorry, but I can't give you more than that right now."

"Maybe I should just get back with my ex, Zack," I muse, turning away from Kaden's stare.

He laughs. "Mr *I don't know how to give a chick an orgasm'*. Seriously?"

"Yeah, at least he can love me and tell me he loves me."

"If that's what you want, I'm not stopping you Lys. But honestly, I don't want you to. I want you, but I can't do love."

I don't reply, instead, I open my car door and get out, leaning in the doorframe to say, "Thanks for the birthday sex, Kaden. I'll talk to you later."

Slamming the car door I run up the path to the front door, letting myself in and falling to the floor in tears.
I'd told him I was falling in love with him, but I'd lied to his face because I'm so crazy in love with him that his words have ripped my heart out.
Why can't he love me back?

Forty-Eight | For Me

It'd been a long arse week, since Elyse's birthday, when she'd practically confessed she's in love with me.

I've not been able to get her off my mind; how she gets to me without even trying.

I feel kinda guilty though, as I didn't tell her about being with Austin and I don't know if I'm going to be able to keep away from him, because he too gets to me without even trying.

Being with him again though certainly brings my feelings for him to the forefront again.

I'd nearly said, *'I love you'* to him when we were together after the threesome, but thankfully I was able to keep my damn trap closed.

I know I'm still feeling something for him and I'm not sure if it's love or just insatiable lust like I feel for Elyse.

I feel so bad about how I treated her on her birthday and I need to make amends.

I haven't told her I'm heading over to hers, but I want to surprise her.

I've bought her flowers, chocolates and a teddy bear.

I know she's a tomboy, but I just hope she'll appreciate the thought regardless.

I'm actually feeling nervous, standing at her doorstep when I knock.

Her sweet bestie answers the door, greeting me with a meek smile.

"Hi Lillie, is Elyse here?"

"Hi, Kaden. Yeah, she's in her room."

She lets me in, eyeing the presents in my arms.

"Are they for her?"

"Yeah, I fucked up on her birthday, so they are I'm sorry gifts."

"She'll like that."
"I hope so," I say smiling at her and heading down the hallway to Elyse's room.

She has music blaring, some chick singing about not being good enough, and holding in my scoff I knock loudly on the door.
The music stops and she calls out, "Yeah, Lil?"
"It's not Lillie. It's me Lys. Can I come in?"
"No! Go away, Kaden!"
"Please Lys, just let me in. I'm sorry ok," I say sighing; my head against the door.
"No! I don't want to talk to you."
"Elyse, please just let me in," I beg, my voice strained.

It seems like an hour passes, but it's barely a minute when she comes to the door, opening it and making me stumble into her room, clutching the gifts tightly so as to not drop them.

She eyes them, as I take in her outfit of short pyjama shorts and a singlet top with built-in bra. Her long dark chestnut hair is down and she looks ravishing; as usual.
"So what do you want? Are those for me?"
"Yeah, belated birthday and I'm sorry presents," I tell her, handing her the teddy bear first, and leaning forward to kiss her on the cheek.

She sniffs the teddy bear, clutching it to her chest before taking the flowers and chocolates which she also sniffs.
"How'd you know that white roses are my fave?"
"I didn't, but they reminded me of you."
She laughs at my stupid words. I'm so out of my depth.
"Really? How?"
"They're beautiful," I mutter, sure that I'm blushing.

She murmurs, stepping around me to close her bedroom door.

"Are you just trying to get into my daks, Kaden?" she says with a teasing tone.

"Maybe, is it working?"

"No, but this is really sweet. And I guess I can forgive you, for now."

She puts the bear down on the bed, and the chocolates and roses on the bedside table, stepping closer to me.

"Just for now?"

"Yeah, if you kiss me I might forgive you. You'll just have to find out."

Grabbing her around the waist I kiss her hard, my breath catching in my chest when her tongue runs along my lips to tease me.

When our lips part, the kiss turning dirty, my cock throbs in my daks, and I push her down onto the bed.

She moans, arching her hips up to mine, before breaking the kiss.

Our foreheads are touching for a moment and she sighs.

"I meant what I said, Kaden."

"I know, Lys," I sigh, rolling off her to lay down beside her.

Brushing her hair from her cheeks, I tell her softly, "But you can't fucking love me Lys."

"Why? I can't help how I feel about you."

"I know, but I can't just be with a girl."

"I get that, but I don't want to share you with anyone, especially a guy."

"Yeah but I'm still struggling with my sexuality Lys. I love being with you, so fucking much."

She mutters something incoherent.

"You know how much you turn me on? How much I love fucking you?"

"Yeah, but why isn't that enough?"

"Because I miss being with a guy."

"I can't begin to understand that, but I...I...um...actually..."

She cuts off her words, blushing.

"Actually what Lys?"

"I um...actually looked up anal."

"Seriously? When?"

"The day after you made me come on the couch when I was on my rags."

"Really? And you didn't tell me?"

"I forgot," she admits, kissing me before she speaks again, "But I kinda want to try it."

"I'd love that Lys and also maybe something else?"

"What? What else is there?"

"Would you wear a strap on to fuck me?"

Her eyes boggle at my question, before she crashes her lips to mine, licking them teasingly again.

"I'll think about it," she whispers against my lips and that's all the confirmation I need for now.

I kiss her back, starting to run my hands all over her body.

At least for now, I can enjoy just being with her, without labels and without expressing feelings.

I know I'm going to have to face how I feel about her and about Austin soon enough, but for now, I'm just going to let my body show her how I feel.

Forty-Nine | Torturous Chatter

Elyse

I'm pissed with myself for giving into Kaden again so easily. We'd spent the arvo before he'd headed to boxing pashing and touching each other in my bedroom.

I'd come at least four times, and my pussy is still throbbing thinking about his touch.

Sitting on the couch next to Lillie, I know the tv is on, but I'm in another world, not sure what we're watching.

Lillie laughs out loud and looks at me out of the corner of her eyes.

"Ely, are you ok? That's literally the funniest line ever and you didn't even crack a smile."

I turn my gaze to the tv, realising that, 'The Big Bang theory' is on and Sheldon has just spat out one of his crazy one-liners.

"Um...I was just thinking about something."

"Did Kaden do something wrong? He said something about stuffing up your birthday."

I laugh at my best friends innocent words, knowing that Kaden most certainly didn't say he stuffed up my birthday.

"Yeah he did fuck up my birthday, but he made up for that."

"So what's wrong then? Are you still angry at him?"

"No, I'm angry at myself," I confess and Lillie gives me a confused look. "Why?"

"Because I gave into him when he barely apologised and he won't call me his girlfriend or tell me how he feels about me."

"Oh right...ok...so you don't think he loves you?"

"I don't know Lil. When we're together physically it seems like he does, but he keeps telling me he can't love me. That he can't just be in love with a girl."

"I don't understand."

"He's bisexual, Lil."

"Oh right, so is it weird being with him?"

"No, the sex is amazing, but he asked me to wear a fake dick to fuck him in the arse." Lillie puts her fingers in her ears. "And he wants to fuck me in…"

She cuts me off, waving her arms at me and shaking her head.

"No way, Ely. I'm not talking about that…sounds like torture. Why would you want to do that?"

"Because Kaden wants me to, Lil. And I'm in love with him."

"Yeah, well love aside, I'd never do that."

"Yeah, I don't know what to do," I reply shrugging and standing up. "I'm gonna hit the hay. Sleep well bestie."

"Sleep better, bestie," she calls out as I close my bedroom door behind me, flopping down on the bed and inhaling Kaden's scent on the sheets. Yep, I'm a fucking goner. I'm in love with a gorgeous guy who won't love me back.

Fifty | Christmas Glee

Bella

Christmas has come around again so quickly, and I'm running around like a chook with my head cut off trying to organise everything.
It hadn't helped that I'd been feeling off for the last couple of months since our Fiji trip, and I'd put on a little weight.

In the kitchen, I'm starting to prep the veggies for lunch tomorrow and feeling really faint.
Travis comes up behind me, wrapping his arms around my waist and kissing the top of my head.

"Honey, you need to stop this craziness. Come into the lounge and open a present with me."
I turn in his arms, kissing him softly. "But it's only Christmas Eve."
"Yeah I know, but that's something we've always done in my family and I want to see if I can give you a special present."
His eyes light up with his words, and he leads me into the lounge room, clutching my hand excitedly.
I sit down on the couch, and he picks up a small wrapped present from under the tree.
It's a rectangle box so I'm thinking it's jewellery of some kind.
"Open it, honey," he says eagerly.

Ripping the paper off, I find a box of pregnancy tests, with a note on top, *'Take one, honey. It will be positive.'*
Tears sting the corner of my eyes.
"Bella, please don't cry."

"But what if I'm not? If it's negative?"

"Honey, it won't be. You've been unwell since we got back from Fiji. I know things with Nora have been worrying, but it's more than that."

"I'm scared, Travis."

"I know honey," he says sitting next to me, and pulling me close into a strong embrace, "But I'm sure if you're pregnant, everything will be fine this time. Go take one and come back."

I give him a quick kiss, and head to the bathroom.

My stomach is in knots as I quickly pee on the stick, and the two pink lines come up immediately before my eyes.

The test line is so much darker than the control.

I burst into tears, jumping up from the toilet and flushing it before I quickly wash my hands and rush back out to Travis.

Tears are streaming down my cheeks, and I'm a sobbing mess.

Travis looks at me, and his face falls.

"Please don't tell me it's negative honey?"

"No, no, it's positive...I...I...just...can't believe it."

"So happy tears then?"

"Very happy tears! I'm pregnant, Travis!"

"I knew it, Bella," he says jumping up from the couch and grabbing me around the waist, lifting my feet off the ground and spinning me around.

"I love you, Bella!" he says with a smile, putting me down and giving me a soft lingering kiss. "And I have another early present for you."

"This is enough of a present."

"I know, but you'll love this one," he says with a laugh, picking up another present.

This time ripping the paper, I open it and smile.

Inside is a yellow onesie with the words, *'Daddy's little monster'* on the front.

I lift it up, admiring it.

"Oh Travis, it's so cute. Thank you."

"You're welcome, honey. So how're we going to spend the rest of our Christmas Eve celebrating?"

I smile, stepping closer to him and wrapping my arms around his neck to pull him closer.

With his forehead against mine, I whisper softly, "Checking in on our little girl and then making love until tomorrow."

"Oh Bella," he moans, his lips brushing mine, "I can't think of anything better than spending the night loving you, my beautiful wife."

He crushes his lips to mine in a hard kiss, and I jump into his arms, wrapping my legs around him as we kiss, hungrily, not able to get enough of each other.

It's the best Christmas Eve in a very long time and I'm excited to share the day tomorrow with my family, the ones already here and the one to come that is growing inside me.

Fifty-One | Christmas Advice

Elyse

After Christmas lunch, we're all sitting around the lounge room, drinking and talking. I don't know if it's the right time to talk to Bella, especially with Tessa—Travis's younger sister—also here; but she's not paying attention to me, busy playing with her baby Tobias.

I wonder for a moment, if he'll be friends with Nora with them being so close in age, but I shake the thoughts aside when Bella elbows me in the side.

"Hey, Ely-bug," she says with a smile, "you ok?"

I scoot up close to Bella on the couch then and she gives me an odd look.

"Um…Bel-bear, I need to talk to you about something."

She ruffles my hair, and I shake my head at her annoyed.

"Stop, Bel-bear, I'm being serious."

"Sorry, Ely-bug. What's up?"

"I've been seeing a guy for most of the year, but we aren't together."

"So you're just sleeping with him?"

"Yeah, but I'm in love with him."

"And he doesn't feel the same?"

"I don't think so, but I'm not really sure. And he's…" I shake my head again, feeling myself blush.

"And he's what Elyse?"

"He's bi."

Her mouth falls open in shock.

"Do you think he's with someone else behind your back?"

"I don't know. Maybe."

"How could you be so stupid Elyse?"

"I don't know Bella. I can't help that I've fallen for him."

"True, but you could have said something sooner Elyse."

"I know. I wanted to tell you months ago, and I kinda did," I confess, biting down on my lip, waiting for her mind to tick over with my confession.

"Oh no, Elyse! You're talking about Kaden?"

"Yeah," I reply meekly, blushing, "I'm so in love with him Bel. I'm sorry."

"You don't have to be sorry, but seriously Elyse I don't think he's the right guy for you."

"I know he's not good for me, but the way he makes me feel I just can't explain it."

"I get you one hundred per cent, but you need to be careful Elyse. Obviously, you've fallen for him, but I don't want to see you get hurt if things don't turn out like you expect them to. I don't know if he's the commitment type."

"I know, I'll be careful. I'm on the shot now and I promise I'll break things off if I don't feel happy."

"You better. Use your super-smart brain, but trust your heart too."

"Is that what you did?"

"Yeah, my body knew Travis was mine before my heart did."

"Well, Bel-bear, I'm glad because he's perfect for you."

As though I've summoned him, he comes back into the room, holding a sleepy Nora against his hip.

"Who's perfect?" he asks with a chuckle.

Bella stands up and goes to give him a kiss.

"You, for me," she taunts, smirking at him, before looking back at me winking.

"Back at you, w...honey," he says with a smirk that has me intrigued about what he was actually going to say.

He whispers something to Bella and she nods before they both come back to sit down.

"Elyse, Tessa, we were going to wait until we had an ultrasound next week, but decided that because it's Christmas and it's just us that we need to tell you something."

I glare at them both, my eyes darting between them.

"What? Are you getting married?"

"No, I'm pregnant. About three months along."

I jump up excitedly wrapping her in an eager hug.

"Oh my god! Bel-bear! That's so exciting! Congrats!" I shriek.

Pulling back from hugging Bella I look at Travis, smiling, "And congrats to you to daddy."

"Thanks, Elyse."

"I'm so excited! I'm going to be an Aunty again. How is this little one doing, anyway?"

I touch Nora's chubby little cheeks and she giggles when I pick her up from Travis's lap.

"She's ok. We have her first chemo appointment in a few weeks."

"I still can't believe it."

"I know. It breaks my heart, but we're keeping positive," Bella says softly.

"Yeah, enough of that. We need to open the rest of the presents now Nor Nor is up."

Nora's eyes light up, and she lets out a little giggle. Taking her from Travis, I carry her against my hip to the Christmas tree and revel in the love in the room.

Nora starts ripping at her presents, and I watch my family around me. Tessa hugging her older brother—and my older sister—in congratulations. Travis takes his nephew from his sister's arms, cooing at the little boy and I can see the love in his eyes and I wonder if this new baby will be a boy or a girl.

Fifty-Two | Hospital Blues

Austin

January 2020

Clutching a crying Nora against my side I'm about ready to break down into tears myself as we walk into the hospital for her first chemotherapy appointment.
Bella had to head to a doctors appointment herself, having just found out she's pregnant and not being able to keep anything down with her bad morning sickness.

My heart is breaking for my little girl, as the doctor informed as the best way forward was to surgically install the catheter to administer the chemo medication. All I really heard was surgery and I'm petrified something is going to go wrong.

At the nurses' station to check-in, I put Nora down at my feet.
She grabs ahold of my leg, looking around anxiously.
"Hello, I'm here to check in my daughter, Nora Mishal."
Saying the word daughter but not my last name feels odd.
"And are you her father?"
"Yes, I believe Doctor Matthias updated the details last time we were in."
The nurse taps on her keyboard furiously, not looking up.
"Ok, you're Mr Austin Belvinz?"
"Yes."

"Do you have some ID and the consent paperwork for Nora?"

"Um, yeah, I have ID, but I haven't filled out any paperwork."

"No problems, I'll sort that out now, and it can be organised whilst Nora is prepped for surgery."

I hand her my licence, and she again taps some details into the computer before handing me a printed document to fill out.

"Take a seat, and start filling that out. The doctors will be with you soon to prep Nora for surgery. Let me know if you have any questions."

"Thank you," I reply, taking a clipboard and pen and hobbling over to the waiting area with Nora still attached to my leg.

I sit down in a chair, putting Nora in one next to me.

Kissing her hair, I soothe her, "It's going to be ok, baby girl. Dada is here."

She lets out little sobs, and I rub her head as I fill out the paperwork as quickly as I can.

I take it up to the desk, before sitting back down with Nora.

Pulling her onto my lap, I hug her tight, inhaling her sweet baby smell.

Barely a minute passes before the doctor comes to prep Nora for surgery.

I watch the whole process, feeling breathless and overwhelmed.

Nora continues her sobbing, but Doctor Matthias calms her with soothing words, helping her calm down when she's put on the stretcher.

Leaning down I kiss her forehead.

"See you soon, baby girl. Dada loves you," I tell her softly before she's wheeled away.

I head back out into the waiting room, to find Bella waiting anxiously with tears streaming down her cheeks.

"Hey, Bel," I greet her as calmly as I can with my heart still beating erratically.

"Hey, is she ok?"

"Yeah, they just took her in. She'll be fine."

"I hope so," she replies softly when I pull her into a hug, trying not to break down into tears again myself.

Again, I'm wishing I could be the one in Nora's shoes, but all I can do is be her father and love her with all my heart.

I may have only recently found out I'm her dad, but I've honestly loved her from the moment I first held her in my arms when she was born.

Fifty-Three | Hospital Drama

Austin

After Nora is out of surgery I'm sitting in the recovery room with Bella, waiting for her to wake up.

We're both silent, staring at each other unsure of what to say, both obviously desperate for Nora to wake up from the surgery and have the all clear to have the chemo started.

It had been a horrible couple of hours, as the doctors nearly lost her small body on the operating table.

Her heart stopped for two minutes and they had to resuscitate her, so now she's out she's hooked up to all sorts of machines that are consistently beeping in the tiny hospital room.

It's the only sound in the room, and it's doing my head in.

I can't think straight and feel trapped.

Stepping outside the room, I curse out a loud *fuck* leaning against the wall.

What I'd do for a fucking joint right now, anything really to calm me down.

I'd even go for a normal ciggie and I don't even smoke.

Even so, I'm about to head to find a cigarette vending machine when Bella steps out of the room closing the door behind her.

She stands in front of me, giving me dagger eyes.

"Are you ok?"

"No, Bella. I'm not fucking ok. Our little girl died today. Like actually died for two minutes and I'm fucking scared shitless that we're going to lose her completely."

"Please Austin. Don't say that, and don't you think I'm scared shitless as well. Every damn second."

"Yeah, I'm sorry. I shouldn't have reacted that way, but I can't stand this Bel. And to think I may have to go through the bone marrow transplant to. It's just fucking scary and unbelievable."

"I know. I don't want that to happen Austin, but we have to be strong to get through this together. Getting angry and upset with each other isn't going to help Nor."

"I know," I say slamming my palms back against the wall, "I um...also think Nora needs to live with me, just in case anything happens."

"No! I'm her mum Austin. I want her with me."

"I get that Bella, but with you being pregnant and Travis not always home because of footy it might be for the best."

"I guess. Can we just get through this arvo and maybe talk about it then?"

"Ok, sounds good," I reply nodding.

Through the door, we hear Nora gasping, quickly heading back in to find her starting to wake up.

Bella presses the call button and Nora's eyes flutter open, locking on me.

"Dada," she says softly through her breathing tube.

"I'm here baby girl. Dada's here," I soothe, taking her hand in mine and squeezing.

Bella looks at me, with a slight smile. I know she's thinking exactly the same thing that I am; that for some reason I'm the person Nora focused on the minute she woke up.

She's turning out to be a daddy's girl. I'm not sure if I'm honestly prepared for Nora to live with me, even though I suggested it to Bella.

Right now, we have to get through the rest of the day with Nora's chemo and then I need to talk to Dana about the possibility of Nora living with us, because our wedding is fast approaching and I don't want any added stress on her or to upset her by rubbing the 'Nora is my daughter card' in her face more.

I take in a deep breath in to calm myself when Doctor Matthias walks in with a smile.
I mentally hope and pray that this is the start of Nora's recovery, not the end of our time with her.

Fifty-Four | Brother Drama

Brennan

My damn motherfucking head is pounding, from coming down hard.
I know I can't go home and face Dad's wrath, so the only place I can
think to go is Kaden's.

Bashing on his front door, I hope he's home, and actually awake come to
think of it considering it's three am.
It's still as hot as blazers outside and I'm sweating like a damn pig.
Wiping my brow with my cotton t-shirt I can feel chunder rising in my
throat from licking my own damn sweat but also the brutal comedown.

Bending over into the nearby bush, I throw my guts the minute Kaden
opens the door.
"Bren, is that you? What the fuck are you doing here at this hour?"
"Hey, bro. I...I need to crash."
"Did you seriously just chunder in the bush?"
"Yeah, I'm...I'm...a bit...rough."
"Looks like it. Get inside dickhead," he berates me, grabbing my t-shirt
and pulling me inside.
"Please...can I...bed?" I ask, knowing the words don't make a damn bit
of sense, but my tongue and brain are not communicating with each
other.
"You know where the spare room is Bren. Sleep it off and we'll talk
tomorrow," my brother says with a tone that is way too fucking fatherly
for my liking.

I don't say anything back this time, because I can't trust my brain to not say something stupid.

Stumbling down the hallway to the spare room, I stop by the bathroom to chunder again and piss Niagara falls before I practically crash into the bed like a plank of wood.

Fuck bed feels good.

Focusing on my breathing, I close my eyes to drift to sleep. I'm going to feel like shit in the morning, and I need to confide in my brother, but I don't know if I'm ready to face my shit head on.

~~

Waking up, I'm feeling a little groggy, but thankfully my comedown isn't too hard since I chundered and my head is not pounding.
Sliding off the bed, stretching I take in a deep breath with a yawn before heading out to the kitchen for a coffee.

Kaden is sitting at the table, sipping coffee and eating cornflakes.
He looks up from his phone in his hand with a sheepish grin.
"Morning, bro," I greet him, a chipper tone in my voice.
"Morning, Bren. You doing better this morning?"
"Yeah, much. Had a ripper night," I tell him, obviously leaving out the details of why my night was so grouse.

"Nice, so what else is happening?" he asks when I sit down next to him with a cup of coffee.
"Not much. Other than Dad being up my arse twenty-four seven. I'm such a disappointment to him; apparently."
"Well, you do need to get your act together, Bren. You can't live at home forever, and bum off them."

"I don't. I might have a shitty retail job at Connor, but at least I'm working. Living at home is just easier, but Dad just does my head in."
"Why do you think I moved out the moment I could?"
"Yeah, so how's ya love life cracking? You fucked ya girl again or you dumped her arse?"
"Yeah, and it was damn good. Fucking ripper actually."
"Really? Cause I thought you were still thinking you're into dudes? And needed to fuck chicks out of your system?"
"I'm bi Bren and she...I don't know she gets to me so bad."
"You confuse me, brother, but honest moment, how do you feel about her?"
"I honestly don't know Bren. Being with her in the bedroom is fucking amazing, but I can't just be with a girl. I like being with guys to and commitment scares the fucking shit out of me."
"You and me both brother. Fuck and dump is my jam."
"Yeah, I can't do that to Elyse. I like her, but I don't want to tie myself down either."
"Wish I could help brother, but I think you're pussy whipped."
"Nah," he laughs, "I'm dickmatised."
"That sounds so wrong, brother."
"I know. I just want to know what to do."
"I think you should just be with her, and get with a guy as well. See which side ya feel more for. If you actually fall in love then power to ya brother. But I'd stay firmly on the fence and forget about ya heart for a while. Let ya dick do the talking."
"Only you'd say that, Bren."

I gulp down the rest of my coffee.
"Just telling it like it is," I reply laughing and standing up, "I'm gonna head to work. Thanks for the crash pad, brother."
He stands up, patting me on the back.

"Thanks for the advice Bren, even though it's shit. And you're always welcome to crash."
"Thanks, Kad. I'll catch ya," I reply heading to the front door.

Heading to the tram to go to work, the word love tumbles in my mind and Lillie pops into my head.
I've thought about her so much lately, and my dick definitely has enjoyed that, but without getting it wet with her I'm never going to feel more than a bad case of lust.

Fifty-Five | Feelings Confession

Starting my firefighter career had been super tough and tumultuous, having had to fight a major factory fire my first official week on the job. I'd been so consumed by it I'd hardly had time for anyone and it was getting me down.

The only thing keeping me going was planning Austin's upcoming bachelor shindig. He wanted something fun and low-key, so I'd been planning something to have at mine.

I hadn't seen Elyse for a few weeks, but we'd talked on the phone, texted or FaceTimed most nights when I didn't fall asleep on the couch. I feel bad for being such a dick to her, but Brennan's advice is still on my mind. And I've been avoiding Elyse especially because I'm scared to face my feelings for her.
I know I'm going to have to face them sooner or later, but I'm hoping it's not today. She's on her way over now, and I'm still in bed even though it's nearly noon.

It's the first Saturday I've had off in ages, the first Saturday I'm not on call and I'm loving staying buried in my bed, stark naked.
Its been a cold few weeks and I've put flannelette sheets on my bed way earlier than normal. It's dirty but I love the feel of the soft fleece on my bare arse and cock.

I'm contemplating a shower when I hear knocking on the door. Knowing it's Elyse I jump out of bed, heading to the door without bothering to get dressed.

Opening it, she smiles at me, her eyes gazing over my nakedness appreciatively.

"Hey, foxy," she greets me seductively.

"Hey, sexy minx. You look hot."

She certainly does look hot, wearing a sexy short halter neck dress.

"I know, I'm wearing a dress," she says with a cheeky laugh that makes my cock stir.

She follows me inside and shutting the door behind her, I pull her close, kissing her zealously.

My cock throbs, becoming hard and pushing against the front of her dress.

She breaks the kiss laughing.

"It seems you like kissing me foxy," she teases with a sexy smirk.

"Oh you know I do sexy minx, but I especially like tasting your pussy and fucking your brains out."

Her smile fades and she walks over to the couch.

Great, I put my fucking foot in it.

Elyse sits down with a sigh, and following I sit opposite her, feeling like she's practically punched me in the guts.

"Lys, did I say something wrong?"

"No, well...it's not what you've said, but what you haven't."

I glance at her confused. "Sorry? What?" I ask with a gulp.

She looks up at me, her eyes darker than normal.

"Kaden, I'm in love with you."

I stand up, wanting to scream at her, but I know I have no reason to be angry.

"I told you Lys. You can't love me. I can't love you back."

"Why not? Am I not good enough?"

"Of course you're good enough Elyse. But I'm not. You deserve someone who can love you back."
"I want that someone to be you, Kaden. I love you."

My breath hitches in my chest, her words hitting me hard in the feels.
I've never had anyone tell me they love me before and it's amazing, but I can't say the words back.
I'm not sure if I feel them for her.
I did for Austin, but he doesn't and never will love me back and now I can't express them again for fear I'll get hurt again.
"Lys, I'm sorry. I...I...don't know what to say."
"Don't worry about it. You don't have to say it back when it's obvious you don't love me."
"Please stop Lys. I wanna be with you, but I'm not ready to use that word."
"Why? Do you honestly not feel anything for me?"
"I don't know what I feel. But honestly I was in love with Austin and I don't know if I want to feel that again. If I can love someone else."

She takes in a deep breath, letting out a deep long exasperated sigh.
"Fine," she says defeated before standing up and heading to the door.
"I'm going home. I can't be around you right now. I do deserve better Kaden and until you can tell me how you feel, that you love me, nothing more is going to happen between us."

I follow her, wanting to tell her the words she needs to hear, wanting to beg her to be with me again but she's gone out the door before I can even get a coherent word to come out of my mouth.

I've definitely fucked up big time again. And this time it's going to take more than flowers, chocolates and a teddy bear to get her forgiveness.

This time I need to use words I'm not sure I'll ever be ready to say, even if I'm possibly feeling them.

Fifty-Six | Show Him
Elyse

The moment I step outside Kaden's door, the tears fall down my cheeks and rushing towards the tram I sniff back sobs.
My heart hurts from Kaden's rejection, his failure to again tell me how he feels when I've poured my heart out to him.

Jumping on the tram I find a seat and close my eyes, trying to rid thoughts of him from my mind.
But it's useless; all I see is him opening the door naked.
All I can think about is kissing him, and fucking him.
My whole body throbs with want and I contemplate jumping off the tram and running back to his house, forgetting all about his lack of words and just being with him.
But I stay seated until I'm closer to Bella's house.

Getting off the tram at the stop closest to my sister's house I swallow back my sobs, walking calmly to her house.
She opens the door almost immediately after I knock, with Nora standing at her feet.

"Hey Bel-bear," I greet her sweetly, before looking down at my niece.
"Hiya, Nor nor."
"An El!" my niece says in her sweet baby voice.
She's just started to say some words, even though most of them make no damn sense.
It's good to see her looking well and being her happy go lucky self.

The last few months with her starting chemo have been tough.
I'm glad she's still living with Bella too, as there was talk of her going to live with Austin, but thankfully that isn't happening yet.

Looking at my sister now, she ushers me inside with a smile.
"Hey Ely-bug, whats going on?"
I follow her inside and into the kitchen.
"I need to ask your advice again."
"Sure, would you like a coffee?"
"Sounds good," I reply, picking Nora up and putting her into her highchair.

As Bella makes our coffee's I give Nora some tiny teddy biscuits and she eats them eagerly.
It makes my heart swell with love for her, and an odd feeling stirs in my stomach when I think back to the pregnancy scare I had when I first slept with Kaden.
It seems like a lifetime ago.

When Bella hands me my coffee, I take a sip, putting it down on the bench in front of me. Bella takes a sip of hers, looking at me over the rim of her mug.
"So Ely-bug, what do you need to chat about?
"I told Kaden I love him."
"How'd that go?" she asks, taking another sip of her coffee.
"Horrible. He practically threw it back in my face."
"How so? Did he not say it back?"
"No, he told me he was in love with Austin and isn't sure if he'll ever love someone again."
"Oh, Ely-bug I hate to say it but I told you so."
"I know, but what should I do?"
"Move on Ely-bug."

"I don't want to, Bel-bear. I love him so much and when I'm with him my whole body is on fire. Even just thinking about being with him gets me hot."

She laughs, a knowing smile curving at the corner of her lips.

"Oh, I know that feeling Ely-bug. But I still think moving on is your best option. You'll find someone else, sis. You're only twenty."

"I don't want anyone else, Bella," I reply harshly.

She doesn't say anything for a moment, taking a final gulp of her coffee, going to put her cup in the dishwasher.

"He actually asked me to do something the other week, and I've been thinking about it."

"What was that?"

"To have…" I start to say, *'fucking'* but change my words so Nora doesn't say the swear word back. "To do it," I say, making talking marks with my fingers, " in his butt with a strap on."

"Oh wow," Bella shrieks, "but yeah I can imagine him making that kinda request."

"Really? Did he do that when you had the threesome?"

"Well, no, but I'm sure he has. Do you honestly really love him, Elyse?"

"Yeah, Bella, so damn much. I've never felt this way about anyone, even Zack and you know how much I loved him. What I feel for Kaden is so much more."

"Then you have to show him with more than just words."

"So, the strap on thing? You think I should?"

"It would certainly show him how much you care about him. That you're willing to please him and show him your love."

"True," I reply, nodding and pulling her into a hug. "Thanks, Bel-bear. I love you so much, sis."

"I love you too," she replies, rubbing her rounded belly softly.

Laughing I ask, "How is the monster today?"

"Kicking me like a damn footballer. I'm sure it's a boy and he's going to take after his father."

"Probably," I laugh, putting my hand against her stomach to feel her baby kick my hand.

"See?" Bella says laughing.

"Yep," I laugh again. "I better head out. I have to go to the library and get some books for my assignment. I'll see you on Sunday."

"No worries, Ely-bug," she says hugging me.

I give Nora a kiss on the cheek. "Bye, Nor nor."

She giggles, blowing me a kiss and doing her little open and shut hand gesture to wave goodbye.

I head out the door to go to the Uni library, my head full of thoughts about showing Kaden how much I love him.

I'm scared, but excited and can't wait to hear the words *'I love you Lys'* falling from his plump lips.

Fifty-Seven | After Party

Austin

Everyone has cleared out, and I'm pretty buzzed and damn horny from watching the strippers and thinking of the threesome with Dana and Kaden.

He's sitting across from me on his couch and takes a big gulp of the beer in his hands.

I can't help but watch his Adam's apple bob when he swallows.

For some reason, watching a guy's Adam's apple has always turned me on.

He gives me a sexy smirk, licking the foam that's collected on his lips.

My cock throbs in my jeans.

"You alright, Aust?" he asks laughing.

"Um, yep, great, buzzed," I say, taking a sip of my own beer.

Kaden watches me, laughing when I put my beer down.

"Aust, you've got some foam on your chin."

I lick my lips and try to lick my chin to get it off.

"Did I get it?"

"Not even close," Kaden replies laughing and leaning closer to me on the couch.

He licks the foam from my chin, groaning before his tongue licks my lips, taking my mouth to his in a kiss.

Moaning I kiss him back for a moment before pulling back.

"Kad, we can't."

"Please, Aust. I fucking want you."

"Yeah I want you to, but I need to tell Dan and she might not be cool with us hooking up."

"Yeah, I know. I just get carried away when I'm near you."

He frowns, looking down at his cock tenting the front of his daks.

"Kad, I'll text her, but are you sure you want to hook up?"

"I do. I want you Aust, but I...I haven't told Lys about us."

Raising my eyebrow at him I ask, "So she doesn't know your bi?"

"No, she knows I'm bi, but I haven't told her about the threesome or us hooking up."

"You should Kad. I don't think Elyse is the type of girl who will care."

"Yeah, I don't know man. She told me she loves me."

"Shit, Kad. How do you feel about her?"

"To be honest I have no fucking idea. I love being with her, and the sex is so fucking good, but letting myself fall for her is too damn scary."

"I get you, completely. I felt the exact same way with Dan, but I think I loved her before my brain knew I did. You have to trust your heart, Kad."

"Yeah, I don't know. Can you just text Dana so we can hook up and I can forget about my feelings for tonight?"

"Yeah, no worries," I reply, grabbing my phone from my pocket.

Quickly I type a text to Dana.

Austin: Dan, hope you're having a great night out. I'm crashing at Kad's. Is it sweet with you if we hook up?

Her reply comes instantly and it's clear she's having a great night.

Dana: grouse night. Fuck his brains out stud. Love you xxx

Austin: ok gorgeous. Slow down and remember I love you. Xxx

Putting my phone down, I dive towards Kaden, my lips a whisper from his when I murmur, "She's cool."

"Mmm, that's good," he moans, cupping my cheeks to pull my face to his for an intense kiss. Licking my lips, he takes my tongue with his, pashing me with such intensity it's like he's fucking my mouth.

Our cocks are hard, rubbing against each other and I just want to get naked together, to touch him and suck him off until we're both moaning so hard his neighbours hear our screams of pleasure.

It still intrigues me how much different being with a guy is.

It turns me on and makes me come in such a different way to when I'm with Dana.

Pulling back from the kiss, I sit up a bit, pulling my T-shirt over my head.

Kaden lets out an appreciative hum, looking at my taut abs.

"God, Aust, you're so fucking hot."

"So are you, Kad. I wanna get naked with you, and suck your cock."

Again he moans, shifting under my body to lift his t-shirt off too.

Grabbing his waist I yank his jeans and boxers down, freeing his hard cock.

Shuffling down the couch, I'm about to put my mouth onto his length when he stops me by yanking my daks down and pulling me back by the waist to kiss me again.

This time as we pash our cocks rub against each other, and it makes my whole body throb with need for my best guy mate.

Being with him feels so good, so good it could never be wrong, despite the fact we both have gorgeous women in our lives.

Kaden telling me he's not sure about his feelings for Elyse isn't a surprise, as I know exactly how he's feeling.

I just hope for her sake he works out how he feels soon before Elyse gets hurt.

I contemplated warning him away from her because Elyse is like another little sister to me, but it's too late and I have to trust my best mate that he'll follow his heart eventually.

He breaks the kiss. "Aust, I wanna try something with you."

"What's that?"

"I got a vibrator the other day. I'd love to suck your cock whilst teasing you with it."

I groan, thinking about his words.

"I love the sound of that Kad, but only if I can suck you at the same time."

"You wanna sixty-nine?"

"Yeah, if you're down for that?"

"Damn straight," he says eagerly, getting up from the couch and grabbing my hand.

Groaning, he pulls me up and kisses me. And we head to his bedroom. Dropping my hand, he opens his wardrobe and I lay down on the bed, watching him, looking appreciatively at his taut round arse.

He turns around, holding a vibrator that has two egg shapes, one on either end. He presses one end and it starts buzzing.

Diving onto the bed chuckling, he kisses me and holds it against my balls.

Against his lips I moan, whispering against his lips as I slowly pull back, "Fuck Kad. That feels amazing."

"Told you, Aust," he teases, sliding down the bed so his face is at my cock.

He moans, taking it into his mouth, and back out again, still rubbing the vibrator under my balls.

My cock is throbbing in his mouth, and I feel like I'm going to come any second.

Fisting his hair, I pull him off my cock and he looks up at me and then down at my cock that is pearling with pre-cum.

"Kad, please I wanna suck you too."

He doesn't reply at first, just moans, licking the tip of my cock.

"Mmm, Aust you taste so good."

"Then suck me. I'm gonna come so hard."

"I bet," he teases scooting up onto his knees and then lying back down so his cock is at my mouth and mine at his.
At the same moment, we take each others cocks into our mouths, sucking and licking each other in a steady rhythm.
His moans are so hot, turning me on so much and the vibrator against my balls is driving me insane.

My cock is spasming, and Kaden licks it, swirling his tongue over my flesh as he sucks me, taking my cock in and out of his mouth.
I'm doing the same with his cock and the pleasure is absolutely unbelievable.
Taking Kaden's cock from my mouth, I scream out, "Kaden, fuck I'm going to come. Oh fuck! I'm coming!"
I moan loudly, my whole lower body spasming as I shoot my load down his throat. He swallows hard, sliding off my cock and sitting up.
"Fuck Austin. You honestly taste delicious."
I laugh, grabbing the vibrator from him.
"Can I tease you with this whilst I finish sucking you too?"
"Oh, yes please," he says chuckling.

Lying back on the bed, he opens his legs wide. I put the vibrator under his balls, and he groans as a rush of pleasure courses through his body.
"That feels so good Aust. Suck me please."

Kneeling on the bed, I take his cock back into my mouth, sucking him eagerly. I swirl my tongue over his flesh, licking the tip.
He moans, louder and louder when I take his whole cock into my mouth.
I feel the vibrator against my chin and it's weirdly arousing too.
His cock is starting to spasm in my mouth and he screams out, "Oh fuck, Austin! I'm coming man, I'm coming!"
I hold his cock steady in my mouth, letting his release pour down my throat before I pull off his cock and swallow his load.

Stretching up over him, I kiss him hard and zealously.
"That was amazing Kad. Thanks for a great end to my bachelor party."
"You're welcome, Aust. I…"
I know he's about to say, *'I love you'* so I cut him off with a kiss.
"Don't say that Kad. You don't feel that way about me anymore."
He sighs, and I lay down next to him, kissing him again.

My thoughts wander to whether Elyse would be happy with us hooking up if she ends up actually being with Kaden, because thinking of not being able to be with him again actually kinda hurts.
I love Dana with all my heart, but I love fucking my best mate too.
It's the best of both worlds.

Fifty-Eight | Best Day

Austin

Standing at the front of the gazebo at Riverwalk I'm nervous.
I can't believe in mere moments at this stunning venue with curtains draped over the ceiling that I'm about to get married.
If you'd told me two years ago that I'd be marrying someone I'd have scoffed at how ridiculous that sounded.
I'd also have thought I was going to marry Annika too, but looking around the venue I know that Anni was never meant to be the one I would be marrying.

Jairus, her husband, is sitting in the front row-next to my family—with their gorgeous twin boys next to him.
Annika is one of our bridesmaids, just as I was a groomsman for her wedding.
I can feel the love evident all around me. And I know my heart is going to damn near explode with love when I see Dana coming down the aisle towards me.
Falling for her had taken me by surprise, but it's real.
In the last year, she'd shown me every day, especially recently that she loves me just as much as I love her. And I love her with my whole damn heart.

Lifting up the sleeve of my navy pinstripe suit I glance at my watch, wary that the time is ticking by and the girls are late.
Looking at Kaden beside me I shuffle on my feet anxiously.
"She'll be here Aust. She loves you, man."

"I know. I'm just so damn nervous. I'm getting married."

"I know. Who woulda thought, huh?" he says with a laugh.

"Exactly, but it's right," I reply, smiling at him, hearing the bridesmaids' entrance music beginning to swell.

He pats me on the back. "Yeah, you're such a lucky bugger to have found such an awesome chick."

He looks at a little down, but I don't have time to question him as Anni has stepped up to the end of the aisle. She starts walking in slowly, a sweet friendly smile on her lips.

She looks absolutely stunning in a dusty pink bridesmaid dress, her short blonde hair framing her heart-shaped face.

Reaching the front of the aisle, she glances across at Jairus and her boys, giving them a wave.

It's so sweet and makes my heart swell with love for my best friend.

Before stepping across to the opposite side of the celebrant she kisses my cheek, whispering in my ear, "Dana looks stunning, Aust. Love you bestie."

I kiss her cheek back. "I bet she does, babe. And you do too. Love you too, bestie."

She giggles and smiles at me.

I look down the aisle as Dana's friend Britney enters the room. She to looks amazing in the dress, with her light brown hair pinned back.

When she reaches the front of the aisle, she gives me a wink, and says with a laugh, "Wait till you see her Austin. You'll cream ya daks."

"I hope not, Brit." I laugh, adjusting myself a little as my cock is hard just thinking about seeing Dana in a wedding dress.

She'd told me nothing about the dress, being completely traditional so I'm desperate to see it, knowing that she'll look incredible.

The music changes to *'Everything I need'* by Picture this, and I see Dana step up to the end of the aisle, her arm linked with her Dad's.

Her dress is stunning, strapless and tight across her breasts, showing a hint of cleavage.

From under her tits it flows down, swishing from side to side as she walks towards me.

Her hair is pinned back, with wispy strands escaping at the front, reminding me of the first time she sent me a picture in her underwear.

I think I'd fallen for her the moment I first saw that picture, even though I didn't make the connection to who she was at first.

But honestly I can't pinpoint what made me fall for Dana.

Reaching me at the front of the aisle, her Dad kisses her cheek, before shaking my hand.

His grip is firm and he nods at me.

"Make her happy son," he says to me with a warning in his tone.

"I will, Mr Ramera," I promise, as he goes to take his seat.

I take Dana's hands in mine after she hands Britney her bouquet of dusty pink roses. She smiles at me, making my heartbeat skip.

"You look so handsome stud," she says to me seductively winking at me.

"You look incredibly beautiful, Dana," I tell her, leaning in close and brushing my lips against the sweet spot on her neck.

She murmurs, and it makes my cock throb in my slacks.

The next time she murmurs like that she'll be my wife and I'll be buried balls deep inside her.

We look to the celebrant then, who gives as a smile, before she starts speaking, "Welcome all, we're here today to celebrate and affirm the love between Austin and Dana. When I met these two a year ago, I could tell that their love was the real deal. They couldn't be more different but they complement each other and are each other's perfect half. Yin and Yang. They have prepared vows for each other, and will then declare their intent with the exchanging of rings."

She looks at me first, nodding to me to begin.

Dana turns to look at me, and I take a deep breath in, exhaling and telling myself to open my mouth.

She smiles wide at me, licking her lips with a teasing glint in her eyes. It's the exact thing I need to see, to be ready to tell her how I feel, to make me open my mouth.

I'd not actually prepared vows, so I'm about to wing it.

"Dana, from the moment I first bumped into you at Uni, I've wanted you in my life. From then as our relationship grew I fell hard for you. I never thought I'd love someone again or as much as I had loved in the past," I pause, smiling at Anni for a moment, "but the love I have for you Dan is so much more, nothing will ever stop my heart beating for you. You are my better half and you're stunningly beautiful. No matter what life throws our way I will be right by your side. I love you Dana, and I give you my heart, always my heart is only yours."

She lets out a little giggle, wiping away the tears in her eyes.

I kiss her forehead and the celebrant nods at her with a smile for her to share her vows.

"Austin, I've loved you from before I even officially met you. And when I actually met you, I fell so in love with you, so hard and quickly. You healed my heart and showed me that love could be amazing when you meet the right person. You're without a doubt my right person, and I'll never stop loving you, Aust. My heart belongs to only you, always."

I wipe tears from my own eyes, resisting the urge to kiss her to seal the deal already.

The celebrant laughs sweetly. "Well, weren't they touching and beautiful words. Austin and Dana have exchanged vows and will share in the exchange of rings to show their commitment to one another. Can Nora please come forward with the rings?"

Everyone lets out a collective *'aww'* as my daughter comes to the front from her seat next to Bella, holding out the tiny pink pillow with the rings tied on it.

She stops at my feet, holding it up to me and announcing rather loudly, "Here dada."

My heart melts and I take the pillow, handing it to the celebrant and picking Nora up I hold her against my hip.

Kissing her forehead softly, I whisper to her, "Thanks, darling. Dada loves you."

She giggles and looks across to Dana with a sweet cheeky smile.

My sweet daughter has been through so much in the last few months with chemotherapy, but thankfully it has worked and she is heading towards remission with her leukaemia.

"Thank you, Nora. You're such a sweetie," the celebrant says with a smile.

"So now Austin will exchange rings with Dana, declaring his intent to marry her, honour her in all things and care for her until her dying breath. If this your intention, Austin, then say, *'I do'.*"

"I do," I declare, sliding the ring awkwardly with one hand onto Dana's finger.

"Dana, do you also declare your intent to marry Austin, to honour him in all things and care for him until your dying breath. If this is your intention, Dana, then say, *'I do'.*"

"I do, I so do," Dana declares, sliding the titanium ring onto my hand, that is still clutching Nora's side.

"Fabulous," the celebrant beams, "now that both Austin and Dana have shared their vows and declared their commitment with the exchanging of rings, it is with great pleasure that I pronounce them husband and wife. Austin, you may kiss the bride."

I smile, chuckling as I lean forward and press a soft sweet kiss to Dana's lips.

Pulling back, the collective *'aww'* of our guests grows louder when Nora softly kisses Dana's cheek.

"Mama, I wuv you," she says sweetly.

"Oh, Nora. I love you too, sweetie," Dana replies to my daughter, giving her a kiss on the forehead.

I put Nora back down and she runs back to Bella and Travis.

He picks her up and kisses her forehead too.

My daughter is incredibly lucky to have such amazing stepparents in her life, as well as her beautiful mother Bella.

What had happened in our lives in the past years, really shows how much we've grown up and how solid our friendships are.

I could have regretted fucking Bella, but if I hadn't Nora wouldn't be here. I wouldn't have my beautiful daughter and just that thought is enough to make my heart ache.

Without a doubt, Travis is the right guy for Bella though. I can tell by the way they look at each other, that they love each other wholeheartedly and that's all I wanted for her.

Her belly is starting to show now, pregnant with her second child and I'm so beyond happy for her.

A pang of hurt hits me, knowing I'll not be able to share that with Dana, but it doesn't mean I'll love her any less.

It actually makes me feel a little guilty because I'm glad to never have to worry about contraception.

I'm broken from my thoughts, realising not even a minute has passed and the celebrant announces, "And now for the very first time I introduce to you, Mr and Mrs Austin and Dana Belvinz."

Taking Dana's hand I pull her close to me, kissing her again harder than before, before I pull back and whisper in her ear, "Tonight Mrs Belvinz, I'm going to make love to you; all night."

My kiss grazes that sweet spot on her neck and she murmurs softly, whispering to me, "Can't wait, Mr Belvinz. I'm so happy to be your wife." And no word—*wife*— has ever sounded sweeter.

I'm married, fucking married and looking around at our families and friends as we sign the register I couldn't be happier to be at this point in my life.

Fifty-Nine | Sweet Night

After getting photos, the bridal party heads inside the decked out reception part of the venue.

I'd only snuck a quick look at Elyse during the ceremony, and had to adjust my daks looking at her.

She looks fucking delectable, her long locks up in a tight ponytail, a wisp of makeup that makes her eyes and lips pop and her outfit; *Fuck,* a leopard print jumpsuit with thin straps that dips into a v at her cleavage. It hides the curve of her hips and her long legs, but fuck it looks sexy on her.

I don't know what I'm feeling towards her; my heart is telling me one thing, my body something else and my brain is telling me to not listen to my damn heart.

It feels like everyone in the damn room is staring at me; that everyone knows my damn secrets; can read my mind.

Taking our seats at the bridal table, Annika elbows me in the side.

"You ok, Kaden?" she asks sweetly.

"Yeah, sweet. But weddings...they...um...get to me."

She smiles, all-knowing.

"Weddings, or your best mates wedding?"

I chuckle. "Ok...you got me. Austin's wedding yes. I...um..."

She laughs this time, touching my arm lightly.

"I know your history together, Kaden. He's my best friend to. You need to let him go."

"I know, but I still..." I nearly say, *'love him'* but I catch another look at Elyse when she stands up from the table she's sitting at with the rest of our friends at the front of the room.

"Love him?" Annika says cheekily.

"Um...no actually. I...don't love him anymore, but I miss the sex."
"Right, well I don't know how to deal with that issue, but not loving him anymore is a big part of moving on."
"Yeah, I just need to find someone new. And I kinda have," I admit, not sure if Annika knows.
I'm not even sure if Bella does, as Elyse and I don't talk about stuff like that when we're together.
I know that's my fault, but she's too damn addictive.
"Yeah, who? Guy or girl?" Annika enquires cheerfully.
"Girl, and um...you know her."
"Oh, really?"
"Yeah, it's um...it's Elyse," I confess.
Annika's mouth drops open, before curving into a smile.
"Oh my God, Kaden, that's great."
"Yeah, but I'm still really confused about how I feel about her."
"I get that, trust me. Just take things as they come."
"Yeah," I reply nodding.

She smiles at me again, licking her lips when our food is bought to the table. It's ravioli bolognese, it looks and smells incredible, so we eat in silence and the whole time I'm eating I watch Elyse, my heart hammering in my chest.
She looks so incredibly gorgeous, beautiful actually. I need to find words to tell her how I feel about her, but I don't know what those words are.

~~

After dinner is finished, and I nearly fuck up my best man speech, because idiot me had decided it was best to wing it, I step up behind Elyse's chair whilst she's focused on the dance floor.
Everyone has started dancing after the official first dance.
Leaning down I whisper in her ear, "Come dance with me sexy minx."
Her breath hitches and she shivers, standing up.

She looks at Bella, who gives her a nod and has an odd knowing look on her face.

Taking Elyse's hand I lead her out to the middle of the dance floor, gripping her hips and pulling her body against mine, my arms wrapped around her; one hand on her hip, the other on her arse.

We start rocking to the music, some new age song I've never heard, but its got a good beat.

Elyse is looking at me sheepishly like she needs to confess something.

"Lys, why are you looking at me like that?"

"Like what?"

"Like you're hiding something from me."

"Oh...um...I told Bella about us."

"Really? Is she cool with us being together?"

"Yeah, she is actually."

"Sweet as. I might have told Annika before," I confess biting my lip.

She doesn't reply, instead leans closer to me, kissing my neck.

Her breath in my ear sends shivers through me, and I hate that the words she whispers make my heart race, as well as make my cock hard.

"I love you, Kaden, and tonight I'm going to show you how much."

Moaning, I grab her ponytail and bring her face back to mine, crashing our lips together in a heated kiss.

I swear time fucking stops, and it's only me and Elyse in that room, our lips locked together whilst our bodies rock to the beat.

It's turning me on so bad. I need her, more than I've ever needed anyone and when the song ends I break the kiss, gazing into her chocolate eyes that are sucking me in with the lust in them.

"Fuck, Lys. You know how to kiss a guy."

"Back at you foxy," she says with a laugh and a wink, "so how about we find the bride and groom to say goodbye and head back to mine?"

"Sounds ripper, Lys. Lead the way." I chuckle, taking her hand and adjusting myself in the front of my slacks with the other.

No chick has ever made me feel the way Elyse does, I've never cracked a fat from just a kiss.
Elyse Mishal is going to be my undoing.
I can feel her getting under my skin. And fuck, it has me both excited and scared.
I think my heart knows how it feels, but my brain is telling me that loving Elyse is a very bad idea.

Sixty | Let Loose

Brennan

Lillie is standing to the side of the dance floor, looking fucking stunning.
She's wearing the world's smallest dress, a strapless knee-length black
number and she's clearly self-conscious in it; obviously not knowing that
just looking at her is making my temperature rise and I want to finally
take her as mine.

I can't do that to Lil though, at least not yet.
She's still so damn innocent. I can't even mention sex without the blush
colouring her cheeks and her whole body. It's damn sexy watching her
creamy white skin colour with a blush that I've given her.
With her fiery hair straight and down over her shoulders, she's a
goddess, and I really want her to be mine completely.

Sauntering up to her, I grab her around the waist to whisper in her ear
with a seductive purr, "Dance with me, Princess."
"Stop Bren, everyone will look at us."
"Only 'cause you're the most stunning girl in the room, Lil."
"Don't tease me, Brennan," she chastises me, her cheeks aflame
because my words set my Lillie on fire.

If only I could actually touch her, pound into her virgin pussy; then she'd
really be on fire.
Taking her hand I drag her into the small crowd on the dance floor.

My brother is dancing with Elyse; well practically dry humping her and pashing her.
It kinda turns me on, like in the room with me porn.
I'd always liked sexy porn, the prelude to the actual event and slow sweet girly sex on my screen.

Yeah, I like dirty sex in reality, fucking a chick until she screams, but nothing beats some sensual slow sex; lovemaking.
And I haven't had that in forever, since Amelia broke my damn heart after high school.
She was my sweetheart, but she broke up with me after confessing she was going overseas for uni because she'd met a guy online and she was in love with him, not me.

Since then, meaningless sex and anything else I can do to block out the feelings for her, the want to jump on a damn plane across the world to find her.
Yeah, I'm that idiot, still pining after the only girl I've loved and sinking my dick into anyone willing. And what makes my attraction to Lillie the worst is the fact she could be Amelia, fiery red hair and gorgeous as fuck.
The only thing that separates them is Lillie is thinner, petite, whereas Amelia had curves for days and was kinda pudgy, squishy I liked to say.

I'm looking at Lillie now; she's still clutching my hand but she's standing rigid, stiff and not moving even though the beat of the music is strong.
Pulling her against my body, I keep a firm grip on her hand and grab her hip with the other to rock our bodies from side to side.

Locking my eyes on hers, she murmurs, a purr kinda sound that sends a jolt to my dick.
"Let loose, Lillie. Feel the music."

"I...I am," she protests with a whimper.

The sexy sounds she makes without trying are like a hit of crack.

I pull her closer, inhaling her scent that's like a red velvet cupcake, sweet with a hint of something else fruity.

My lips find her ear, and nibbling it, I whisper to her, "Lillie, I want to fuck you."

She whimpers, pulling back from me, blushing and showing her shy side.

"Um...I...um...Brennan...I..." she stammers, biting down on her thin pink lip.

God, she's gorgeous.

Chuckling I say softly, a husky whisper, "Do you know what you do to me, princess?"

"Um, no..." she snaps, her glistening blue-grey eyes looking me up and down.

I poke her in the belly, teasing her, "Come on Lillie, you must be able to tell you turn me on."

She scoffs and steps back from me, seeing now that I have a mega hard on.

Her eyes boggle at me, a glint in them when she looks up from my dick.

"Is your d...d...d...ick h...h...hard? She stammers at me, not able to tear her eyes from my want for her in my slacks.

Her appreciative but innocent stare honestly makes my dick harder.

I don't reply and she walks off, leaving me with a tent in my slacks in a crowd full of people.

I contemplate chasing after her, but all that would give me is a bad case of blue balls so instead I wander up to the bar, pulling up a stool next to a chestnut-haired chick.

She gives me an appreciative once over whilst I order a whisky. And I practically jump out of my skin when she holds up a packet with a couple of white pills in it.

"Hey sexy, you up for some fun?"
"Sure gorgeous, just the 'E' on offer, or are you on the menu too?"
"Play ya cards right, and both for you."

I nod, taking the tablet she hands me and downing it with my whiskey in one quick gulp.
It takes longer for a hit to give me a buzz now, but I down the rest of the whiskey before I look at the chick next to me.
"Thanks, gorgeous. You wanna stay here or find a better party?"
"Whatever you want, I'm easy."
I chuckle under my breath.

I bet you are. Easy as and most likely going to cost me a packet, but beggars can't be choosers. I need pussy tonight.

"Sweet, let's bounce then."
She smiles at me, and even though it doesn't make my whole body throb with longing I want her, even if it's just to let loose for the night.
Kaden isn't going to be home tonight, he's staying at Elyse's so there's no better place to take this chick than back to his, where I can sink my dick inside her without a care in the fucking world.

Sixty-One | Dirty Girl

On the tram, I'm barely able to keep my hands off Elyse, so much so that I pull her off the tram at my stop instead of hers.

Pulling her against me, I kiss her furiously.

"Damn, Lys."

"Why are we getting off at your stop? I thought we were going to mine."

"I can't wait Lys. I need you now."

I take her hand again, and we run across the road to my apartment.

We barely make it inside before we're pashing again, and I'm feeling her up, running my hands all over her clothed body.

I moan against her lips, and she responds deepening the kiss with her tongue dancing with mine.

It makes my cock throb and my heart pound. Lys is the only one who can set me on fire so completely.

She breaks the kiss, dropping her small handbag from her arm and stepping back from me for a moment, before kneeling down to fish through the bag for something.

"I have a surprise for you," she says with a giggle standing up with a rather large black silicone dildo in her hand.

I gulp, licking my lips before asking, "Has that been in your bag all day?

"Yep," she replies with a seductive wink.

"Fuck, Lys you're dirty. God, I want you."

"I want you to, Kaden. And I want to do this for you."

I'm about to kiss her when she giggles and starts to sashay towards my bedroom, still holding the dildo in her hand. Following her, she stops at my door jam.

"You coming foxy?" she asks teasingly, walking backwards into my room.

Throwing the dildo on the bed she hooks her fingers into the straps of the leopard print jumpsuit, sliding them down her arms.

I watch, absolutely fucking mesmerised by her as the fabric falls from her alluring body.

She's wearing black lacy knickers with an o-ring in the front, and some weird tape things are covering her nipples, holding up her tits a little.

I step closer to her, tugging off my jacket and shirt so quick, like they're burning my damn skin.

Lys yanks the nipple covers off, and her perfect pink nipples are hard, so ready to take into my mouth.

"God, Lys, you're fucking stunning. And those fucking knickers look so naughty on you."

"Mmm, Kad, you look fucking hot in a suit."

I again step closer to her grabbing her around the waist.

She steps out of the jumpsuit pooled at her feet, and all she's wearing now are the arousing knickers and strappy black high heels.

Lifting her foot she's about to take them off, but I shake my head at her.

"Keep them on Lys. You look so fucking luscious right now."

"Mmm, well when I said you look hot in a suit, I meant your birthday suit."

"Oh, sexy minx...I...fuck," I curse loudly, undoing my belt and tugging my slacks and jocks to the floor in one swift movement.

My cock springs forward, so hard from thinking about what Elyse is going to do to me.

We stare at each other, our eyes locked on each other full of desire.

My heart is pounding, and my whole body is throbbing with need and longing for the stunning woman half-naked in front of me, offering me something to show she cares.

She licks her lips, and softly hisses, "Kiss me, Kaden, please."

I let out a moan before crashing my lips to hers, taking her mouth as mine and slipping a hand into the front of the knickers to tease her.

Flicking her clit, I slide a finger inside, pulling back from the kiss a little.

With my lips brushing against hers I tease, "Damn Lys, you're so damn wet. I want you to get off too, sexy minx."

She moans, kissing me in a hard bruising kiss that completely sets me on fire.

I'm fucking aching for her.

She takes my lips harder against hers, fisting my hair and pulling me down with her to fall against the bed.

Again I pull away from her kiss, this time kissing down over her collarbone and down to her tits.

Taking a nipple into my mouth, I roll my tongue over the sensitive bud and she bucks her hips up towards me, sweet moans escaping her lips.

"God, Lys, you're going to kill me," I taunt, tugging on the edge of the knickers.

She lets out a dirty snigger.

"They're crotchless Kad."

She spreads her legs wide, and I slide down to my knees.

"Oh god, Lys. Please sit on my face, and then fuck my arse."

Standing up I sit down on the bed pulling her onto my lap.

"Tonight was supposed to be about you," she teases, rocking her pussy over the tip of my cock, coating it in her arousal.

"I want to make you feel good first, Lys."

"You don't have to, Kaden."
"Yeah, I damn well do, so get up here and ride my face sexy minx."

Again she lets out a delicious moan, stretching her body like a cat.
I slide down underneath her and she crawls up the bed, gripping the headboard and lining her pussy up with my mouth.
Softly I press a kiss to her clit, and she moans loudly.
I then bite it, and she screams out, "Oh fuck, Kaden...more...more."

Slowly I slip my tongue into her pussy, licking and lapping up her arousal.
She's rocking her pelvis against my chin, moaning and screaming her pleasure, "Oh...oh...so good...Kaden...more...fuck!"
I bite her clit again. "Come for me Lys. Come on my face."

Torturously she rocks her pussy over my face again, and I tease her, flicking my tongue over her clit before slipping it inside her pussy again and fucking her with it.
She tastes absolutely fucking amazing, a taste I'll never get enough of and when she releases suddenly with a lascivious moan all over my face I lap it up, sucking and kissing her pussy dry.
She slides down my body, kissing me to taste herself on my lips.
Her kiss is fierce, and it's making my cock throb.
Breaking the kiss I sit up a bit.

"Elyse, that was fucking incredible."
"Yeah," she says blushing, "and now I'm going to make you feel incredible."
Reaching behind her, she grabs the dildo, pushing it into the front of the knickers.
Slipping her fingers in her pussy she moans and then rubs them over the dildo.

Lining it up with my arse, she rocks her pelvis back and forth a little; tentative.
"Is that good?"
"Yeah, sexy minx. Kneel and push it in, all the way."

She follows my instruction, pushing the dildo all the way into my arse and then out again, just to the tip.
At the same time I stroke my cock, and watch her body as she fucks me.
Her tits are bouncing, and she looks absolutely provocative.

Pounding in and out of me she leans over my body to kiss me, zealously, her tongue fucking my mouth.
"Mmm, Lys, fuck that feels good...so good."
"Good to know, foxy," she teases pulling all the way out. "Wanna ride my cock, Kad?" she asks seductively.
"Oh yeah, sexy minx," I taunt back.

She lies down next to me and I climb onto her lap, impaling myself on the dildo.
I lift my pelvis up and down, and Elyse takes my cock in her hands, stroking it as I get myself off.

"That's it, fuck me, Kaden," she calls out, driving me wild.
"Elyse, fuck...so...oh my god...so good."
"Come for me Kaden," she taunts still stroking my cock.
"Don't stop, Lys...I'm gonna come...fuck I'm gonna come," I scream out, pushing myself hard down on the dildo and spurting my load over her stomach.

Sliding off the dildo I lay down next to her, pulling her close.
"Fuck Lys, that was awesome. I fucking loved it."
I kiss her forehead softly and she murmurs.

"I'm glad you loved it. I did it for you."
"I know Lys, and thank you."
"I love you, Kaden.

I hear her words, looking across at her and I say them back in my head, giving her a soft lingering kiss that again makes her murmur.
"Mmm, Elyse I...I...lo...fuck....I..."
I can't get the words out and go to try to kiss her again instead, but she turns away.

"I can't believe you Kaden. even after doing that for you, you still can't tell me how you feel about me. I'm so fucking in love with you and you can't even tell me that you like me, let alone love me."

She gets out of the bed, picking up my shirt from the floor and pulling it on.
She looks fucking sexy but I know it's not the time to tell her that.
"I'm sorry Lys, I am. But I...I...don't know how I feel. You make me feel so much."
"Then why can't you fucking tell me those feelings?"
"I don't know. I just fucking can't."
"Yeah, well I can't be with you then. I can't do this anymore Kaden."
"Please Lys. I want you."
"No, you just want sex, Kaden. And I want..." she pauses, taking the dildo out from the front of the knickers and throwing it at me.
"You want what?"
"Forget it, Kaden, ok, just fucking forget it."

And with those words, she walks out of my room, leaving her clothes on the floor. And I let her because my dirty girl completely shattered my world and even though I can't tell her how I feel I'm pretty fucking sure she's taken my heart with my shirt on her back.

Sixty-Two | Man Up

Brennan

Getting up the next day, I find Kaden sitting in the kitchen eating toast smothered with Vegemite.

"Morning, bro," I greet him, "was Elyse fucking your brains out last night or what?"

He gives me an odd look like he doesn't want to share what's on his mind.

"Kaden, did something else happen?"

"Yeah Bren, we had a fight."

"I kinda thought so. What about?"

"Nothing. It's stupid. Wanna come out with me? Austin and Dana are having a post-wedding brunch."

"Sure, sounds ripper. Is Elyse going to be there?"

"Unfortunately, can we not talk about her now."

"Fine, don't get ya knickers in a knot, you pansy arse."

I laugh and he runs at me slapping me in a boxing stance.

"Sorry, bro, don't hit me," I protest playfully.

He laughs then. "Just go get dressed, wanker."

"You better put ya big boy knickers on, pansy."

~~

Getting out of Kaden's commodore, we walk casually into the pub together. I'm half expecting to see Lillie, since she's Austin's little sister, but I'm surprised that only some mates are gathered around the bar, and no chicks are in sight.

Kaden steps up to Austin at the bar.

"Hey man, where's ya wife and the rest of the chicks?"

Austin laughs, taking a sip of his beer and signalling the barman with a nod to get us both a drink.

I probably shouldn't be drinking, as my damn head is still throbbing with a comedown headache from the 'E' last night.

The hit wore off way to damn quick and I kicked the chick out before Kaden realised she was there.

She wasn't worth the fuck, not even getting me off and only because she wasn't my firecracker redhead.

I'm ashamed with myself that I wanked after the chick left and only thoughts of Lillie got me off.

I'd thought about shimmying off the little black dress, exposing her creamy skin and taking my time kissing every inch of her, before making her mine completely.

I've never really been into virgins—well since Amelia—and we lost our virginity to each other.

It's stupid, but I think that's part of the reason I'm still in love with her—never forget and can't damn well let go of your first love bullshit—even when you want to.

Our drinks are slid down the bar, and taking a big sip I nod when Austin replies to Kaden.

"They're down the road, having a high tea girly brunch."

Kaden laughs, replying, "I bet Lys is loving that."

Austin glares at him, before laughing. "Yeah, her worst nightmare. She'd probably rather be here with us."

"Yeah, probably," Kaden muses, taking a big gulp of his beer and swallowing it hard.

It's clear he doesn't want to talk about Elyse, but mentioning her clearly gets to him and as though Austin can read my mind, he asks, "What's with you and Elyse now? Are you actually together?"

Kaden gulps again, looking at me for help, but I throw my brother under the bus.

"Yeah, Kad, whats going on with you and Lys? She's just a fuck buddy, huh?"

My older brother glares at me, anger building, but I laugh, taunting him, "Don't get angry Kad. I didn't tell you earlier that I heard every word of your fight with her last night."

"Fight? What happened, Kaden?" Austin asks, elbowing Kaden in the side.

"She um...she pegged me, and told me..." he takes another sip of beer, cutting his words off.

"She told you what?" Austin questions.

"Nothing, just forget it."

"No, Kad, brother she's totally in love with you."

"Yeah, but I can't tell her how I feel."

Austin shakes his head. "Kaden, seriously she's in love with you and you're pushing her away," he says accusingly but calm at the same time.

"I have to. I can't be the guy for her."

"Why the hell not? You love her don't you?"

"Yeah, I do. I don't think I've ever loved a chick...not even my first girlfriend who I thought I did love," he pauses, taking in a deep breath before he blurts out words, "I'm in love with Elyse."

He takes a final gulp of his beer. "But that doesn't mean I can be with her."

Austin and I both chuckle. "Um Kad, that's exactly what it means. She's in love with you and you need to get your act together and tell her you love her too before its too late."

"Exactly brother, she's clearly got it bad for you, despite your switch-hitting tendencies."

"I know Bren, but that's what I'm worried about. That I'll want to be with a guy again and I'll fuck things up; cheat on her."

I laugh so hard I feel like I'm gonna piss my daks when Austin speaks, "Kad, mate, I can't see that happening, and honestly she fucked you in the arse with a strap on dick. I think she's a keeper."
"Yeah, I guess you're right. And maybe she'll be cool with us hooking up."
"Don't know if you don't ask."
"Or if you don't tell her how you feel."
"True, thanks for the kick up the arse."
"You gonna tell her how you feel?"
"Yeah, I've got an idea of when."
"Good," Austin replies before ordering another round, "so tell me Kad, what was it like being pegged?"

I tune out of the conversation, not wanting to hear any more about their weird sex life.
I'd heard enough the night before, my brother's weird moans as Elyse fucked him in the arse.
If I'd had something else to take a hit of I'd have taken it.
I scull my second beer, the alcohol making my head pound harder.
Slapping a hand on Kaden's back I tell him, "I'm gonna skip out brother. I'll catch a tram back and get my bike."
"No worries, Bren. I'll catch ya next week before we head to the parentals for Easter."
I laugh and scoff at the same time. "Don't remind me of that torture...but yeah, I'll come over before so I don't have to hear dad's lectures."
"Sweet, bro, catch ya then," he replies giving me a side bro-hug that is a little too endearing.

My damn brother has fallen in love, and I can swear if I didn't know he was bi, I'd think he'd fallen for a dude because he's acting like a pansy.

Sixty-Three | Happy Easter

It took a helluva lot of convincing, grovelling and begging on my part to get Lys to agree to come to my parents for Easter.
I sent her flowers, sweet words via text without quite confessing how I really feel about her.
What sealed the deal was an L-word confession, not the actual L-word, love but I like you.
Her response back was a heart eyes emoji and about five kisses.
I really want to tell her that I love her, but I'm not sure I'm ready to utter the words; to actually confess them to her face.

Pulling up in front of her house, I'm about to get out and go in, when she comes running out the front door.
Brennan is sitting next to me in the passenger seat, and I elbow him in the side. "Get in the back, dickwad."
"Fine, fuckwit, but don't you dare try any funny business with me in the car."
"I'm not a dirty tosser like you, Brennan," I taunt as he gets out, holding the passenger door open for Elyse and grabbing her bag from her grip.
Elyse gets in, and he shuts the door behind him before putting her bag in the boot and getting back in the car.

"Well, aren't you the perfect gentlemen Bren," I jeer, laughing.
Elyse is looking between us, trying not to laugh.
"I'm a good guy, sometimes," he says back with a laugh, clipping his seatbelt in.
I look across at Lys, who's smile is so wide.

"Hey, sexy minx. Love the dress," I comment, leaning over the console to kiss her.

I hear Brennan scoff in the backseat.

"Thanks, I thought I better attempt to show I'm a girl."

I start to pull out into traffic. "Are you nervous?"

"Yeah, I'm not good at the whole parent meeting thing."

"It'll be fine Lys, I promise they'll love you as much as I..." I snap my mouth shut, realising what I was about to confess.

It's not the time with my brother in the car; plus I want to show her, tell her how I feel in a big grand gesture.

I've been such an arse and I need to make it up to her.

Reassuringly, after slipping the gears, I rub her thigh.

"They'll love you Lys. Don't stress."

"Ok, I'll try not to," she replies with a smile, turning her attention to the radio to turn up the volume.

'Looking Hot' by No Doubt starts to play, and she sings along, practically purring the words.

I want to say so much, that of course, she's looking hot; that she's the most gorgeous chick on the fucking planet and that my stupid brain has finally realised that hearts don't steer us wrong.

I'm driving on autopilot and stealing glances at her.

The emotions hitting me hard in the feels are my heart telling me that it was in love with her months ago, practically from the first time I fucked her at the beach, but I'd been too daft to realise it and put us both through unnecessary angst.

She continues singing along to the radio, knowing the words to every song that comes on.

Looking in the rearview mirror I lock eyes with Brennan and he sniggers at me, before laughing.

He mouths the words, *'tell her you love her'*.
I mouth back, *'not yet wanker'*.
He shrugs and turns to look out the window, and again I touch Elyse's thigh smiling at her when she turns to look at me.

We're only about ten minutes from my parents now, so I ask softly, "You ready Lys?"
"As ready as I'll ever be, Kad."
I nod, turning into the cul-de-sac my parents live on.

No sooner than a minute after I've pulled up out the front Mum is running down the front path, calling out, "Happy Easter my darlings". She's so peppy.
Getting out of the car, I'm about to open Elyse's door when Mum envelopes me in a hug, squeezing me so tight I gasp for air.
"Mum, please...I can't breathe," I pant and she releases me.

She looks behind me, noticing that Elyse is out of the car.
Mum's smile is about to break her face.
"Oh, hi dear, you must be Elyse. We've heard so much about you from our Kaden."
"Hi, Mrs Abbett. It's nice to meet you."
"You too dear. Very much. Our Kaden here hasn't bought a girl home before. We were beginning to think he may have batted for the other team."
Elyse gives me a knowing look, and I pull her to my side.
"Please Mum, stop."

I take Elyse's hand, and we all head up the front path still listening to Mum rambling.

Once inside, she shows Elyse to the guest room, and I share a laugh with her at the traditional old school nature of my parents, not letting us sleep in my old room together even though I have a double bed.

Mum and I leave Elyse to get settled, and head to the kitchen to make coffees.

"So dear, have you told her how you feel about her?"

I shake my head, not able to meet Mum's intense gaze.

"Why not, dear? You are in love with her, aren't you?"

I don't reply, my head in a spin.

"Kaden, it's as clear as day dear."

"Yes, Mum, I'm in love with her, but I haven't told her because I want to make a big grand gesture of it. I've been a dufus and I need to make it up to her."

"Oh my dear son, that's wonderful."

She smiles at me, and I can't help but smile back, especially when Elyse walks into the kitchen.

"Were you talking about me?" she asks, hugging me, her arms around my waist.

"Never," I say with a laugh, kissing her hair, "why would I be talking about you?"

She giggles, and I notice the Cheshire cat grin on Mum's face as she busies herself with finishing off making the coffee's.

I know she wants to say something else, but I glare at her, telling her not to without words.

I give Elyse a soft kiss, pulling back and taking a coffee from Mum. And as we head into the lounge room to enjoy our coffees and Easter chocolate, Mum whispers to me, "I've never seen you this happy Kaden. You need to tell her how you feel before it's too late."

"I know Mum. I am happy. And I will."

And that I will. I have the perfect plan already ticking over in my mind with my birthday only a couple of weeks away, I want to celebrate it with telling Elyse that I'm arse over tits in love with her.

Who woulda thought I'd fall for a chick?

Sixty-Four | Beach Love

Grabbing Elyse's hand the moment we're out of the commodore at St Kilda beach sends a giddy rush through my body.
I know she feels it too, the connection between us, and today it's making my heart race.

Over the past few weeks, my feelings for her have hit me head on.
And even though she insisted that she wanted to take me out for my birthday I said no; so I could share how I feel about her—with her—at the place where I fell in love with her months ago.
It hit me like a tonne of bricks; all these months I've been fighting a battle between my head and my heart because I'd fallen in love with Elyse the first time I fucked her.
Our first time together had been so intense, and overwhelming that I told myself those feelings were all just because of the phenomenal sex, but I finally got my stupid brain to realise that the sex is so fucking amazing because I love her.

It's still warm for early May, and running down the beach she's pulling me with her.
Getting closer to the water, she kicks off her thongs and pulls her oversized t-shirt off before shimmying out of her jeans.
She's wearing her red bikini again, and my dick tents in the front of my jeans looking at her in that again, memories flooding my mind.
And now I'm inwardly screaming for joy that she's mine; well she will be completely when I confess how I feel about her.
Walking backwards towards the sea, she beckons me with a finger and a sexy smirk.
"Well, Kaden, are you coming in or what?"

"Oh I'm coming sexy minx, and so are you," I say undressing quickly and running towards her in just my boxer shorts.
I hadn't planned on going swimming and the thought crosses my mind that I'm going to be getting out of the water after our swim sans jocks, but I don't fucking care.
All I want now is to be with my girl, and tell her that I'm absolutely arse over tits in love with her.

She's stopped moving and is just staring at me with that smirk that makes my stomach flip.
Reaching her I grab her around the waist, and she giggles, squirming in my arms when I tickle her.
"Don't foxy, don't," she protests through her giggles.
"Don't what, sexy minx?" I tease, slipping a hand into the bikini bottoms and brushing it against her clit when I tease again, "Touch you?"
"Yes, yes...oh...fuck," she says loudly, moaning, my finger sliding inside her wet pussy.

She's putty in my arms, and it's damn arousing.
She lets out a hiss of pleasure, before kissing me hard and taking my breath away. Her kiss is fierce, hungry and sending my heart racing.
Telling her how I feel about her now, probably isn't the best idea, but when she tears her mouth from mine, shuddering around my fingers with her orgasm rocking through her body—on a public beach—I can't help the words that fall from my lips.
"God, Lys, I love you."
Her eyes boggle and her mouth drops open in shock.
"What? You what?" she mutters, licking her lips before biting down on the bottom one.
"I said, I love you."
She lets out a sweet laugh. "I heard you, but um...do you mean it?"

"Of course I fucking mean it Lys. I'm arse over tits in love with you. And I'm sorry it's taken me so long to grow a pair to tell you. I've loved you since that day I first fucked you; I just didn't trust my heart to steer me right."

"Yeah, hearts don't steer us wrong, Kad. And you know what?"

"What? Are you pregnant for real or something?"

"No, nothing like that. I um...I think I've been in love with you since we first kissed. Maybe even before that."

"Aww, Lys, I'm sorry I strung you along, but I'm all in now."

She smiles at me, laughing and freeing herself from my arms around her and running into the surf.

Following her, I laugh and smile.

I'm diving into the fucking waves for her.

And fuck does it feel amazing.

I can't even remember why I was so afraid to fall in love again in the first place.

Sixty-Five | After Fun

Getting out of the surf, Elyse runs in front of me, cacking herself laughing because just as I'd thought my jocks washed away in the sea and now I'm starkers.

Holding a hand over my junk I stumble up the beach. Elyse stops where we left our clothes on the sand, grabbing my jeans and holding them with a seductive smirk on her face.
"You want these, foxy?" she taunts, picking up the rest of our clothes and running towards the car.

I want to run faster, but the only way to do that is to take my hand off my junk and bolt.
"Lys, come on yeah? Give me my damn jeans!" I call out to her, but she shakes her head, stopping at the car and leaning against the door, still smirking at me wickedly.
It's now or never; I drop my hand from my cock, glancing around for a moment before I sprint up the beach.
It's kinda weird, and oddly arousing to have my cock swishing from side to side in the breeze.
Elyse's gaze on me doesn't help the situation; my cock starting to harden from her eyes locked on me.

Reaching her at the car, I push her against the door. "You play dirty, sexy minx."
She laughs, winking at me. "What can I say? I've told you before that your birthday suit is your best outfit."
"True, but I just had to sprint up the beach starkers, Lys. I think I deserve a kiss for that."

Again she laughs at me, before crashing her lips to mine in a bruising kiss, that takes my breath away and makes my cock harden more, teasing her pussy through her bikini bottoms. She bites my bottom lip, pulling it back between her teeth and then licking it to soothe the sting before her tongue teases mine. My head is in a spin, I'm drowning in her kiss and the whole world has ceased to exist until I hear a wolf whistle behind us from some cock sucker.

I break the kiss, realising I'm still naked and the cock sucker was obviously whistling about my bare arse being on display.
Elyse laughs. "See, foxy? He liked your peachy arse too."
"Yeah, haha, Lys. Not funny. Give me my damn jeans now and just wait until we get back to mine."
I step back from her and she hands me my jeans, which I quickly—albeit awkwardly as my dick is still hard—slip them up my legs. Walking around to the driver's side, Elyse slaps my arse playfully, giggling.

We both slide into the Commodore and I reverse out of the parking spot, onto the esplanade.
My cock is still hard, bordering on painful pressing against the fly of my jeans.
Elyse keeps glancing at it, which of course doesn't help. Her eyes on me full of lust can instantly make me rock hard.
She reaches over the console, grabbing it in her hand.
I groan, electricity pulsing through my body. "God, Lys, please....please...touch me."

She doesn't reply, instead, licks her lips and with her eyes on me, she slips her hand into my jeans.
Slowly, she starts to stroke my cock, flipping it out over the hem and a moan escapes her lips.

Her hand starts to caress my cock faster and it throbs. I almost want to pull over and fuck her right here, but tonight I also want to take things slow, and make slow sweet love to her.

"Lys, fuck that feels good, but if you don't stop I'm gonna come and tonight I only want to come from making love to you."

She gasps, her breath hitching in her throat. There are no words to say. I know what she's thinking. I just told her I want to make love to her, not to fuck her, and even though those words sound foreign from my lips I mean them.

~~

Fifteen minutes later we're back at my apartment and racing inside. We've barely stepped inside the front door before I yank my jeans off and kick them aside. I'm about to kiss Elyse, but she taunts me, shaking her head and reaching behind her back to untie the bikini top.

It falls from her tits, and I groan looking at her; the pink buds hard and just begging to be in my mouth.

She turns me on fucking much.

She's taunting me and I can't take much more, so grab her around the waist, smashing my lips to hers and sliding my hands into the bikini bottoms to palm her perfect round arse cheeks.

Her skin feels so soft against my callous hands, and when she moans against my lips, I slide the bikini bottoms over her arse cheeks, pushing them to the floor.

"Mmm, Kaden," she moans against my lips, licking them and deepening the kiss more.

Grabbing her arse I lift her into my arms, carrying her down the hallway to my bedroom.

I need to have her now.

Once in my room, we stumble back towards the bed, still pashing and when her legs hit the edge of the bed she falls backwards, pulling me down with her.

My cock is teasing her pussy, so hard the tip is at her entrance; one small thrust and I'd fill her.

Breaking the kiss, she gives me a shy smile before frowning and panic fills me.

"Lys? Are you ok?"

"Yeah, but I um...forgot to get my shot."

"Oh, shit," I reply, rolling off of her to go and grab some frangers from the bathroom.

When I come back into the bedroom, she's sitting up in my bed, looking utterly heartbroken.

Sitting next to her I kiss her forehead, softly.

"I'm sorry, Kaden. I ruined the moment. I want to be with you again, but I don't want to risk it."

I chuckle slightly. "You didn't ruin anything, Lys. Better safe than sorry."

"Yeah, do you still want to fuck?" she asks, looking at me sheepishly.

"Is my cock still hard?" I say laughing and grabbing her hand to touch me.

"Yeah, rock hard," she replies laughing and smiling at me.

"Exactly, and sexy minx, you know I don't want to fuck you tonight."

"I know, but I kinda want to fuck you, reverse cowgirl."

She blushes with her confession, and I swear it makes my cock harder.

"Oh fuck yeah," I bellow, ripping open a franger packet and sliding it down onto my cock.

Edging back onto the bed I pull Elyse onto my lap, giving her a quick, hard kiss, before I murmur, "Ride me, sexy minx."

Turning around she impales herself on my cock, sitting right down so our bodies meet; her arse cheeks meeting my hips.
She lets out a lascivious moan of pleasure, rocking up and down on my cock.
"That's it, sexy minx, fuck me hard."
Her moans increase, louder and louder, making my cock throb inside her.
It's been an age since I fucked a chick reverse cowgirl, but I know it was never this amazing.
Just watching Elyse enjoying herself and her arse bouncing on my cock makes me want to come.
"Kaden, fuck, fuck….oh my god…I'm gonna come."
"Not yet, Lys, hold it for me, sexy minx," I tell her, pressing my thumb against her arse hole.
Another illicit, screaming moan escapes her lips and she stops bouncing on my cock a moment when I push my thumb deeper inside her arse.
"Oh god, Kaden…fuck that…feels…amazing…I'm gonna come so hard."

Again she starts bouncing up and down on my cock, with my finger teasing her arse. It's barely a minute, before I feel her pussy clenching around me and she moans, a bellowing 'fuck' escaping her lips as she comes apart around me.

When she slides off my cock, I pull her down next to me, kissing her passionately.
Wrapping my arms around her, I slip my cock inside her, holding her close and rocking our bodies together.
Soft murmurs escape her lips against mine and my heart is hammering in my chest.
Without a doubt I've never felt like this—never had sex like this—with anyone else; this is making love.
Against my lips, she moans, and whispers, "I love you, Kaden, so much."

I break the kiss, brushing her hair from her face and still rocking my cock inside her pussy I lock my eyes on hers.

"I love you too, Elyse."

"Mmm," she murmurs, kissing me and as usual taking my breath away. No one before her has ever left me breathless, and pounding hard into her pussy I murmur against her lips, a whisper, "Lys, my sexy minx, come with me, for me."

Her hands find my face and she deepens the kiss with her tongue, pushing her body closer to mine.

I've never felt so close to someone before, so connected as one.

Sex has never felt so amazing and breaking the kiss panting I thrust inside her core hard, hitting the sweet spot inside her that makes her moan so loud I swear my neighbours will hear.

"Kaden, god...I'm...coming...again," she says huskily, trembling in my arms when her second release rocks through her body and my come fills her in a hard throbbing release.

I pull out, quickly discarding the condom in the bin beside my bed.

Elyse snuggles into my side, looking up at me. "That was phenomenal, Kaden. The best sex ever."

"Yeah, Elyse, but that wasn't sex."

"Huh? What do you mean?"

"Lys, that was slow sweet lovemaking, and I've never made love to anyone."

"Me either, just you."

"I'm glad to hear that, sexy minx," I reply sweetly, kissing her hair and wrapping her in my arms again.

She kisses me softly, a sweet goodnight kiss with the promise of forever.

Being with her feels so incredibly right. I want to ask her a question, but it will have to wait until the morning as she's fallen asleep in my arms; my beautiful sexy minx, my forever love.

Sixty-Six | Morning Questions

Waking up the next morning my heart is still racing, and my dick is hard as steel from sleeping with Elyse naked beside me.

Even now in the light of day, our bodies are wrapped around each other, our legs entangled and my arms enveloping her. It's absolute fucking bliss.

Elyse murmurs in her sleep, before moaning and rocking her naked pussy against my dick.

Laughing I kiss her forehead softly.

"Lys, wake up beautiful."

She startles, her eyes opening wide. "Huh, what?" she mutters looking at me worriedly, before smiling. "Did you just call me beautiful?"

"You bet I did, sexy minx. You know you're damn beautiful, Lys."

She laughs softly. "I never thought I'd love hearing a guy say that to me."

"I better say it again then," I reply laughing and kissing her lips softly.

She deepens the morning kiss with her tongue, stirring up the lust for her in my belly, but it's so much more now. It's longing and love and against her lips, I ask with a whisper, "Wanna marry me, beautiful?"

Biting down on her lip, she tries to hide the smirk on her face.

"I'm serious, Lys."

"Yeah...but what about when you get sick of me and wanna be with a guy?"

I chuckle, then reply, "Then you'll just let me fuck that hot arse of yours or peg me hard."

She appears to ponder my statement for a moment, and I caress her cheek with my palm, brushing her long hair aside.

"So? Is it a yes, sexy minx?"

"Fine, yes...I'll marry you but after Bella and Travis get married."

"Are they even engaged yet?"

"Fucked if I know. She hasn't told me, but they will. Especially if I tell her that we are."

"Ok, so now that we're engaged will you move in with me then?" I ask wickedly, not even caring to hide my smirk.

Lys frowns back at me, making my heart sink.

"I don't want to ditch Lil."

Playfully I poke her in the ribs. "Fair enough...so I guess I'll have to shack up with you both then."

"Sounds fun," she says with a sweet laugh.

Giving her a kiss I whisper against her lips, "I love you, Elyse."

She breaks the kiss, looking at me with the widest smile.

"I love you too, Kaden."

She honestly looks so stunning lying in my arms naked, and as much as I want to stay in bed all day, I also want to take her out and get her a diamond ring, to show the whole damn world she's mine.

"So, sexy minx, how about we get up for some brekkie and go get you a ring?"

"Brekkie does sound good. We kinda skipped dinner last night."

"Yeah, fuck, we did. No wonder my guts are rumbling."

She stands up getting out of bed, and I lie there a moment admiring her hot as sin body.

She turns to look back at me.

"Kad, do you have anything I can wear? I really don't want to put my dress on."

"Yeah, sure sexy minx. I'll see what I can find."

I get out of bed, heading to my walk in to find her something to wear. It turns me on so bad, that my girl is a tomboy.

Seeing her in my clothes is going to make keeping my cock tame a tad difficult.

Opening my drawers I pull out a pair of grey trackies and a black v-neck Nike t-shirt.

Lys steps up behind me, wearing her bikini bottoms that she ran out to collect from the lounge room.

Holding the clothes up to her I ask, "Will these be ok, sexy minx?"

"Yeah, great, thanks," she replies taking them and giving me a quick kiss.

I watch her get dressed, gulping when she slips the t-shirt on and I realise she's planning to go braless.

"Um, sexy minx, are you hoping to torture me?"

She laughs. "No, what do you mean?"

"No bra, Lys. How do you expect me to keep my hands off you?"

"Maybe I don't want you to keep your hands to yourself."

"Oh really? It's like that is it?"

"Yep, it is," she says with a laugh before running a finger up the middle of my abs; all the way to my lips.

I take her finger into my mouth, licking it and moaning.

"Damn Lys, you're gonna kill me."

Her eyes lock on mine and she moans before pushing me against the drawers. I can barely think before she kisses me, hard and hot, again making me breathless.

Elyse taking control of a kiss is the biggest fucking turn on ever and grabbing her around the waist I pull her against me more.

Our lips are locked together, and her tongue slips inside my mouth; teasing me in a delicious battle.

Again a moan escapes my lips against hers and I break the kiss.

She's smirking at me and grabs my cock in her hand.

"You're still alive, foxy."

"That I am, sexy minx, but that was some kiss. You're gonna be the death of me though, Lys."

She laughs cheekily, letting go of my cock and dropping to her knees in front of me.
Looking up at me her eyes are hooded with lust, and she slides her lips onto my cock, taking my length in and out of her pretty pink lips.
"Fuck, Lys!" I bellow, feeling my release building.
To tease me more, she takes my cock all the way out, just to the tip, swirling her tongue into my slit.
It's so damn arousing and when she takes my cock back into her mouth again, I can't help exploding down her throat in a shattering release.

She swallows before standing up and kissing me without a word.
Breaking the kiss she walks out, leaving me dumbfounded.
She calls back to me, "Get dressed foxy. I'm starving."
Quickly I collect my thoughts and pull on some jocks, with trackies and a t-shirt.

Elyse is in the ensuite, helping herself to my toothbrush and I laugh at how domestic it feels; like we've shacked up together.
We continue getting ready together, glancing at each other and laughing, before we head out for breakfast and buying the ring.
Elyse can't stop smiling, so obviously excited and that warms my heart.
I'm so in love with her.
Who woulda thought I'd ever be buying a chick an engagement ring?
Not me, not ever, but it's happening and I'm excited for all that comes after today.

Sixty-Seven | House Crasher

Closing the door of my Hawthorn apartment behind me for the last time, a tonne of feels hit me hard in the chest.

I'm excited to be moving in with Elyse but scared as hell about taking such a big step in our lives.

Leaving the apartment behind is surreal kinda, like the end of an era, finally growing up.

And it makes me feel like a man.

It helped that my parents approved of Elyse and of us getting married. If they didn't I have no idea what I'd do.

Elyse's mum thankfully also approved, and getting into the commodore that's loaded up with all my belongings I think back to the FaceTime chat we'd had with Mrs Mishal telling her we are engaged.

I dutifully apologised for not asking her to marry her daughter, but I needn't have worried as she was that elated that both her daughters are happy she squealed the moment we told her the news and Elyse held up the diamond ring on her finger to the screen.

Pulling away from the kerb, I sigh, preparing myself for the next steps.

The whole drive over to Elyse and Lillie's, my heart hammers in my chest.

I'm really doing this, I'm letting go of the bachelor life and crashing into my fiancee's house.

It still feels weird to say that and my head still spins thinking about getting married.

Once outside the apartment, my house now, I make a mental note to discuss some wedding plans with Elyse.

I'm barely out of the car before Elyse is out the door and running down the path toward me in trackies and a jumper, with ugg boots on her feet. They clomp on the ground, and she looks like a complete dag running towards me but at the same time, she looks absolutely fucking stunning, her tomboy side clearly showing.

Laughing I pull her into a hug, kissing her hair that is pulled up in a messy bun on her head.
"You look like a dag, Lys."
She laughs. "I try."
"You don't have to dress up to be beautiful Lys. In fact I quite like it when you let your tomboy side out."
She eyes me, giggling. "Really? My tomboy side? Do you like that side of me, because you like boys, Kaden?"

Her questions come at me like lightning and I love the teasing tone of her voice.
"Yeah, I like boys Elyse. But I'm in love with the best girl. She just so happens to dress like a boy."
Again she laughs, but doesn't tease me more, just demands, "Shut up and kiss me, boy lover."
Taking her lips to mine, her tongue instantly licks along my lips to deepen the kiss and I moan against her lips.
It's the kinda kiss that you feel through your entire body and pulling back a moment I find myself panting.

"Fuck, Elyse. I love you, and when you kiss me like that you make a guy wanna fuck you right here, right now."
She laughs at me, teasing, "Well I had to convince you that you shouldn't love boys anymore."
"Oh really? And why is that?"
"Because I'm in love with you, Kaden."

The way she purrs my name stirs the butterflies and that flip flop feeling in my stomach, as well as making my cock ache to fuck her again.

"I'll never get tired of hearing you say that,Lys."

"I love you, Kaden, I love you, I love you!" She calls out, giggling.

"Music to my ears, sexy minx. How about some help getting my shit out of the car and we can celebrate moving in together?"

She laughs, her eyebrows raising up at me slightly when she asks, "And how might we celebrate that, foxy?"

"Fucking in our bed of course." I air quote 'our' smirking at her.

"Oh yeah, we better hurry the fuck up and get you settled then."

I don't reply, just walk back over to my car, and pop the boot to pull out my suitcase.

Elyse follows, taking a small gym bag and heading back inside.

I grab a few more things, falling into the open boot when Brennan skids to a halt at the kerb behind me on his bike. He lifts off his helmet to greet me, "Hey big bro. Need some help?"

"Yeah, Bren, but no funny business with Lillie when we get inside."

"Never, Kad. I'm here to help my pussy whipped big brother move in with his chick."

"Fiancée, Brennan."

"You weren't fucking kidding about that? You're seriously getting married?"

"Yep, haven't set a date yet, but yes I'm dead serious. I'm not letting Elyse go."

"Good for you, bro. I hope I can honestly find a chick I can feel that way about."

"You will, Brennan. But now can you get off ya bike and help bring in some of my shit?"

"Yeah, of course. Anything I can grab from the back? You've got the com loaded to the brim."

"Yeah, maybe grab the bedding from the back seat." He follows my instruction and we head inside together.

Crossing the threshold of the open front door, I take a look around, grinning from ear to ear.

Memories hit me hard, the times I shared with not only Austin but Elyse, and I'm excited to make more memories in this house and with Elyse no matter where we are.

Sixty-Eight | Hello Princess

Brennan

Following Kaden inside his new digs, I can't help but glance around, wondering where Lillie sleeps. My dirty mind is so going there, thinking about her naked in her bed, which is probably just a dirty thought. Lillie is way too innocent to sleep naked, but I can't help but think about it. Kaden's warnings to keep away from her only make me want her more, but I know I have to keep away. I can't drag an innocent chick like Lillie into my fucked up life.

Stopping at the first bedroom, behind Kaden I throw the bedding in a pile and give Elyse a smile.

"Congrats on getting engaged, Elyse," I tell her.

"Thanks, Brennan," she replies with a smile, pulling my brother into a side hug, and kissing his cheek.

My stomach lurches at how sickly sweet it is, but the pang of jealousy hits me harder in the chest.

"I hope you know what you're getting yourself into with my brother. He's a dirty fucker."

"I know," she laughs, "but I love him, and his dirty side."

"Yeah, ok, way to make me wanna chunder. I'm out. I'm just gonna take a leak and leave you to it. Have a good first night together, lovers."

I laugh hard, slapping my brother on the back before I walk out of the room to head down the small hallway to the main bathroom.

The other bedroom door is open, and I take a quick squiz into Lillies room.

It screams girly, pretty pink bedding with Ballerinas on it.
And a small mountain of stuffed animals piled high.
There are no posters of bands or half-naked hot guys on the wall, like in
Elyse's room and I laugh at another sign of Lillie's innocence.

I hate myself for the fact that I've thought about taking Lillies innocence
away, her sexy as fuck body is like dick crack. And way too many dirty
thoughts have gone through my head since I met her months ago.

Thinking she must be out, I step across the hallway to the bathroom,
opening the door, and shutting it hastily when I hear a soft shriek of
panic.

No fucking way!

Lillie is in the bathroom; naked.

Oh god, I want to look, but I can't do that.

"Sorry," I call out.
She opens the door, in just a towel. And slinks out on her tiptoes trying
to push past me; I don't let her move, instead pin her against the wall.
"Hello, Princess," I purr in her ear.

Her body betrays her; I feel her shiver in delight.
I don't doubt her pussy is humming, wet and god do I want to kiss her
and have the small towel fall to the floor between us.
She huffs at me.
"Hi," is the only meek reply she gives me, biting down on her lip.

Fuck, she's gorgeous, step the fuck away from the girl, you fucker.

For once I obey my conscience, feeling like my brother is screaming in my head, as well as Elyse.

"Sorry Princess," I mutter, stepping aside and watching her rush across the hallway to her room.

Her pert arse is almost visible at the bottom of the towel, and I have to resist the temptation to reach out and grab it.

She slams the door behind her, and I quickly rush into the bathroom to drain my snake, which is a little bit difficult with a hard on starting to tent my daks.

I know I can't have Lillie, but god do I fucking want her.

Exiting the bathroom, I rush out of Kaden's house, not even bothering to say goodbye as the bedroom door is now shut and I swear I can hear kissing sounds.

I need a hit or a chick to sink my cock into, to rid my mind of innocent minx's named Lillie.

Sixty-Nine | Lovers Night

I'm pretty sure Brennan has left, but honestly I couldn't give a rats arse.
All I care about right now is celebrating moving in with Elyse.
She closes the bedroom door and looks at me with lust flaring in her dark brown eyes.
She bites down on her lip a moment, and then says, "So, foxy how are we going to celebrate this occasion?"
"By fucking, sexy minx," I taunt her, invading her personal space to pin her against the wall.
She whimpers, but it's so hot; it makes my cock ache.

"Where? Right here? Against the wall," she taunts me, her fingers clutching the hem of my t-shirt.
I groan, pleasure coursing through my body.
She lifts my t-shirt off and lets out an appreciative hum glaring at my body.
"You're so fucking hot, Kad," she teases, moaning before kissing me, hard and leaving me breathless.

Our hands roam each other's bodies as we kiss, frantically as though we'll never be able to get enough of each other. And I'm positive I will never get enough of Elyse.
No chick has ever turned me on as much as she does; all she needs to do is look at me with her mesmerising sienna eyes and my body wants her.

Breaking the kiss, she's panting for breath and locks her eyes on mine, lifting her jumper over her head.

She's wearing one of those bralette things again and seductively slips the straps down her arms.

I can't bear to look away, watching her strip for me is so damn sexy.

She slides it down her torso, pushing it and her trackies to the floor, exposing her lace g-string.

"Fuck, Lys, you're so fucking sexy and damn beautiful."

She actually blushes and it makes my cock jolt in my daks.

Locking my eyes on hers, I lean in close, grabbing her arms and pinning her against the wall, before kissing her neck.

Pants and whimpers escape her lips, turning me on even more, and I know her pussy is going to be so wet.

Kissing her ear, I take a deep breath in and exhale, whispering, "Are you wet for me, sexy minx?"

"Yes, yes, so wet, for you," she pants, fisting my hair and pulling my lips to hers for a brazen, dirty kiss.

My cock is so hard, her pussy is rubbing against it between us as we kiss.

I feel like I'm gonna come just from that.

Breaking the kiss, I rest my forehead on hers. "You're going to kill me Lys."

"Not if you kill me first. Please, Kaden, fuck me now."

I don't reply, instead take a step back, yanking my trackies and boxers to the floor.

My cock is harder than ever.

Elyse whimpers looking at me naked in front of her. "Condom?" she says huskily.

I laugh, bending down to grab the franger I put in my trackies pocket earlier.

Handing it to her, she rips it open and slips it onto my cock, stroking me at the same time.

Reaching forward I shove the skimpy fabric of her g-string aside, slipping a finger inside her pussy to make her moan.

"You want my cock inside you, sexy minx?"

"Yes, yes, foxy, fuck me now, please," she begs, tipping her head back in pleasure.

Taking out my finger I lick it clean, moaning at how good she tastes.

I yank the g-string down her legs, over her arse and without warning, when her eyes are back on mine I push my cock inside her pussy, making her arse hit the wall hard.

She lets out a hot whimper.

"Oh god, Kaden, fuck!

"Mmm, Elyse, tell me how good it feels."

"So fucking good," she says barely audible as a loud moan rocks her body.

"Are you gonna come on my cock, sexy minx?"

"Yes, oh yes, fuck," she pants making me drive my cock into her harder.

When she lets out another loud moan, I silence her with a kiss, a hard deep kiss that makes my cock throb inside her.

Breaking the kiss, she moans and says, "I love you, Kaden."

"I love you too, Elyse. Do you trust me?"

She nods, and says a meek, "Yes."

I slow my thrusts into her, reaching down and grabbing her arse, and hooking her thighs in the crook of my elbows.

Holding her in my arms I step away from the wall and thrust my cock into her harder.

Her arms wrap around my neck and she starts to bounce on my cock, screaming moans of pleasure escaping her lips.

"Oh fuck, fuck, fuck! Kaden! Fuck!"

I kiss her again, rendering as both breathless, as we pant against his others mouths, lacing our tongues together as our bodies rock together. I've never fucked a chick like this, and it's so fucking amazing.

Elyse moans against my mouth, her whole body trembling with her impending release.
She breaks the kiss, her mouth falling open in an 'o,' a hot as fuck moan on her lips as her pussy clenches around me with her release.
"Oh Kaden, fuck," she says softly, before kissing me.
My cock is still rock hard inside her but I don't want to release in the condom and I want to taste her arousal; make her orgasm again on my tongue.

Stepping back towards the bed, I pull her down with me.
I'm still inside her and she rocks her pussy over my cock, kissing me again for a moment before I pull back.
"Lys, I wanna taste you," I tell her with a smirk.
"Yeah, only if I can taste you to," she teases biting down on her lip.
"You telling me you want to sixty-nine?"
"Yeah, up for it?"
"Oh, you bet sexy minx," I jeer as she climbs off me.

She turns around, scooting back a bit so her pussy is in my face.
Again without giving her any warning I kiss her clit, licking her slowly and sucking her pussy lips into my mouth.
Her pussy bucks against my face and she takes the condom off my cock, sliding her lips over my length.
It feels so fucking amazing, making me moan against her wet pussy.
"Mmm, fuck, Lys, so good. Suck me, sexy minx."
She takes her mouth off of my cock for a moment, swirling her tongue in the tip, and pushing her pussy onto my face more.
"Fuck, Kad, taste my pussy, so good," she teases.

We continue sucking and licking each other until I can feel my release building.

"Lys, I'm gonna come," I tell her, before slipping a finger inside her pussy with my tongue circling her clit.

She sucks me harder when her release starts to build and together we come, my release shooting into her mouth, her pussy spasming with her squirting orgasm all over my face.

She swallows my load, and I lick her pussy dry, before grabbing her by the hips and turning her body around.

She's still straddling me and I pull her down for a kiss, that makes her moan when she tastes herself on my lips.

"That was so fucking good, Kad."

"Tell me about it, Lys. You know you squirted yeah?"

"Really? Is that why it felt so good?"

"Yeah, beautiful. And I'm gonna make you feel that good for the rest of our fucking lives."

"Sounds like bliss. I love you so much."

"I'll never get tired of making you feel bliss or hearing you say you love me, Elyse Abbett."

She laughs. "That's not my name, Kaden."

"Yet," I say laughing and kissing her forehead, "and I want it to be soon."

"Me too, but for now, I just wanna lie here in your arms, and kiss you, and fuck you again."

"Sounds like bliss, " I say, teasing her back with her own words, making her laugh before I kiss her again.

Against her lips, I softly say, "I love you, my beautiful sexy minx."

She moans, deepening the kiss, entangling our legs together.

I'm already ready to have her again, my cock starting to harden just from kissing her.

The first night of us living together, a lovers night and most definitely
bliss that I can't wait to spend the rest of my life enjoying.
It's most definitely true that hearts don't steer us wrong, and I can't help
but think that players don't fall quietly either.
I most certainly fell for Elyse louder than ever, and my heart is hers.

Epilogue | The Day

Elyse
5 months later

It feels surreal and an absolute whirlwind that this day is here. I'm getting married, to Kaden. If you'd told me five months ago that he would have made any kind of commitment to me, let alone be marrying me on a balmy November day I'd have told you, you were dreaming. But it's happening.

Bella steps up behind me, helping me step into the wedding jumpsuit. Part of me wanted to wear a dress for Kaden—knowing how much he loves me wearing dresses—but I know he also loves my tomboy side and every dress I tried on didn't feel right.
The moment I tried on the jumpsuit I knew it was perfect. It hugs my hips and shows just a peek of cleavage, and has a chiffon billowy train skirt over the top.
I feel unbelievably gorgeous and sexy in it, especially when I slip my feet into my strappy white stiletto heels.

"Aww Ely-bug, you look beautiful. I can't believe my little sister is getting married."
"Thanks, Bel-bear. Kinda crazy huh? I still can't believe you eloped though Bella."
"I know Ely-bug, but it was the right thing for me and Travis. I didn't really want the big fanfare, and he knew that."
"Yeah, I'm kinda excited to be the centre of attention."

"I bet you are, and you're certainly going to be in this."

"You don't look too bad yourself. Blue suits you," I tell her stepping back from the mirror so she can take in her appearance in the short tight blue shift dress.

"Yeah, I didn't think I'd fit in this, so soon after having Taylor."

"Speaking of my nephew...I can't wait to see him walk down the aisle in his little tux. And Nora in her little dress."

"Yeah, I know. They're going to look so cute," she says in a tone that seems a little sad.

"Bel-bear, you ok?"

"Yeah, I just...I'm just so glad we didn't lose Nora."

She starts to sob and I wrap her into a hug.

"Don't cry Bella, you'll ruin your makeup."

She sniffs, pulling back from my hug. "I know, I know, I just...love her and miss her so badly, but her living with Austin is the best thing."

"Yeah, she's a real daddy's girl. Must take after her aunty," I say with a laugh.

"Yeah and Ely-bug, I'm so sorry Dad can't be here for you. He loved you so much."

"Yeah, but regardless I'm surrounded by family and friends. I'm so happy."

"I'm so glad Ely-bug. It's funny how things work out." Her tone is soft again.

"Bel-bear, is that part of the reason you eloped? Because of the whole dad situation?"

"Yeah, and I know I need to find him, my real dad, especially now I've got my own kids."

"Yeah, let me know if you want some help. I love you, big sis."

"I love you too, little sis."

We hug again and break apart when a couple soft knocks come from the door.

"That's probably Lil," I say eagerly, rushing over to the door and opening it in a haste.

My best friend and my mum are standing in front of me.

I hug Lil, and then Mum, ushering them inside.

"Oh Elyse dear, you look beautiful."

"Thanks, Mum. We're just about ready to go."

I look to Lillie, and she laughs at me. "I wasn't expecting this outfit Ely, but I love it. So you, bestie."

"Thanks, Lil. The blue dress looks sexy on you. Brennan will die seeing you."

"Yeah," she says blushing.

We all laugh, before making sure we have everything—including my bouquet of white roses, and greenery—before we head out the hotel room door to the ceremony space downstairs.

I'm feeling giddy, and excited.

Lillie

The music fills the small chapel, and I tentatively take steps down the aisle, thankful that Elyse let me wear flats. I'd have been falling all over the place in heels.

Reaching the front of the aisle I smile at Brennan, stepping up to him and Kaden for a moment.

Brennan gives me a kiss on the cheek.

"You look sexy, Princess," he purrs, slurring the words slightly.

He's probably drunk, having had too much whiskey to calm his nerves,
but when I step back across the aisle to wait for Bella and Elyse to enter
I can't help but notice the glazed look in Brennan's eyes.

He stumbles a bit on his feet—next to his brother—and Kaden elbows
him the side, whispering something to him that makes him nod and
salute in jest.
I'm so focused on watching him, I barely notice Bella coming in and
stepping up beside me.
She takes my hand in hers, and I smile at her as we watch Elyse come in.

Her two kids are at our feet, bouncing up and down to the music.
I glance at Brennan again, my eyes on him the entire ceremony, listening
to Elyse exchange vows with Kaden.
Brennan is watching me too, but he's not focused on me completely.
And it hurts, that I'm not going to be able to have this with him when
I'm hopelessly in love with him.
He's never going to want to marry me.

Something is definitely not right with him, and I'm scared shitless—yes I
said, 'shitless' in my head—that I'm going to lose him.
He's completely spaced out, even when the ceremony ends and he takes
Bella's hand to walk down the aisle.

He's stumbling all over the place, just like he was at Austin's wedding
and I know that only means one thing now.
He's not drunk, he's high.
And I'm angry at him, for getting high again, and at his brother's
wedding when he's the best man, but I'm also completely scared shitless
that this time I'm going to lose him.

It should be a happy day, but my heart is breaking for my beautiful broken Brennan.

I haven't even told him I love him.

I don't want this to be goodbye, but I'm scared it is.

The End (for now)

Australian Slang Glossary

Ute-Truck

Bludger- someone lazy, doesn't do much and possibly relies on social security benefits

Ripper- something really good/great

Ridgy-Didge- Cool

Bonzer-Great, awesome

Pash/ing/ed- to kiss/make out

Arvo- afternoon

Chunder- Vomit, throw up

Gobby- Blowjob

Aussie Kiss- going down on a girl

Daks- pants/trousers/underwear

Undies/Knickers/Jocks-underwear (female knickers, male Jocks, undies both)

Dakking/ed- to pull or have pulled someone daks down (see above)

Bathers- universal name for female swimwear

Budgie Smugglers- small male swimmer that looks like underwear (google this one to see)

Thongs- Footwear, otherwise known as flip flops

Esky- Cooler-you keep drinks cool in it

Dunny- toilet

Bogan-white trash/trailer trash

Old Fella- Your father/Dad

Franger- Condom, Trojan etc

Milo- a malt chocolate powered drink mix (can be made hot or cold)

Macca's-MacDonalds

Fair Dinkum- used to emphasise or seek confirmation of the genuineness or truth of something

Fucking/Bloody oath- similar to above, but an extreme or emphasised way of saying yes.

Shark Week/Rags- A woman's monthly cycle

Stuffed if I know- a nicer way to say fucked if I know

AFL- Australian Rules Football

Playlists

Kaden

https://open.spotify.com/playlist/0LpKgUYmC6Hg6mES3yS7ov?
si=1YH8U5-SSf6tTzGBYGqEPA

Elyse

https://open.spotify.com/playlist/3FbzRazJtW9lvpthHtsK1E?
si=ykK_4CorReqYnssM8VWUnA

Other

https://open.spotify.com/playlist/6sVABCXfGHDcua14SdA2JP?
si=hLEdzeu_T3mFisFDSTNy3Q

About the Author

Caz May is a librarian/teacher by trade, but was always destined to be an author from a young age.

In her spare time, she can be found devouring books or writing her own stories with characters that may not be the typical romance heroes but are loveable just as much.

Caz is married to her own real-life bearded hero and has two fur babies.

She lives for Iced coffee, especially from Gloria Jeans or a Farmers Union but pretty much just loves food in general.

When she's not writing, or reading a book most likely she can probably be found asleep or binge-watching shows on Netflix.

Check out her Instagram or other socials to get in touch.

Instagram- @cazmayauthor

Facebook- @CazMayAuthor

Spotify- cazcat25

Website- https://cazcat25.wixsite.com/cazmay-author

Wattpad- https://www.wattpad.com/user/Caz-May

Acknowledgments

Well, here we are! Acknowledgements for Book Four! Holy fucking wow! The end of Book Four! I can't quite believe we're here!

I really don't know what to say this time around, except a massive shoutout to every single person who has read my books thus far or supported me on Instagram with likes, comments and shares.
When close to the end of writing this book, I was ready to give up on publishing my books but YOU all lifted my spirits and told me not to give up and for that I'm truly grateful.
There are way too many of you to name here, but know that I see you and appreciate every bit of your encouragement and support.

I need to make a mega shoutout to my bestie, B. She read this story as I wrote it, chapter by chapter and her encouragement that Kaden's story is worth reading is why you're hear reading these acknowledgements.
I love you, B. I'll always keep writing for you.

As always I need to send a huge thanks to my husband Cam. He teases me constantly about my writing, but is really my biggest supporter. If he could write me a million reviews he would.

So lovelies, I leave you for another book. And take heart that if you love my stories, this one certainly won't be the last.

Signing off! For now!

Caz May

xx

Look out for Book Five

PDFQ

(Brennan's Story)

Coming Soon

See below for a teaser

Prologue   Black Out

It's so damn shit being at my brother's wedding, watching him being a pussy confessing his love to Elyse. I most certainly didn't want that for myself, especially because I'm never going to actually be with the chick I want.

She looked so fucking stunning, the tight blue bridesmaids dress hugging her tight dancer's body. It even makes her small perky tits look so amazing and I wanted to touch her all over, to find out if she purrs when she comes.

When I kissed her a couple of months back, the moans she made have been like a hit but I can't bring her into my fucked up life.

I hate that I'm an addict, that I need cocaine, weed or ecstasy to get through a week. And I hate the fact even more that I was clean for months until Amelia came back.

I never could resist her when she handed me a tablet, naked and ready to fuck whilst we were high. She'd always told me that her orgasms were more intense when she was high and even though I agreed I always regretted the comedown from our high induced fucks; especially when she'd get violent and teary.

But idiot me put up with her shit because I loved her until she ripped my heart out, again.

I'd only taken a hit of coke before the ceremony, but washing it down with my whiskey flask it'd given me an odd buzz and watching Lillie laughing and happy without me, whilst looking like a red-headed goddess that hit was nowhere enough to make me forget all my feelings for Amelia and the reality that I cant have Lillie when I'm fucked up.

I need another hit, to block out all the feelings of wanting her and thoughts of Amelia fucking me over again. I rush into the bathroom, leaning against the sink and looking at myself in the mirror.

Yep I look like shit, I need to feel good

Quickly I swallow down—with a swig of whiskey—the 'e' pills I'd stashed in my jacket pocket. The whiskey burns my throat but I swallow it and the pill down with a gulp.
I stand there, letting the high take over for a moment, wondering if I should head out to see what is happening.
Something doesn't feel right about this hit. It's made me feel a little off, but I suck it up splashing some water on my face and I push the bathroom door open.
It swings back at me, and I curse at it, slamming my fists into it. I can hear the music pounding from in the main part of the reception now and I stumble out the door.
Yeah, this is not good, something is so not good right now.
The walls are closing in on me and I can't see straight; there are colours and weird creatures in the reception venue. My stomach feels like there's nothing in it and I can feel my blood pumping through my veins.
I see Lillie walking towards me; at least I think it's my redhead goddess but everything is blurry, my vision is fucked up and my body feels weightless.

There's a moment when you know you've fucked up, hit rock bottom and I'm so there. This is not how I should be feeling when a high hits.
My world is closing in on me, I've fucked up and I've hit the floor, the world going black.
I've gone and done it. Completely fucked up my life, just for a damn hit.
I'm gonna fucking die.
And I'm not getting any of that life flashing before my damn eyes bullshit. What a damn waste.
I can hear voices, a sweet angel talking to me, "Brennan, wake up, it's me. It's Lillie."

I moan like a wounded dingo, or at least it sounds like that in my pounding head. I want to open my eyes to look at Lillie or the angel who is telling me she's my Lillie but my eyes are glued shut.
Other voices surround me now, *'Austin, he won't wake up. Help him.'*
'Call an ambulance. He's...'
That's the last words I hear, completely blacking out.

Brennan checking out. Goodbye Princess.